PENGUIN CLASSICS

UNDER THE GREENWOOD TREE

Thomas Hardy was born at Higher Bockhampton, near Dorchester, on 2 June 1840. He was educated locally at the village school and later in Dorchester. At sixteen he was articled to the Dorchester architect and church restorer, John Hicks, although he continued his studies under the guidance of Horace Moule, a Cambridge graduate, whose later suicide affected Hardy and his writing deeply. In 1862 he went to London to pursue his architectural career and also began writing. He returned to Dorset in 1867 to become assistant to John Hicks, at the same time beginning his first novel, *The Poor Man and the Lady*, of which only fragments remain. In 1870 Hardy was sent to St Juliot in Cornwall and it was here that he met his first wife, Emma Gifford, whom he married in 1874; in the same year *Far from the Madding Crowd* was published and met with considerable success. In the previous three years he had published *Desperate Remedies* (1871), *Under the Greenwood Tree* (1872) and *A Pair of Blue Eyes* (1873). In 1878 Hardy moved back to London and in this year *The Return of the Native* appeared. His reputation as a writer grew and he became a well-known figure in London's literary circles. In 1885 he returned to Dorset to live at Max Gate and over the next three years he published *The Mayor of Casterbridge* (1886), which many regard as his greatest tragic novel, *The Woodlanders* (1887) and his first collection of short stories, *Wessex Tales* (1888). In 1891 *Tess of the D'Urbervilles* appeared and in 1895 his last novel, *Jude the Obscure*. During the latter part of his life Hardy devoted himself to poetry, publishing his first collection of verse, *Wessex Poems*, in 1898. He also worked on his autobiography, *The Early Life of Thomas Hardy* (published posthumously in 1928), at the same time burning his old letters, notebooks and private papers. Thomas Hardy died on 11 January 1928.

David Wright's collected poems, *To the Gods the Shades*, appeared in 1976. He has edited *The Penguin Book of Romantic Verse*, *The Penguin Book of Everyday Verse*, *Longer Contemporary Poems*, *Thomas Hardy: Selected Poems*, Edward Thomas's *Selected Poems and Prose*, Trelawny's *Records of Shelley, Byron and the Author* and De Quincey's *Recollections of the Lakes and the Lake Poets* for Penguins. He has also translated *Beowulf* and *The Canterbury Tales*, and published an autobiography, *Deafness*.

Under the Greenwood Tree

OR

The Mellstock Quire

A RURAL PAINTING OF THE DUTCH SCHOOL

* *Thomas Hardy* *

EDITED WITH AN

INTRODUCTION AND NOTES BY

DAVID WRIGHT

PENGUIN BOOKS

Penguin Books Ltd, 27 Wrights Lane, London w8 5tz (Publishing and Editorial)
and Harmondsworth, Middlesex, England (Distribution and Warehouse)
Viking Penguin Inc., 40 West 23rd Street, New York, New York 10010, USA
Penguin Books Australia Ltd, Ringwood, Victoria, Australia
Penguin Books Canada Ltd, 2801 John Street, Markham, Ontario, Canada l3r 1b4
Penguin Books (NZ) Ltd, 182-190 Wairau Road, Auckland 10, New Zealand

First published 1872
Published in the Penguin English Library 1978
Reprinted 1979, 1981, 1982 (twice), 1984 (twice)
Reprinted in Penguin Classics 1985, 1986, 1987

Made and printed in Great Britain by
Hazell Watson & Viney Limited,
Member of the BPCC Group,
Aylesbury, Bucks
Set in Intertype Lectura

CONTENTS

1839 Thomas Hardy, builder and mason of Higher Bockhampton near Dorchester, marries Jemima Hand, cook and servantmaid, at Melbury Osmund on 22 December.

1840 Their eldest son Thomas Hardy born at Higher Bockhampton, 2 June.

1848 He attends village school at Bockhampton built by the lady of the manor, Mrs Julia Martin of Kingston Maurward. His mother gives him Dryden's *Virgil*, Johnson's *Rasselas*. First visit to London about this time.

1849–56 Goes to school at Dorchester to learn Latin. Sees traditional harvest-supper and dance in Kingston Maurward barn. Plays fiddle at weddings and dances; begins learning French and German; reads the novels of Harrison Ainsworth and Dumas père.

1856–62 He is articled to one of his father's employers, the architect and church-restorer John Hicks, whose office in Dorchester is next door to the school kept by the Rev. William Barnes, the Dorset poet and philologist. Witnesses the public execution of Martha Brown outside Dorchester County Gaol. Horace Moule, a university educated classical scholar and eight years Hardy's senior, becomes his mentor. Studies Greek dramatists with Moule. Reads Darwin's *Origin of Species* (1859). Writes his first poem, *Domicilium*.

1862–7 Leaves Dorchester for London in the year of the Exhibition, 1862. Works as assistant-architect to Arthur Blomfield. Attends operas and theatre, explores London, visits National Gallery almost daily, dances at Willis's Rooms, sees Cremorne and the Argyle. Reads Spencer, Huxley, J. S. Mill, Shelley, Browning, Scott and Swinburne. In 1865 publishes his first article, 'How I Built Myself a House' (*Chamber's Journal*). Buys Walker's *Rhyming Dictionary* and begins sending poems to periodicals (they are rejected).

1867–70 Returns to Higher Bockhampton to assist Hicks at Dorchester. Begins his first novel (now lost) *The Poor Man and the Lady*. May have had an understanding with his cousin Tryphena Sparks, the model for Fancy Day and Sue Bridehead. (She went to London to train as a teacher in 1870, married seven years later, and died in 1890.) Completes *The Poor Man* in 1868; it is accepted by Chapman and Hall, but their reader, George Meredith, advises Hardy not to publish. Hicks dies, and Hardy moves to Weymouth to work for his successor, Crickmay. Begins writing *Desperate Remedies*. In 1870 Crickmay sends Hardy to St Juliot, Cornwall, to make plans for the restoration of the church. Here he meets his future wife, Emma Lavinia Gifford, the rector's sister-in-law.

1870–85   Publishes *Desperate Remedies* in 1871, followed by *Under the Greenwood Tree*, 1872, and *A Pair of Blue Eyes*, 1873. Leslie Stephen serializes *Far from the Madding Crowd* in *The Cornhill Magazine*. Horace Moule commits suicide at Cambridge. Publication and success of *Far from the Madding Crowd* in 1874. Hardy marries Emma Lavinia Gifford at St Peter's church, Paddington, and encouraged by her abandons architecture for novel-writing. They take a short continental honeymoon and after brief residences at Surbiton, Swanage and Yeovil, settle at Sturminster Newton in 1876. In this year *The Hand of Ethelberta* is published. 1878 sees publication of *The Return of the Native* and the end of Hardy's 'Sturminster Newton idyll'. They remove to Upper Tooting. Hardy joins Savile Club and becomes a well-known literary figure in London, attending parties and 'crushes'. In 1880 publishes *The Trumpet-Major*, falls seriously ill and is bedridden for six months while writing *A Laodicean*. In 1881 Hardy publishes *A Laodicean*, and takes a house at Wimborne Minster. Visits Paris in 1882 after publication of *Two on a Tower*. Moves to Dorchester in 1883 to supervise the building of his house at Max Gate, taking occupation in 1885.

1885–97   The next three years see the publication of *The Mayor of Casterbridge*, 1886, *The Woodlanders*, 1887, and his first collection of short stories, *Wessex Tales*, 1888. In the spring of 1887 the Hardys tour Italy, visiting Genoa, Pisa, Florence, Rome, Venice, and Milan, returning via London, where Hardy meets Browning and Arnold. From now on they usually visit London in the spring, and sometimes the Continent or Scotland. *A Group of Noble Dames* and *Tess of the D'Urbervilles* are published in 1891; and in the following year Hardy's father dies. In 1893 the Hardys visit Dublin at the invitation of Mrs Henniker (authoress, a daughter of Richard Monckton Milnes). In 1894 publishes *Life's Little Ironies*. About this time strain manifests itself in Hardy's home life, especially during the writing of *Jude the Obscure* (published 1896). Hardy resolves to write no more novels, though he publishes *The Well-Beloved* (written ten years earlier) in 1897.

1898–1912   In 1898 Hardy publishes his first collection of verse, *Wessex Poems*, and in 1902 *Poems of the Past and Present*. In this year he begins *The Dynasts*, of which the first part appears in 1904, the year of his mother's death. Two subsequent parts are published in 1906 and 1908, in which year he also brings out a selection of William Barnes's poems. In 1909 he publishes *Time's Laughing-Stocks*, and in the following year is awarded the Order of Merit and the freedom of Dorchester. He makes a final revision of his novels in 1912, and in November his wife suddenly dies.

1913–28   In March 1913 Hardy makes a pilgrimage to St Juliot and his wife's birthplace at Plymouth. He marries in February 1914 Florence Emily Dugdale, whom he had met through Mrs Henniker in 1904 and who had acted as his secretary and general assistant since 1912. In 1913 receives honorary degree of Litt. D. from Cambridge University (in 1920 Oxford University was to follow suit) and publishes *A Changed Man and Other Tales*. In 1914 publishes *Satires of Circumstance* (including 'Poems of 1912–13'). In 1915 his sister Mary dies. *Moments of Vision* published 1917; *Late Lyrics and Earlier*, 1922; and in 1923 a verse play, *The Famous Tragedy of the Queen of Cornwall*. *Human Shows*, the last collection of poems to appear in his lifetime, is published in 1925. During these years he works at his autobiography, *The Early Life of Thomas Hardy*, supposedly written by Florence Emily Hardy (published posthumously in 1928); at the same time burning his old letters, notebooks and private papers. Dies 11 January 1928, and his ashes are laid in Poets' Corner of Westminster Abbey at the same time that his heart is buried in the grave of his first wife at Stinsford, next to the tombs of his parents. This year sees the publication of his posthumous collection of poems, *Winter Words*.

Under the Greenwood Tree was Hardy's second published novel and the foundation of his career as a writer of fiction. He wrote it when he was thirty-one, a struggling provincial architect planning to marry, like the hero of his book, a little above himself. Though he was the son of a prospering mason and builder, Hardy's next-of-kin included working-folk and even servants, whereas his future wife, Emma Lavinia Gifford, could and did claim to be the niece of an archdeacon.

Hardy wrote novels to make money. He wanted to get married, and he wanted to write poetry. Architecture does not seem to have really engaged him and he was not very good at it (the house he designed for himself, Max Gate near Dorchester, turned out ugly to look at and uncomfortable to live in). The publication of *Under the Greenwood Tree* in 1872 set him on the way to make a living as a novelist. It also inaugurated the great run of Wessex novels, annals of the disintegration of rural England, a series which ended with the appearance of *Jude the Obscure* almost a quarter of a century later. By then Hardy had become famous; *Jude*, because it dealt too uncompromisingly with sexual realities, made him notorious. Thereafter he never wrote another novel, but lived on their royalties and devoted the last thirty years of his life to writing verse. He had always been a poet.

Hardy's first effort at novel-writing was *The Poor Man and the Lady*. This would seem to have been a somewhat melodramatic tale of the ill-fated love of a peasant lad for the squire's daughter. The book was turned down by Macmillan's, but accepted by the next publisher he sent it to, Chapman and Hall. Nonetheless their reader, no less a person than the novelist George Meredith, begged Hardy not to publish the book. Its satire of the upper classes and socialistic 'message' would, Meredith warned him, lead to its being violently attacked by the reviews, and thus damage Hardy's future career as a writer. Would it not be better if the author were 'to put it away for the present and attempt a novel with a purely artistic purpose, giving it a more complicated "plot" '? Hardy followed the latter part of Meredith's advice. He produced *Desperate Remedies*, his first published book, a Wilkie Collins-type murder mystery with a plot so complicated that it resembled clockwork. Its elaboration must have taught Hardy a lot about novel-construction. The book appeared anonymously and at the author's expense in 1871. The publishers were a firm called Tinsley Brothers, whose list sparkled with such best-sellers as *Lady Audley's Secret*, the novels of Ouida, and the works of George Augustus Sala. No doubt Hardy hoped that the sales of *Desperate Remedies* would emulate these, but such expectations were soon dashed. The *Spectator* greeted the book with a review that began:

This is an absolutely anonymous story; no falling back on previous works which might give a clue to the authorship, and no assumption of a *nom de plume* which might, at some future time, disgrace the family name, and still more, the Christian name of a repentant and remorseful novelist, and very right too. By all means let him bury the secret in the profoundest depths of his own heart, out of reach, if possible, of his own consciousness. . .

Half a century later, in *The Early Life of Thomas Hardy*, Hardy recalled 'how he had read this review as he sat on a stile leading to the eweleaze he had to cross on his way home to Bockhampton. The bitterness of that moment was never forgotten; at the time he wished he were dead.' Despite the savage preamble of the *Spectator* review, it went on to praise very highly Hardy's descriptive powers, and his 'unusual and very happy facility in catching and fixing phases of peasant life', demonstrating both with long quotations from the book, particularly a cidermaking episode in the eighth chapter. This praise tallied with that of John Morley, who had read *The Poor Man and the Lady* for Macmillan's and remarked that the country scenes were the best thing in the book. At any rate Hardy took notice. Within a month or two the resilient young author had started writing a new novel – 'a short and quite rustic story' to exploit what his critics agreed was his forte. Of *The Poor Man and the Lady* Morley had said that 'the opening pictures of Christmas Eve in the tranter's house are really of good quality.' This was the genesis of *Under the Greenwood Tree*. Hardy built his new novel round the tranter's Christmas party, cannibalized from his unpublished MS. (Some of *The Poor Man and the Lady* had been re-used in *Desperate Remedies*; what was left after Hardy pillaged it for *Under the Greenwood Tree* went into a story called *An Indiscretion in the Life of an Heiress*, published many years later.) *

He called his new work 'The Mellstock Quire' to begin with, but changed the title to *Under the Greenwood Tree*, taken from the song in *As You Like It*, 'because titles in poetry were in fashion just then'. Tinsley published the novel in 1872, paying Hardy £30 for the copyright. Afterwards he gave Hardy another £10 as his share of the continental copyright for a Tauchnitz edition. Obviously Tinsley did well out of the transaction, for many years later he held out for £300 when Hardy wanted to buy back the copyright. But in the meantime it must have sold well, perhaps very well. The Tauchnitz paperback edition is a pointer to a considerable popularity, to say nothing of the fact that a pirated edition appeared in America the year after its publication in England. Even the reviews were good, though the best was by a friend – Horace Moule, who had been Hardy's literary and intellectual guide and mentor.† Nonetheless Moule made some pertinent criticisms. He said that Hardy's rustic characters sometimes express themselves 'in the language of the author's manner of thought, rather than their own' and gave examples. It is interesting to see that Hardy altered some of these passages in deference to Moule's criticisms when he came to revise the novel for publication in the uniform edition

---

* See also Hardy's poem *A Poor Man and a Lady*, 'intended to preserve an episode in the story "The Poor Man and the Lady", written in 1868'.

† Moule's suicide in the following year may have affected Hardy profoundly. Robert Gittings points out that after Moule's death the tragic and defeated hero arrives for good in all Hardy's novels. Thereafter 'Hardy never portrayed a man who was not, in some way, maimed by fate'.

of his works in 1896. However, the important thing was that *Under the Greenwood Tree* attracted the notice of Leslie Stephen, then the editor of *The Cornhill*, who was later to initiate the *Dictionary of National Biography*, edit the 'English Men of Letters' series, and become the father of Virginia Woolf. In a word, Stephen was a panjandrum of Victorian letters, and when he asked Hardy to contribute to *The Cornhill*, Hardy was launched. *Under the Greenwood Tree* was the last book that he was to publish anonymously.

In many ways the novel was a tuning-up for Hardy's main work in prose fiction. It is the first of his books to introduce 'Wessex' – a geographical term revived by Hardy which has since re-entered the language – and the 'Wessex' pseudonyms such as 'Mellstock' for Stinsford, 'Casterbridge' for Dorchester and so on; place-names now as familiar as the real ones to readers of Hardy's prose and verse. The village musicians of the 'Mellstock Quire', whose fortunes are central to the book, are prototypes of the Wessex rustics characterized in the later novels, where some of them even appear in *propria persona*.

Indeed, Dick Dewy and Fancy Day, the ostensible hero and heroine, are less interesting than the Mellstock rustics: Dick's father the village 'tranter' or carrier, Robert Penny the shoe-maker, Leaf the simpleton; to say nothing of Fancy's game-keeper father, Geoffrey Day, a man of eloquent silences, and the singular Mrs Day ('She d'belong to that class of woman-kind that become second wives; a rum class rather'). These are sharply-drawn individuals, and their talk is a delight. Hardy was reacting to the contemporary view that countryfolk were *ipso facto* inarticulate yokels. In his essay *The Dorsetshire Labourer*, published some ten years after *Under the Greenwood Tree*, he was particularly biting about middle-class Victorians who saw the rural worker 'personified by the pitiable picture known as Hodge . . . a degraded being of uncouth manner and aspect, stolid understanding, and snail-like movement. His speech is such a chaotic corruption of regular language that few persons of progressive aims consider it worth while to enquire what views, if any, of life, of nature, or of society are conveyed by these utterances.' Were an urban visitor with such prejudices to go to Dorset, adds Hardy,

He would, for one thing, find that the language, instead of being a vile corruption of cultivated speech, was a tongue with a grammatical inflection rarely disregarded by his entertainer, though his entertainer's children would occasionally make a sad hash of their talk. Having attended the National School they would mix the printed tongue as taught therein with the unwritten, dying, Wessex English that they had learned of their parents.

As for the conditions of existence that would be encountered by the supposed inquirer, Hardy is at his most Hardyesque when he says 'He would have learnt that wherever a mode of supporting life is neither noxious nor absolutely inadequate, there springs up happiness, and will spring up happiness, of some sort or other. Indeed, it is among such communities as these that happiness will find her last refuge on earth, since it is among them that a perfect insight into the conditions of existence will be longest postponed.'

Under the Greenwood Tree might almost have been written to illustrate that thesis, even though the members of the Mellstock choir are not farm-labourers but village craftsmen and traders, the class to which Hardy's parents belonged. This, however, was the class which did most to keep village culture alive. Hardy later confessed that he felt he had rather burlesqued members of the Mellstock choir. There is certainly a good deal of fun and not altogether subdued slapstick in the chapter describing the interview between the village choir and the new vicar. But the conversation of Hardy's rustics is full of observation as well as humour. Now and then one is reminded by its rhythm of the talk outside Justice Shallow's house in Gloucestershire. It is not surprising that of all Shakespeare's plays the two parts of *Henry IV* are the ones to which most reference is made in Hardy's novels. Though he never set out to reproduce Dorset dialect with the philologic fidelity of his friend and neighbour William Barnes,* Hardy modelled the idiom and

---

* See (reprinted in the Appendix) Barnes's poem *A Bit o' Sly Coorten*, which has sometimes been compared with the chapter called 'Driving out of Budmouth'.

characters of his rustics on real persons whom he had known intimately from childhood. Indeed their graves are to be seen to this day a few yards from the tomb in which Hardy's heart lies buried near his parents in Stinsford ('Mellstock') church-yard.

Though there are no children in the book, the evocative power of this minor masterpiece comes from its being a re-creation of Hardy's childhood environment, of the people and surroundings where he spent the most impressionable years of life. Tranter Dewy's cottage in 'Upper Mellstock' is the cottage in which Hardy was born and grew up in Higher Bockhampton; indeed, it is where *Under the Greenwood Tree* was written. According to Hardy the individual Dewys were not modelled on members of the Hardy family – but the Hardys, like the Dewys, were all members of the Stinsford ('Mellstock') church choir. This comprised Hardy's grandfather, who had founded it, his two sons, and their brother-in-law James Dart. Hardy's first memory was of his father giving him an accordion. While very young he learned to play the fiddle, and though the Stinsford choir came to an end when Hardy was a year old, he was more or less brought up in its ambience. As a youth studying archi-tecture in Dorchester he would, according to his disguised autobiography, *The Early Life of Thomas Hardy*, often go out in the evening

with his fiddle under his arm, sometimes in the company of his father as first violin and uncle as 'cellist, to play country-dances, reels, and hornpipes at an agriculturist's wedding, christening, or Christmas party ... not returning sometimes till nearly dawn, the Hardys being traditionally string-bandsmen available on such occasions, and having the added recommendation of charging noth-ing for their services.

Hence the singular vividness and authoritative circumstan-tiality of his evocation of the carol-singing and the Christmas party at the tranter's cottage. Other childhood memories con-tribute, e.g. to the tranter's discourse on cider-apples, to the beekeeping scenes and the exhaustively detailed description of the chimney-corner in Geoffrey Day's front room. This chimney-corner once existed in the Hardy cottage at Higher

Bockhampton; but the description is paralleled in another of Barnes's poems. *The Settle an' the Girt Wood Vire*, to which it may owe something.*

At least Barnes pointed the way. Almost as Joyce recorded Dublin in such detail in *Ulysses* that, so he said, were it destroyed his book would furnish the evidence for its reconstruction, so Hardy recorded the Dorset of his childhood. As for the general setting of *Under the Greenwood Tree*, the relevant exactness of its opening sentence: 'To dwellers in a wood almost every species of tree has its voice as well as its feature' comes immediately to mind when one visits the Hardy birthplace at Higher Bockhampton, a brick and thatch cottage still hidden and bowered in the thick embrace of Yellowham ('Yalbury') Wood. The book is divided into the four seasons of the year; and, like remembered happy childhood, a tranquil timelessness and Arcadian appropriateness is established in each. It is the only one of Hardy's novels unshadowed by tragic happening.

Yet for all that its feet are firmly on the ground. The character of the heroine Fancy Day is only a sketch, but a sketch by the novelist who perhaps understood and liked women better than any male writer of the nineteenth century, including Tolstoy and the Portuguese Eça de Quieroz. 'You praised me, and praise is life to me,' she tells the vicar, Maybold, in trying to explain why she had accepted his offer of marriage although already engaged to Dick. She is quite conscious of her position. Her father, who has progressed from ordinary keeper to become head gamekeeper and timber-steward to a great landowner, is a cut above Dick's, who is a local carrier and haulier; and she has been educated in order to rise in the world, perhaps to marry a gentleman. Therefore she hesitates to prefer Dick in the face of the social position offered by a rival suitor, the farmer Shiner. The Rev. Maybold is an even greater temptation. There is a fine ironic touch when Dick, having unwittingly put an end to the Rev. Maybold's courtship of Fancy by revealing his own engagement to her, implicitly solicits custom by handing the vicar his tradesman's card. As if to underline the social

* See appendix for this poem.

difference, Hardy seems here to have deliberately rusticated Dick's speech. It is probable that the character of Fancy Day, like that of Sue Bridehead in *Jude the Obscure*, was based on Hardy's cousin Tryphena Sparks. Like Fancy and Sue, Tryphena had bettered herself by becoming a certificated teacher. Hardy wrote several poems about Tryphena, and was almost certainly in love with her before he met Emma Gifford; but there seems to be nothing but sexual speculation in the recently promoted scandal that Tryphena bore him an illegitimate child *à la* Wordsworth and Annette Vallon.* The rather brittle characters of both Fancy Day and Sue Bridehead would appear to suggest that Hardy 'saw through' Tryphena, if it is indeed her personality which these two characters reflect.

To this day *Under the Greenwood Tree* has been the best-loved if not the most highly-regarded of Hardy's novels. Minor in scale, it has often been called 'a prose idyll'. One critic even described it, rather incongruously, as 'a modern and exquisite version of *Daphnis and Chloe*'.

But Dick Dewy and Fancy Day are no Arcadians innocent of the facts of life. Their environment is not a pastoral ideal but rural reality. In this early work, for all its charm – and charm is a quality not automatically associated with Hardy – the author strikes, however *pianissimo*, notes that will be heard in his later and greater Wessex novels. Its theme points to the main theme of Hardy's fiction: the clash between agrarian and urban ways of life, between traditional rural culture and that of the new metropolitan *déracinés*.

For Hardy's grand subject, as he perhaps discovered during the writing of this book, was the decline and fall of the rural culture of England. No fugitive or insular concern: one of the fundamental revolutions of his time and ours has been the replacement of organic by technological cultures. *Mutatis mutandis* this has happened or is happening everywhere now. The industrial or technological revolution had its birth in Eng-

---

* See *Providence and Mr Hardy* by Lois Deacon and Terry Coleman (Hutchinson, 1966) for the evidence that Tryphena Sparks had a son by Thomas Hardy; and for its refutation, Robert Gittings: *The Young Thomas Hardy* (Heinemann, 1975).

land, which naturally became the first country in the world to feel its consequences. The impact of these on urban life – huge and growing conglomerations centred on the new factories, the new kind of mass-society produced by rootless congeries of too many people – was first reflected in the novels of Charles Dickens. But, apart from the polemic of Cobbett, it was poets like Goldsmith, Crabbe, Wordsworth, John Clare and William Barnes who first recorded the concomitant erosion of the traditional English rural way of life. This had continued almost unchanged up to the beginning of the nineteenth century and the enclosure of common lands. Later George Eliot, in *Adam Bede* and *Silas Marner*, Mrs Gaskell, even Anthony Trollope in one or two of his novels, took up or touched upon the theme of rural decline. To this list one might add Disraeli's *Coningsby* and *Sybil*, Charles Kingsley's *Yeast* and *Alton Locke*, George Borrow's *Lavengro* and *The Romany Rye*. But leaving aside literary merit, no novelist ever handled it with anything like the scope, authority, intimate knowledge and realistic balance of Hardy.

The scope of Hardy's Wessex novels is broad: they cover all but the last decade of the nineteenth century, from *The Trumpet-Major*, set in Nelson's day, to *Tess of the D'Urbervilles*, where the action takes place in the late 1880s. Moreover, unlike his predecessors and coevals in this field, Hardy belonged to the milieu that he depicted. Though he liked to believe, with Tess Darbeyfield's father, that he was a 'downstart' of a family of gentlefolk, at the time of his birth the Hardys were barely a rung above peasants or artisans. Hardy's father began as a self-employed mason; his mother had been a servant and was brought up as a pauper on parish relief. This accounts for Hardy's realistic balance: first-hand observation and experience of rural life stopped him from becoming a blind enemy to progress or, despite nostalgia, a nurser of illusions about the recent or remote past.* After all, the Tolpuddle Martyrs of 1834 – the six Dorset farm labourers transported for trying to form a trades union – had come from a village only a few

---

* Equally Chekhov, a descendant of liberated serfs, could never go along with the aristocratic Tolstoy's disbelief in the benefits of progress.

miles from Higher Bockhampton, where Hardy had been born in 1840. In an essay written in 1883 Hardy was explicit:

Progress and picturesqueness do not harmonize. They [the labouring class] are losing their individuality, but they are widening the range of their ideas, and gaining in freedom. It is too much to expect them to remain stagnant and old-fashioned for the pleasure of romantic spectators. (*The Dorsetshire Labourer*)

If *Under the Greenwood Tree* – 'A Rural Painting of the Dutch School' – has a touch of the picturesque, and if in classic pastoral tradition it has practically nothing to say about work on the land, nevertheless it inaugurates a pattern, one that Lionel Johnson was first to detect. Here, as in the great Wessex novels that were to follow, the protagonists are countryfolk brought up to a traditional rural way of life; Hardy brings into relation with them people from outside the agricultural world, their betters in education and status. But not in worth: as the rural landscape and the ways and traditions of its inhabitants are elaborated and realized, the urban disruption of it is better seen. There comes a clash between urban and rural values and modes of life; the latter is inevitably defeated.

In Hardy's later novels this defeat is ever more manifest and overwhelming, as if to keep pace with the worsening of agricultural conditions during his lifetime. For example, in 1840 agriculture was still the most important industry in England, but by 1900, a few years after the publication of Hardy's last novel, its labour force had dwindled by more than half. Thus in *Under the Greenwood Tree*, set in the period around 1840, the rural defeat is sketched lightly; there is nothing to match the later doom of a Henchard in *The Mayor of Casterbridge* or of Tess in *Tess of the D'Urbervilles*. All that happens in *Under the Greenwood Tree* is the substitution of a harmonium in the parish church for the music made by the old-fashioned choir of village instrumentalists with their bass-viols and clarinets.

There is almost no 'story' to this event. Yet when the harmonium replaces the choir, with Fancy Day at its keyboard, it is one of the climaxes of the book. An alienation is seen to have begun. The villagers' involvement with their church has been thereby lessened, and an autochthonous culture diminished.* This small affair manages to overshadow the love-story that is the seeming *raison d'être* of the novel. The two narratives are adroitly made interdependent. It is a member of the choir, Dick Dewy, who falls in love with Fancy Day, who has been 'educated'. The new and progressive-minded vicar, the Rev. Maybold (like Fancy representative of a more sophis-ticated culture), asks her to play the harmonium that is to replace the village musicians. The members of the old choir, which consist of three generations of Dewys and two or three other villagers, somewhat supinely acquiesce to the harmon-ium. The old ways are not vigorous enough to resist the new. Meanwhile Dick's courtship of Fancy runs predictably if not smoothly, disturbed only by one or two tiffs over her flirta-tiousness, and the gamekeeper's reluctance to have his outlay on her education wasted on marriage to a villager. There is a moment that threatens melodrama when Fancy, already affi-anced to Dick, is surprised into accepting the Rev. Maybold's unexpected proposal of marriage. But all's well that ends well. The final chapters even hint at an accommodation between the old and the new, with Fancy consenting to the traditional wedding-procession round the parish ('respectable people don't nowadays'), and the villagers dancing six-hand reels to the music of the choir under the greenwood tree. As for the Rev. Maybold, Dick never hears what passed between him and Fancy. So the book ends with Hardy allowing himself one characteristic touch:

Dick was talking to his companion.

'Fancy,' he said, 'why we are so happy is because there is such full confidence between us. Ever since that time you confessed to that little flirtation with Shiner by the river (which was really no flirta-tion at all), I have thought how artless and good you must be to tell me o' such a trifling thing, and to be so frightened about it as you

* Cf. Hardy's comment in his 1896 preface to the novel: 'One is in-clined to regret the displacement of these ecclesiastical bandsmen by an isolated organist.' As Merryn Williams remarks in *Thomas Hardy and Rural England*, 'the word "isolated" carries several shades of meaning here.'

were. It has won me to tell you my every deed and word since then. We'll have no secrets from each other, darling, will we ever? – no secret at all.'

'None from today,' said Fancy. 'Hark! what's that?'

From a neighbouring thicket was suddenly heard to issue in a loud, musical, and liquid voice –

'Tippiwit! swe-e-et! ki-ki-ki! Come hither, come hither, come hither!'

'O, 'tis the nightingale,' murmured she, and thought of a secret she would never tell.

Not only is *Under the Greenwood Tree* the happiest of Hardy's books, it is the one novel in which his prose is free and natural throughout. Few of the stilted circumlocutions that sometimes infect his style are to be found in it, perhaps because Hardy is here dealing with a social milieu in which he was thoroughly at home, perhaps because the small scale of the work made it seem unnecessary to put on the grand manner. It is quite free of the melodramatics and literarysms that Hardy seems to have caught from that poor man's Walter Scott, Harrison Ainsworth, whose popular novels he enjoyed too well in his nonage. These occasional exasperating portentousnesses (exasperating because Hardy had so fine an ear for the rhythm of prose) have also been put down to his diffidence and over-caution as a self-educated man. Though it would be as well to remember that Hardy gave himself a better education in the 'two cultures' than most university graduates, including the present writer, can boast in the twentieth century.

Under the Greenwood Tree – it was Ezra Pound's favourite of the novels – remains the best and certainly the most inviting introduction to Hardy's *oeuvre*. Slight as it may seem, the work is in every sense a prologue to the five great 'Wessex' novels – *Far from the Madding Crowd*, *The Return of the Native*, *The Mayor of Casterbridge*, *The Woodlanders*, and *Tess of the D'Urbervilles*. Their epilogue is *Jude the Obscure*; and if the latter is Hardy's *Il Penseroso*, then *Under the Greenwood Tree*, a half-pastoral prelude to the survey of the rural world of nineteenth-century England, is his *L'Allegro*.

DAVID WRIGHT.

HARDY'S WESSEX

HARDY'S Wessex is so familiar that it is hard to realize how odd it is that a novelist should have tied himself by so many strings to a particular tract of territory. Many novelists have set their scenes in real places, or have written with some features of a familiar landscape always before them. But Hardy has done something different. Almost every step taken by his characters is taken along real roads or over real heaths; the towns and villages, the hills, even many of the houses are identifiable. It is as if Hardy's imagination could not work unless with solid ground under its feet, with solid objects to be seen around it. Many of the characters, there is little doubt, contain more or less of one real person, more or less of another, with elements drawn purely from imagination or from the accumulated layers of experience, which comes to much the same thing. But with the topography, Hardy was rarely satisfied with anything less than a one-to-one correspondence between the fictional and the real.

While the detail of Hardy's topographical nomenclature may become tedious, the fact that the landscape is identifiable does give the novels a special quality, as of a day-dream, with half-real figures moving over a real world. One might say – if it can be said with respect – that it is this which leaves the novels with a touch of the magazine-story still, in which the ingenuous reader may lose himself – or herself – in vicarious adventures. And part of the immense popularity of Hardy certainly derives from the interest of the places written about, and particularly the more picturesque.

Hardy's WESSEX

Bristol

Bat

Bristol Channel

Mendip Hills

Fountall

Prospect Hotel

Exon Moor

Stancy Castle

Quantock Hills

Poldon Hills

Glaston

Cliff Martin

Dunkery Beacon

Will's Neck

Marshal's Elm

Downstaple

Sedgemoor

WESSEX

Stourhe

Toneborough Deane

R. Parret

Toneborough

OUTER

Ivelchester

Ivell

Stourcast

Sherton Abbas

Tivworthy

Exe Valley

LOWER

WESSEX

Silverthorn

King's Hintock

SOUTH

Vale of Bla

High

Bulba

Stoy

Flintco

Evershead

Abbots

As

Cernel

Upp

Long

Exonbury

R. Otter

Emminster

Pilsdon

Chalk Newton

Egd

Weatherbury

Idmouth

Port Bredy

Casterbridge

R.

W

Blackon

Nethe

Widon Val

Bue

mo

Deadmans Bay

Isle of Slingers

The Beal

The Race

Tor-upon-Sea

The

NORTH

R. Thames
Lumsdon
Christminster

The Brown House
Alfredston
Cresscombe
Marygreen

WESSEX

MID

Marlbury Downs

Castle Royal

Kennetbridge
Gaymead
Aldbrickham

Batton Castle
Inkpen Beacon

WESSEX

The Great Plain

Stoke Barehills
Icenway House
Quartershot

Weydon Priors

UPPER

Stonehenge

WESSEX

Melchester

Wintoncester

Fernel Hall
Deansleigh Park

...denton
...on
Wingreen
The Chase
The Slopes
Trantridge Cross
Chaseborough
ESSEX
Shottsford Forum
Lornton Inn
Badbury Rings
...ton
Yewsholt
...ney Welland
...bere
Chene Manor
Warborne
Heath
...othays
Havenpool

Southampton

The Great Forest

Bramshurst

Solentsea
Portsmouth

...ridge
...ryesgate
Anglebury
Sandbourne

The Island

...wind Cove
...hip
Knollsea

N

channel

0   10   20   30 miles

Fictitious names: Exonbury
Real names: Portsmouth

H. A. Shelley

Key to Place-Names

HARDY'S NAME	REAL NAME
Abbot's-Cernel	Cerne Abbas
Abbotsea	Abbotsbury
Aldbrickham	Reading
Alfredston	Wantage
Anglebury	Wareham
Badbury Rings	A hill near Wimborne Minster
Budmouth	Weymouth
Bulbarrow	A hill near Sturminster Newton
Casterbridge	Dorchester
Chalk Newton	Maiden Newton
Chaseborough	Cranborne
Christminster	Oxford
Cresscombe	Letcombe Basset
Damer's Wood	Came Wood near Dorchester
Dogbury	A hill near High Stoy
Durnover	Fordington
Egdon Heath	A composite of the heaths between Bournemouth and Dorchester
Emminster	Beaminster
Evershead	Evershot
Exonbury	Exeter
Fensworth	Letcombe Regis
Flintcombe-Ash	Nettlecombe-Tout
Greenhill	Woodbury Hill near Bere Regis
Hope Cove	Church Hope
Kennetbridge	Newbury
Kingsbere and *King's Bere*	Bere Regis
Leddenton	Gillingham
Longpuddle	Piddlehinton (also called by Hardy *Upper Longpuddle*)
Lulwind Cove	Lulworth Cove
Lumsdon	Cumnor
Marlott	Marnhull

Marygreen	Fawley
Melchester	Salisbury
Mellstock	Stinsford and Lower and Higher Bockhampton
Middleton Abbey	Milton Abbas
Nether-Moynton	Overmoigne
Norcombe Hill	A hill near Toller Down
Nuttlebury	Hazelbury Bryan
Oxwell Hall	Poxwell
Port Bredy	Bridport
Pos'ham	Portisham
Quartershot	Aldershot
Rainbarrow	Rainbarrows, a mound north of the Dorchester-Wareham road
Ridgeway	A road between Dorchester and Weymouth
Roy Town	Troy Town
St Aldhelm's Head	St Alban's Head
Sandbourne	Bournemouth
Shaston	Shaftesbury
Sherton	Sherborne
Shottesford and *Shottsford Forum*	Blandford
Stoke-Barehills	Basingstoke
Stourcastle	Sturminster Newton
Upper Longpuddle	Piddlehinton
Weatherbury	Puddletown
Wellbridge	Wool
Wintonchester	Winchester
Yalbury Wood	Yellowham Wood

UNDER THE
GREENWOOD TREE

OR

THE MELLSTOCK QUIRE

A RURAL PAINTING OF THE
DUTCH SCHOOL

CONTENTS

CONTENTS

Part The Fourth · Autumn

Part The Fifth · Conclusion

THIS story of the Mellstock Quire and its old established west-gallery musicians, with some supplementary descriptions of similar officials in *Two on a Tower*, *A Few Crusted Characters*, and other places, is intended to be a fairly true picture, at first hand, of the personages, ways, and customs which were common among such orchestral bodies in the villages of fifty or sixty years ago.

One is inclined to regret the displacement of these ecclesiastical bandsmen by an isolated organist (often at first a barrel-organist) or harmonium player; and despite certain advantages in point of control and accomplishment which were, no doubt, secured by installing the single artist, the change has tended to stultify the professed aims of the clergy, its direct result being to curtail and extinguish the interest of parishioners in church doings. Under the old plan, from half a dozen to ten full-grown players, in addition to the numerous more or less grown-up singers, were officially occupied with the Sunday routine, and concerned in trying their best to make it an artistic outcome of the combined musical taste of the congregation. With a musical executive limited, as it mostly is limited now, to the parson's wife or daughter and the school-children, or to the school-teacher and the children, an important union of interests has disappeared.

The zest of these bygone instrumentalists must have been keen and staying, to take them, as it did, on foot every Sunday after a toilsome week through all weathers to the church, which often lay at a distance from their homes. They usually received so little in payment for their performances that their efforts were really a labour of love. In the parish I had in my mind when writing the present tale, the gratuities received yearly by the musicians at Christmas were somewhat as follows: From the manor-house ten shillings and a supper; from the vicar ten shillings; from the farmers five shillings each;

from each cottage-household one shilling; amounting altogether to not more than ten shillings a head annually – just
enough, as an old executant told me, to pay for their fiddle-
strings, repairs, rosin, and music-paper (which they mostly
ruled themselves). Their music in those days was all in their
own manuscript, copied in the evenings after work, and their
music-books were home-bound.

It was customary to inscribe a few jigs, reels, hornpipes, and
ballads in the same book, by beginning it at the other end, the
insertions being continued from front and back till sacred and
secular met together in the middle, often with bizarre effect,
the words of some of the songs exhibiting that ancient and
broad humour which our grandfathers, and possibly grand-
mothers, took delight in, and is in these days unquotable.[1]

The aforesaid fiddle-strings, rosin, and music-paper were
supplied by a pedlar, who travelled exclusively in such wares
from parish to parish, coming to each village about every six
months. Tales are told of the consternation once caused among
the church fiddlers when, on the occasion of their producing a
new Christmas anthem, he did not come to time, owing to
being snowed up on the downs, and the straits they were in
through having to make shift with whipcord and twine for
strings. He was generally a musician himself, and sometimes a
composer in a small way, bringing his own new tunes, and
tempting each choir to adopt them for a consideration. Some
of these compositions which now lie before me, with their
repetitions of lines, half-lines, and half-words, their fugues and
their intermediate symphonies, are good singing still, though
they would hardly be admitted into such hymn-books as are
popular in the churches of fashionable society at the present
time.

August 1896

Under the Greenwood Tree was first brought out in the summer of 1872 in two volumes. The name of the story was originally intended to be, more appropriately, *The Mellstock Quire*,
and this has been appended as a sub-title since the early

editions, it having been thought unadvisable to displace for it the title by which the book first became known.

In rereading the narrative after a long interval there occurs the inevitable reflection that the realities out of which it was spun were material for another kind of study of this little group of church musicians than is found in the chapters here penned so lightly, even so farcically and flippantly at times. But circumstances would have rendered any aim at a deeper, more essential, more transcendent handling unadvisable at the date of writing; and the exhibition of the Mellstock Quire [2] in the following pages must remain the only extant one, except for the few glimpses of that perished band which I have given in verse elsewhere.

T. H.

April 1912

PART THE FIRST

WINTER

I

Mellstock-Lane

To dwellers in a wood almost every species of tree has its voice as well as its feature. At the passing of the breeze the fir-trees sob and moan no less distinctly than they rock; the holly whistles as it battles with itself; the ash hisses amid its quiverings; the beech rustles while its flat boughs rise and fall. And winter, which modifies the note of such trees as shed their leaves, does not destroy its individuality.

On a cold and starry Christmas-eve within living memory a man was passing up a lane towards Mellstock Cross in the darkness of a plantation that whispered thus distinctively to his intelligence. All the evidences of his nature were those afforded by the spirit of his footsteps, which succeeded each other lightly and quickly, and by the liveliness of his voice as he sang in a rural cadence:

> With the rose and the lily
> And the daffodowndilly,
> The lads and the lasses a-sheep-shearing go.[3]

The lonely lane he was following connected one of the hamlets of Mellstock parish [4] with Upper Mellstock and Lewgate, and to his eyes, casually glancing upward, the silver and black-stemmed birches with their characteristic tufts, the pale grey boughs of beech, the dark-creviced elm, all appeared now as black and flat outlines upon the sky, wherein the white stars twinkled so vehemently that their flickering seemed like the flapping of wings. Within the woody pass, at a level anything lower than the horizon, all was dark as the grave. The copse-wood forming the sides of the bower interlaced its branches so densely, even at this season of the year, that the draught from the north-east flew along the channel with scarcely an interruption from lateral breezes.

After passing the plantation and reaching Mellstock Cross the white surface of the lane revealed itself between the dark hedgerows like a ribbon jagged at the edges; the irregularity being caused by temporary accumulations of leaves extending from the ditch on either side.

The song (many times interrupted by flitting thoughts which took the place of several bars, and resumed at a point it would have reached had its continuity been unbroken) now received a more palpable check, in the shape of 'Ho-i-i-i-i!' from the crossing lane to Lower Mellstock, on the right of the singer who had just emerged from the trees.

'Ho-i-i-i-i!' he answered, stopping and looking round, though with no idea of seeing anything more than imagination pictured.

'Is that thee, young Dick Dewy?' came from the darkness.

'Ay, sure, Michael Mail.'

'Then why not stop for fellow-craters – going to thy own father's house too, as we be, and knowen us so well?'

Dick Dewy faced about and continued his tune in an under-whistle, implying that the business of his mouth could not be checked at a moment's notice by the placid emotion of friendship.

Having come more into the open he could now be seen rising against the sky, his profile appearing on the light background like the portrait of a gentleman in black cardboard. It assumed the form of a low-crowned hat, an ordinary-shaped nose, an ordinary chin, an ordinary neck, and ordinary shoulders. What he consisted of further down was invisible from lack of sky low enough to picture him on.

Shuffling, halting, irregular footsteps of various kinds were now heard coming up the hill, and presently there emerged from the shade severally five men of different ages and gaits, all of them working villagers of the parish of Mellstock. They, too, had lost their rotundity with the daylight, and advanced against the sky in flat outlines, which suggested some processional design on Greek or Etruscan pottery. They represented the chief portion of Mellstock parish choir.

The first was a bowed and bent man, who carried a fiddle

under his arm, and walked as if engaged in studying some subject connected with the surface of the road. He was Michael Mail, the man who had hallooed to Dick.

The next was Mr Robert Penny,[5] boot- and shoe-maker; a little man who, though rather round-shouldered, walked as if that fact had not come to his own knowledge, moving on with his back very hollow and his face fixed on the north-east quarter of the heavens before him, so that his lower waistcoat-buttons came first, and then the remainder of his figure. His features were invisible; yet when he occasionally looked round, two faint moons of light gleamed for an instant from the precincts of his eyes, denoting that he wore spectacles of a circular form.

The third was Elias Spinks, who walked perpendicularly and dramatically. The fourth outline was Joseph Bowman's, who had now no distinctive appearance beyond that of a human being. Finally came a weak lath-like form, trotting and stumbling along with one shoulder forward and his head inclined to the left, his arms dangling nervelessly in the wind as if they were empty sleeves. This was Thomas Leaf.

'Where be the boys?' said Dick to this somewhat indifferently-matched assembly.

The eldest of the group, Michael Mail, cleared his throat from a great depth.

'We told them to keep back at home for a time, thinken they wouldn't be wanted yet awhile; and we could choose the tuens, and so on.'

'Father and grandfather William have expected ye a little sooner. I have just been for a run round by Ewelease Stile and Hollow Hill to warm my feet.'

'To be sure father did! To be sure 'a did expect us – to taste the little barrel beyond compare that he's going to tap.'

' 'Od rabbit it all! Never heard a word of it!' said Mr Penny, gleams of delight appearing upon his spectacle-glasses, Dick meanwhile singing parenthetically –

The lads and the lasses a-sheep-shearing go.

'Neighbours, there's time enough to drink a sight of drink now afore bedtime?' said Mail.

'True, true – time enough to get as drunk as lords!' replied Bowman cheerfully.

This opinion being taken as convincing they all advanced between the varying hedges and the trees dotting them here and there, kicking their toes occasionally among the crumpled leaves. Soon appeared glimmering indications of the few cottages forming the small hamlet of Upper Mellstock for which they were bound, whilst the faint sound of church-bells ringing a Christmas peal could be heard floating over upon the breeze from the direction of Longpuddle and Weatherbury parishes on the other side of the hills. A little wicket admitted them to the garden, and they proceeded up the path to Dick's house.

II

The Tranter's

IT was a long low cottage with a hipped roof of thatch,[6] having dormer windows breaking up into the eaves, a chimney standing in the middle of the ridge and another at each end. The window-shutters were not yet closed, and the fire- and candle-light within radiated forth upon the thick bushes of box and laurestinus growing in clumps outside, and upon the bare boughs of several codlin-trees hanging about in various distorted shapes, the result of early training as espaliers combined with careless climbing into their boughs in later years. The walls of the dwelling were for the most part covered with creepers, though these were rather beaten back from the doorway – a feature which was worn and scratched by much passing in and out, giving it by day the appearance of an old keyhole. Light streamed through the cracks and joints of outbuildings a little way from the cottage, a sight which nourished a fancy that the purpose of the erection must be rather to veil bright attractions than to shelter unsightly necessaries. The noise of a beetle and wedges and the splintering of wood was periodically heard from this direction; and at some little distance further a steady regular munching and the occasional scurr of a rope betokened a stable, and horses feeding within it.

The choir stamped severally on the door-stone to shake from their boots any fragment of earth or leaf adhering thereto, then entered the house and looked around to survey the condition of things. Through the open doorway of a small inner room on the right hand, of a character between pantry and cellar, was Dick Dewy's father Reuben, by vocation a 'tranter', or irregular carrier. He was a stout florid man about forty years of age, who surveyed people up and down when first making their acquaintance, and generally smiled at the horizon or other distant object during conversations with friends, walking about with a steady sway, and turning out his toes very considerably. Being now occupied in bending over a hogshead that stood in the pantry ready horsed for the process of broaching, he did not take the trouble to turn or raise his eyes at the entry of his visitors, well knowing by their footsteps that they were the expected old comrades.

The main room, on the left, was decked with bunches of holly and other evergreens, and from the middle of the beam bisecting the ceiling hung the mistletoe, of a size out of all proportion to the room, and extending so low that it became necessary for a full-grown person to walk round it in passing, or run the risk of entangling his hair. This apartment contained Mrs Dewy the tranter's wife, and the four remaining children, Susan, Jim, Bessy, and Charley, graduating uniformly though at wide stages from the age of sixteen to that of four years – the eldest of the series being separated from Dick the firstborn by a nearly equal interval.

Some circumstance had apparently caused much grief to Charley just previous to the entry of the choir, and he had absently taken down a small looking-glass, holding it before his face to learn how the human countenance appeared when engaged in crying, which survey led him to pause at the various points in each wail that were more than ordinarily striking, for a thorough appreciation of the general effect. Bessy was leaning against a chair, and glancing under the plaits about the waist of the plaid frock she wore, to notice the original unfaded pattern of the material as there preserved, her face bearing an expression of regret that the brightness had passed away from the visible portions. Mrs Dewy sat in a brown settle by the side of the glowing wood fire – so glowing that with a heedful compression of the lips she would now and then rise and put her hand upon the hams and flitches of bacon lining the chimney, to reassure herself that they were not being broiled instead of smoked – a misfortune that had been known to happen now and then at Christmas-time.

'Hullo my sonnies, here you be, then!' said Reuben Dewy at length, standing up and blowing forth a vehement gust of breath. 'How the blood do puff up in anybody's head, to be

sure, a-stooping like that! I was just going out to gate to hark
for ye.' He then carefully began to wind a strip of brown paper
round a brass tap he held in his hand. 'This in the cask here is a
drop o' the right sort' (tapping the cask); ' 'tis a real drop o'
cordial from the best picked apples – Sansoms, Stubbards, Five-
corners, and such-like – you d'mind the sort, Michael?'
(Michael nodded.) 'And there's a sprinkling of they that grow
down by the orchard-rails – streaked ones – rail apples we
d'call 'em, as 'tis by the rails they grow, and not knowing the
right name. The water-cider from 'em is as good as most
people's best cider is.'[7]

'Ay, and of the same make too,' said Bowman. ' "It rained
when we wrung it out, and the water got into it," folk will say.
But 'tis on'y an excuse. Watered cider is too common among
us.'

'Yes, yes; too common it is!' said Spinks with an inward
sigh, whilst his eyes seemed to be looking at the case in an
abstract form rather than at the scene before him. 'Such poor
liquor do make a man's throat feel very melancholy – and is a
disgrace to the name of stimmilent.'

'Come in, come in, and draw up to the fire; never mind your
shoes,' said Mrs Dewy, seeing that all except Dick had paused
to wipe them upon the doormat. 'I am glad that you've stepped
up-along at last; and, Susan, you run down to Grammer
Kaytes's and see if you can borrow some larger candles than
these fourteen.[8] Tommy Leaf, don't ye be afeard! Come and
sit here in the settle.'

This was addressed to the young man before mentioned,
consisting chiefly of a human skeleton and a smock-frock, who
was very awkward in his movements, apparently on account of
having grown so very fast that before he had had time to get
used to his height he was higher.

'Hee – hee – ay!' replied Leaf, letting his mouth continue to
smile for some time after his mind had done smiling, so that his
teeth remained in view as the most conspicuous members of his
body.

'Here, Mr Penny,' resumed Mrs Dewy, 'you sit in this chair.
And how's your daughter, Mrs Brownjohn?'

'Well, I suppose I must say pretty fair.' He adjusted his spectacles a quarter of an inch to the right. 'But she'll be worse before she's better, 'a b'lieve.'

'Indeed – poor soul! And how many will that make in all, four or five?'

'Five; they've buried three. Yes, five; and she not much more than a maid yet. She do know the multiplication table onmistakable well. However, 'twas to be, and none can gainsay it.'

Mrs Dewy resigned Mr Penny. 'Wonder where your grandfather James is?' she inquired of one of the children. 'He said he'd drop in tonight.'

'Out in fuel-house with grandfather William,' said Jimmy.

'Now let's see what we can do,' was heard spoken about this time by the tranter in a private voice to the barrel, beside which he had again established himself, and was stooping to cut away the cork.

'Reuben, don't make such a mess o' tapping that barrel as is mostly made in this house,' Mrs Dewy cried from the fireplace. 'I'd tap a hundred without wasting more than you do in one. Such a squizzling and squirting job as 'tis in your hands! There, he always was such a clumsy man indoors.'

'Ay, ay; I know you'd tap a hundred beautiful, Ann – I know you would; two hundred, perhaps. But I can't promise. This is a' old cask, and the wood's rotted away about the tap-hole. The husbird [9] of a feller Sam Lawson – that ever I should call'n such, now he's dead and gone, poor heart! – took me in completely upon the feat of buying this cask. "Reub," says he – 'a always used to call me plain Reub, poor old heart! – "Reub," he said says he, "that there cask, Reub, is as good as new; yes, good as new. 'Tis a wine-hogshead; the best port-wine in the commonwealth have been in that there cask; and you shall have en for ten shillens, Reub," – 'a said says he – "he's worth twenty, ay, five-and-twenty, if he's worth one; and an iron hoop or two put round en among the wood ones will make en worth thirty shillens of any man's money, if –" '

'I think I should have used the eyes that Providence gave me to use afore I paid any ten shillens for a jimcrack wine-barrel;

a saint is sinner enough not to be cheated. But 'tis like all your family was, so easy to be deceived.'

'That's as true as gospel of this member,' said Reuben.

Mrs Dewy began a smile at the answer, then altering her lips and refolding them so that it was not a smile, commenced smoothing little Bessy's hair; the tranter having meanwhile suddenly become oblivious to conversation, occupying himself in a deliberate cutting and arrangement of some more brown paper for the broaching operation.

'Ah, who can believe sellers!' said old Michael Mail in a carefully-cautious voice, by way of tiding-over this critical point of affairs.

'No one at all,' said Joseph Bowman, in the tone of a man fully agreeing with everybody.

'Ay,' said Mail, in the tone of a man who did not agree with everybody as a rule, though he did now; 'I knowed a' auctioneering feller once – a very friendly feller 'a was too. And so one hot day as I was walking down the front street o' Caster-bridge, jist below the King's Arms, I passed a' open winder and see him inside, stuck upon his perch, a-selling off. I jist nodded to en in a friendly way as I passed, and went my way, and thought no more about it. Well, next day, as I was oilen my boots by fuel-house door, if a letter didn't come wi' a bill charging me with a feather-bed, bolster, and pillers, that I had bid for at Mr Taylor's sale. The slim-faced martel [10] had knocked 'em down to me because I nodded to en in my friendly way; and I had to pay for 'em too. Now, I hold that that was coming it very close, Reuben?'

' 'Twas close, there's no denying,' said the general voice.

'Too close, 'twas,' said Reuben, in the rear of the rest. 'And as to Sam Lawson – poor heart! now he's dead and gone too! – I'll warrant, that if so be I've spent one hour in making hoops for that barrel, I've spent fifty, first and last. That's one of my hoops' – touching it with his elbow – 'that's one of mine, and that, and that, and all these.'

'Ah, Sam was a man,' said Mr Penny, contemplatively.

'Sam was!' said Bowman.

'Especially for a drap o' drink,' said the tranter.

'Good, but not religious-good,' suggested Mr Penny.

The tranter nodded. Having at last made the tap and hole quite ready, 'Now then, Suze, bring a mug,' he said. 'Here's luck to us, my sonnies!'

The tap went in, and the cider immediately squirted out in a horizontal shower over Reuben's hands, knees, and leggings, and into the eyes and neck of Charley, who, having temporarily put off his grief under pressure of more interesting proceedings, was squatting down and blinking near his father.

'There 'tis again!' said Mrs Dewy.

'Devil take the hole, the cask, and Sam Lawson too, that good cider should be wasted like this!' exclaimed the tranter. 'Your thumb! Lend me your thumb, Michael! Ram it in here, Michael! I must get a bigger tap, my sonnies.'

'Idd it cold inthide te hole?' inquired Charley of Michael, as he continued in a stooping posture with his thumb in the cork-hole.

'What wonderful odds and ends that chiel has in his head to be sure!' Mrs Dewy admiringly exclaimed from the distance. 'I lay a wager that he thinks more about how 'tis inside that barrel than in all the other parts of the world put together.'

All persons present put on a speaking countenance of admiration for the cleverness alluded to, in the midst of which Reuben returned. The operation was then satisfactorily performed; when Michael arose and stretched his head to the extremest fraction of height that his body would allow of, to restraighten his back and shoulders – thrusting out his arms and twisting his features to a mass of wrinkles to emphasize the relief acquired. A quart or two of the beverage was then brought to table, at which all the new arrivals reseated themselves with wide-spread knees, their eyes meditatively seeking out any speck or knot in the board upon which the gaze might precipitate itself.

'Whatever is father a-biding out in fuel-house so long for?' said the tranter. 'Never such a man as father for two things – cleaving up old dead apple-tree wood and playing the bass-viol. ' 'A'd pass his life between the two, that 'a would.' He stepped to the door and opened it.

'Father!'

'Ay!' rang thinly from round the corner.

'Here's the barrel tapped, and we all awaiting!'

A series of dull thuds, that had been heard without for some time past, now ceased; and after the light of a lantern had passed the window and made wheeling rays upon the ceiling inside the eldest of the Dewy family appeared.

The Assembled Quire

WILLIAM DEWY — otherwise grandfather William — was now about seventy; yet an ardent vitality still preserved a warm and roughened bloom upon his face, which reminded gardeners of the sunny side of a ripe ribstone-pippin; though a narrow strip of forehead, that was protected from the weather by lying above the line of his hat-brim, seemed to belong to some town man, so gentlemanly was its whiteness. His was a humorous and kindly nature, not unmixed with a frequent melancholy; and he had a firm religious faith. But to his neighbours he had no character in particular. If they saw him pass by their windows when they had been bottling off old mead, or when they had just been called long-headed men who might do anything in the world if they chose, they thought concerning him, 'Ah, there's that good-hearted man — open as a child!' If they saw him just after losing a shilling or half-a-crown, or accidentally letting fall a piece of crockery, they thought, 'There's that poor weak-minded man Dewy again! Ah, he's never done much in the world either!' If he passed when fortune neither smiled nor frowned on them, they merely thought him old William Dewy.

'Ah, so's — here you be! — Ah, Michael and Joseph and John — and you too, Leaf! a merry Christmas all! We shall have a rare log-wood fire directly, Reub, to reckon by the toughness of the job I had in cleaving 'em.' As he spoke he threw down an armful of logs which fell in the chimney-corner with a rumble, and looked at them with something of the admiring enmity he would have bestowed on living people who had been very obstinate in holding their own. 'Come in, grandfather James.'

Old James (grandfather on the maternal side) had simply called as a visitor. He lived in a cottage by himself, and many people considered him a miser; some, rather slovenly in his habits. He now came forward from behind grandfather William, and his stooping figure formed a well-illuminated picture as he passed towards the fire-place. Being by trade a mason, he wore a long linen apron reaching almost to his toes, corduroy breeches and gaiters, which, together with his boots, graduated in tints of whitish-brown by constant friction against lime and stone. He also wore a very stiff fustian coat, having folds at the elbows and shoulders as unvarying in their arrangement as those in a pair of bellows: the ridges and the projecting parts of the coat collectively exhibiting a shade different from that of the hollows, which were lined with small ditch-like accumulations of stone and mortar-dust. The extremely large side-pockets, sheltered beneath wide flaps, bulged out convexly whether empty or full; and as he was often engaged to work at buildings far away – his breakfasts and dinners being eaten in a strange chimney-corner, by a garden wall, on a heap of stones, or walking along the road – he carried in these pockets a small tin canister of butter, a small canister of sugar, a small canister of tea, a paper of salt, and a paper of pepper; the bread, cheese, and meat, forming the substance of his meals, hanging up behind him in his basket among the hammers and chisels. If a passer-by looked hard at him when he was drawing forth any of these, 'My buttery,' he said, with a pinched smile.

'Better try over number seventy-eight before we start, I suppose?' said William, pointing to a heap of old Christmas-carol books [11] on a side table.

'Wi' all my heart,' said the choir generally.

'Number seventy-eight was always a teaser – always. I can mind him ever since I was growing up a hard boy-chap.'

'But he's a good tune, and worth a mint o' practice,' said Michael.

'He is; though I've been mad enough wi' that tune at times to seize en and tear en all to linnit.[12] Ay, he's a splendid carrel – there's no denying that.'

'The first line is well enough,' said Mr Spinks; 'but when you come to "O, thou man," you make a mess o't.'

'We'll have another go into en, and see what we can make of the martel. Half-an-hour's hammering at en will conquer the toughness of en; I'll warn it.'

' 'Od rabbit it all!' said Mr Penny, interrupting with a flash of his spectacles, and at the same time clawing at something in the depths of a large side-pocket. 'If so be I hadn't been as scatter-brained and thirtingill as a chiel [13] I should have called at the schoolhouse wi' a boot as I cam up along. Whatever is coming to me I really can't estimate at all!'

'The brain has its weaknesses,' murmured Mr Spinks, waving his head ominously. Mr Spinks was considered to be a scholar, having once kept a nightschool, and always spoke up to that level.

'Well, I must call with en the first thing tomorrow. And I'll empt my pocket o' this last too, if you don't mind, Mrs Dewy.' He drew forth a last, and placed it on a table at his elbow. The eyes of three or four followed it.

'Well,' said the shoemaker, seeming to perceive that the interest the object had excited was greater than he had antici-pated, and warranted the last's being taken up again and ex-hibited; 'now, whose foot do ye suppose this last was made for? It was made for Geoffrey Day's father, over at Yalbury Wood. Ah, many's the pair o' boots he've had off the last! Well, when 'a died, I used the last for Geoffrey, and have ever since, though a little doctoring was wanted to make it do. Yes, a very queer natured last it is now, 'a b'lieve,' he continued, turning it over caressingly. 'Now, you notice that there' (pointing to a lump of leather bradded [14] to the toe), 'that's a very bad bunion that he've had ever since 'a was a boy. Now, this remarkable large piece' (pointing to a patch nailed to the side), 'shows a' acci-dent he received by the tread of a horse, that squashed his foot a'most to a pomace.[15] The horse-shoe came full-butt on this point, you see. And so I've just been over to Geoffrey's, to know if he wanted his bunion altered or made bigger in the new pair I'm making.'

During the latter part of this speech Mr Penny's left hand wandered towards the cider-cup as if the hand had no connec-tion with the person speaking; and bringing his sentence to an abrupt close all but the extreme margin of the bootmaker's face was eclipsed by the circular brim of the vessel.

'However, I was going to say,' continued Penny, putting

down the cup, 'I ought to have called at the school' – here he went groping again in the depths of his pocket – 'to leave this without fail, though I suppose the first thing tomorrow will do.'

He now drew forth and placed upon the table a boot – small, light, and prettily shaped – upon the heel of which he had been operating.

'The new schoolmistress's!'

'Ay, no less, Miss Fancy Day; as neat a little figure of fun as ever I see, and just husband-high.'

'Never Geoffrey's daughter Fancy?' said Bowman, as all glances present converged like wheelspokes upon the boot in the centre of them.

'Yes, sure,' resumed Mr Penny, regarding the boot as if that alone were his auditor; ' 'tis she that's come here schoolmistress. You knowed his daughter was in training?'

'Strange, isn't it, for her to be here Christmas-night, Master Penny?'

'Yes; but here she is, 'a b'lieve.'

'I know how she comes here – so I do!' chirruped one of the children.

'Why?' Dick inquired with subtle interest.

'Pa'son Maybold was afraid he couldn't manage us all tomorrow at the dinner, and he talked o' getting her just to come over and help him hand about the plates, and see we didn't make pigs of ourselves; and that's what she's come for!'

'And that's the boot, then,' continued its mender imaginatively, 'that she'll walk to church in tomorrow morning. I don't care to mend boots I don't make; but there's no knowing what it may lead to, and her father always comes to me.'

There, between the cider-mug and the candle, stood this interesting receptacle of the little unknown's foot; and a very pretty boot it was. A character, in fact – the flexible bend at the instep, the rounded localities of the small nestling toes, scratches from careless scampers now forgotten – all, as repeated in the tell-tale leather, evidencing a nature and a bias. Dick surveyed it with a delicate feeling that he had no right to do so without having first asked the owner of the foot's permission.

'Now, neighbours, though no common eye can see it,' the shoemaker went on, 'a man in the trade can see the likeness between this boot and that last, although that is so deformed as hardly to recall one of God's creatures, and this is one of as pretty a pair as you'd get for ten-and-sixpence in Casterbridge. To you, nothing; but 'tis father's voot and daughter's voot to me, as plain as houses.'

'I don't doubt there's a likeness, Master Penny – a mild likeness – a fantastical likeness,' said Spinks. 'But *I* han't got imagination enough to see it, perhaps.'

Mr Penny adjusted his spectacles.

'Now, I'll tell ye what happened to me once on this very point. You used to know Johnson the dairyman, William?'

'Ay, sure; I did.'

'Well, 'twasn't opposite his house, but a little lower down – by his paddock, in front o' Parkmaze Pool. I was a-bearing across towards Bloom's End, and lo and behold, there was a man just brought out o' the Pool, dead; he had un'rayed for a dip, but not being able to pitch it just there had gone in flop over his head. Men looked at en; women looked at en; children looked at en; nobody knowed en. He was covered wi' a sheet; but I catched sight of his voot, just showing out as they carried en along. "I don't care what name that man went by," I said, in my way, "but he's John Woodward's brother; I can swear to the family voot." At that very moment up comes John Woodward, weeping and teaving,[16] "I've lost my brother! I've lost my brother!"'

'Only to think of that!' said Mrs Dewy.

' 'Tis well enough to know this foot and that foot,' said Mr Spinks. ' 'Tis long-headed, in fact, as far as feet do go. I know little, 'tis true – I say no more; but show *me* a man's foot, and I'll tell you that man's heart.'

'You must be a cleverer feller, then, than mankind in jineral,' said the tranter.

'Well, that's nothing for me to speak of,' returned Mr Spinks. 'A man lives and learns. Maybe I've read a leaf or two in my time. I don't wish to say anything large, mind you; but nevertheless, maybe I have.'

'Yes, I know,' said Michael soothingly, 'and all the parish knows, that ye've read sommat of everything a'most, and have been a great filler of young folks' brains. Learning's a worthy thing, and ye've got it, Master Spinks.'

'I make no boast, though I may have read and thought a little; and I know – it may be from much perusing, but I make no boast – that by the time a man's head is finished 'tis almost time for him to creep underground. I am over forty-five.'

Mr Spinks emitted a look to signify that if his head was not finished, nobody's head ever could be.

'Talk of knowing people by their feet!' said Reuben. 'Rot me, my sonnies, then, if I can tell what a man is from all his members put together, oftentimes.'

'But still, look is a good deal,' observed grandfather William absently, moving and balancing his head till the tip of grandfather James's nose was exactly in a right line with William's eye and the mouth of a miniature cavern he was discerning in the fire. 'By the way,' he continued in a fresher voice, and looking up, 'that young creature, the schoolmis'ess, must be sung to tonight wi' the rest? If her ear is as fine as her face, we shall have enough to do to be up-sides with her.'

'What about her face?' said young Dewy.

'Well, as to that,' Mr Spinks replied, ' 'tis a face you can hardly gainsay. A very good pink face, as far as that do go. Still, only a face, when all is said and done.'

'Come, come, Elias Spinks, say she's a pretty maid and have done wi' her,' said the tranter, again preparing to visit the cider-barrel.

* IV *

Going the Rounds

SHORTLY after ten o'clock the singing-boys arrived at the tranter's house, which was invariably the place of meeting, and preparations were made for the start. The older men and musicians wore thick coats, with stiff perpendicular collars, and coloured handkerchiefs wound round and round the neck till the end came to hand, over all which they just showed their ears and noses, like people looking over a wall. The remainder, stalwart ruddy men and boys, were dressed mainly in snow-white smock-frocks, embroidered upon the shoulders and breasts in ornamental forms of hearts, diamonds, and zigzags. The cider-mug was emptied for the ninth time, the music-books were arranged, and the pieces finally decided upon. The boys in the meantime put the old horn-lanterns in order, cut candles into short lengths to fit the lanterns; and, a thin fleece of snow having fallen since the early part of the evening, those who had no leggings went to the stable and wound wisps of hay round their ankles to keep the insidious flakes from the interior of their boots.

Mellstock was a parish of considerable acreage, the hamlets composing it lying at a much greater distance from each other than is ordinarily the case. Hence several hours were consumed in playing and singing within hearing of every family, even if but a single air were bestowed on each. There was Lower Mellstock, the main village; half a mile from this were the church and vicarage, and a few other houses, the spot being rather lonely now, though in past centuries it had been the most thickly-populated quarter of the parish. A mile north-east lay the hamlet of Upper Mellstock, where the tranter lived; and at other points knots of cottages, besides solitary farmsteads and dairies.

Old William Dewy, with the violoncello, played the bass; his grandson Dick the treble violin; and Reuben and Michael Mail the tenor and second violins respectively. The singers consisted of four men and seven boys, upon whom devolved the task of carrying and attending to the lanterns, and holding the books open for the players. Directly music was the theme old William ever and instinctively came to the front.

'Now mind, neighbours,' he said, as they all went out one by one at the door, he himself holding it ajar and regarding them with a critical face as they passed, like a shepherd counting out his sheep. 'You two counter-boys, keep your ears open to Michael's fingering, and don't ye go straying into the treble part along o' Dick and his set, as ye did last year; and mind this especially when we be in "Arise, and hail." Billy Chimlen, don't you sing quite so raving mad as you fain would; and, all o' ye, whatever ye do, keep from making a great scuffle on the ground when we go in at people's gates; but go quietly, so as to strike up all of a sudden, like spirits.'

'Farmer Ledlow's first?'

'Farmer Ledlow first; the rest as usual.'

'And, Voss,' said the tranter terminatively, 'you keep house here till about half-past two; then heat the metheglin [17] and cider in the warmer you'll find turned up upon the copper; and bring it wi' the victuals to church-hatch, as th'st know.'

Just before the clock struck twelve they lighted the lanterns and started. The moon, in her third quarter, had risen since the snowstorm; but the dense accumulation of snow-cloud weakened her power to a faint twilight which was rather pervasive of the landscape than traceable to the sky. The breeze had gone down, and the rustle of their feet and tones of their speech echoed with an alert rebound from every post, boundary-stone, and ancient wall they passed, even where the distance of the echo's origin was less than a few yards. Beyond their own slight noises nothing was to be heard save the occasional bark of foxes in the direction of Yalbury Wood, or the brush of a rabbit among the grass now and then as it scampered out of their way.

Most of the outlying homesteads and hamlets had been

visited by about two o'clock; they then passed across the out-skirts of a wooded park toward the main village, nobody being at home at the Manor. Pursuing no recognized track, great care was necessary in walking lest their faces should come in con-tact with the low-hanging boughs of the old lime-trees, which in many spots formed dense overgrowths of interlaced branches.

'Times have changed from the times they used to be,' said Mail, regarding nobody can tell what interesting old panoramas with an inward eye, and letting his outward glance rest on the ground because it was as convenient a position as any. 'People don't care much about us now! I've been thinking we must be almost the last left in the county of the old string players? Barrel-organs, and the things next door to 'em that you blow wi' your foot, have come in terribly of late years.'[18]

'Ay!' said Bowman shaking his head; and old William on seeing him did the same thing.

'More's the pity,' replied another. 'Time was – long and merry ago now! – when not one of the varmits was to be heard of; but it served some of the quires right. They should have stuck to strings as we did, and kept out clarinets, and done away with serpents.[19] If you'd thrive in musical religion, stick to strings, says I.'

'Strings be safe soul-lifters, as far as that do go,' said Mr Spinks.

'Yet there's worse things than serpents,' said Mr Penny. 'Old things pass away, 'tis true; but a serpent was a good old note: a deep rich note was the serpent.'

'Clar'nets, however, be bad at all times,' said Michael Mail. 'One Christmas – years agone now, years – I went the rounds wi' the Weatherbury quire. 'Twas a hard frosty night, and the keys of all the clar'nets froze – ah, they did freeze! – so that 'twas like drawing a cork every time a key was opened; and the players o' 'em had to go into a hedger-and-ditcher's chimley-corner, and thaw their clar'nets every now and then. An icicle o' spet hung down from the end of every man's clar'net a span long; and as to fingers – well, there, if ye'll believe me, we had no fingers at all, to our knowing.'

'I can well bring back to my mind,' said Mr Penny, 'what I said to poor Joseph Ryme (who took the treble part in Chalk-Newton Church for two-and-forty year) when they thought of having clar'nets there. "Joseph," I said says I, "depend upon't, if so be you have them tooting clar'nets you'll spoil the whole set-out. Clar'nets were not made for the service of the Lard; you can see it by looking at 'em," I said. And what came o't? Why, souls, the parson set up a barrel-organ on his own account within two years o' the time I spoke, and the old quire went to nothing.'

'As far as look is concerned,' said the tranter, 'I don't for my part see that a fiddle is much nearer heaven than a clar'net. 'Tis further off. There's always a rakish, scampish twist about a fiddle's looks that seems to say the Wicked One had a hand in making o'en; while angels be supposed to play clar'nets in heaven, or som'at like 'em if ye may believe picters.'

'Robert Penny, you was in the right,' broke in the eldest Dewy. 'They should ha' stuck to strings. Your brass-man is a rafting [20] dog – well and good; your reed-man is a dab at stirring ye – well and good; your drum-man is a rare bowel-shaker – good again. But I don't care who hears me say it, nothing will spak to your heart wi' the sweetness o' the man of strings!'

'Strings for ever!' said little Jimmy.

'Strings alone would have held their ground against all the new comers in creation.' ('True, true!' said Bowman.) 'But clarinets was death.' ('Death they was!' said Mr Penny.) 'And harmonions,' William continued in a louder voice, and getting excited by these signs of approval, 'harmonions and barrel-organs' ('Ah!' and groans from Spinks) 'be miserable – what shall I call 'em? – miserable –'

'Sinners,' suggested Jimmy, who made large strides like the men and did not lag behind with the other little boys.

'Miserable dumbledores!' [21]

'Right, William, and so they be – miserable dumbledores!' said the choir with unanimity.

By this time they were crossing to a gate in the direction of the school which, standing on a slight eminence at the junction of three ways, now rose in unvarying and dark flatness against the sky. The instruments were retuned, and all the band entered the school enclosure, enjoined by old William to keep upon the grass.

'Number seventy-eight,' he softly gave out as they formed round in a semicircle, the boys opening the lanterns to get a clearer light, and directing their rays on the books.

Then passed forth into the quiet night an ancient and time-worn hymn, embodying a quaint Christianity in words orally transmitted from father to son through several generations down to the present characters, who sang them out right earnestly:

> Remember Adam's fall,
>   O thou Man:
> Remember Adam's fall
>   From Heaven to Hell.
> Remember Adam's fall;
> How he hath condemn'd all
> In Hell perpetual
>   There for to dwell.
>
> Remember God's goodnesse,
>   O thou Man:
> Remember God's goodnesse,
>   His promise made.
> Remember God's goodnesse;
> He sent His Son sinlesse
> Our ails for to redress;
>   Be not afraid!
>
> In Bethlehem He was born,
>   O thou Man:
> In Bethlehem He was born,
>   For mankind's sake.
> In Bethlehem He was born,
> Christmas-day i' the morn:
> Our Saviour thought no scorn
>   Our faults to take.

Give thanks to God alway,
    O thou Man:
Give thanks to God alway
    With heart-most joy.
Give thanks to God alway
On this our joyful day:
Let all men sing and say,
    Holy, Holy!

Having concluded the last note they listened for a minute or two, but found that no sound issued from the schoolhouse.

'Four breaths, and then, "O, what unbounded goodness!" number fifty-nine,' said William.[22]

This was duly gone through, and no notice whatever seemed to be taken of the performance.

'Good guide us, surely 'tisn't a' empty house, as befell us in the year thirty-nine and forty-three!' said old Dewy.

'Perhaps she's jist come from some musical city, and sneers at our doings?' the tranter whispered.

''Od rabbit her!' said Mr Penny, with an annihilating look at a corner of the school chimney, 'I don't quite stomach her, if this is it. Your plain music well done is as worthy as your other sort done bad, a' b'lieve, souls; so say I.'

'Four breaths, and then the last,' said the leader authoritatively. ' "Rejoice, ye Tenants of the Earth," number sixty-four.'

At the close, waiting yet another minute, he said in a clear loud voice, as he had said in the village at that hour and season for the previous forty years –

'A merry Christmas to ye!'

V

The Listeners

WHEN the expectant stillness consequent upon the exclamation had nearly died out of them all, an increasing light made itself visible in one of the windows of the upper floor. It came so close to the blind that the exact position of the flame could be perceived from the outside. Remaining steady for an instant, the blind went upward from before it, revealing to thirty concentrated eyes a young girl framed as a picture by the window architrave, and unconsciously illuminating her countenance to a vivid brightness by a candle she held in her left hand, close to her face, her right hand being extended to the side of the window. She was wrapped in a white robe of some kind, whilst down her shoulders fell a twining profusion of marvellously rich hair, in a wild disorder which proclaimed it to be only during the invisible hours of the night that such a condition was discoverable. Her bright eyes were looking into the grey world outside with an uncertain expression, oscillating between courage and shyness, which, as she recognized the semicircular group of dark forms gathered before her, transformed itself into pleasant resolution.

Opening the window, she said lightly and warmly —

'Thank you, singers, thank you!'

Together went the window quickly and quietly, and the blind started downward on its return to its place. Her fair forehead and eyes vanished; her little mouth; her neck and shoulders; all of her. Then the spot of candlelight shone nebulously as before; then it moved away.

'How pretty!' exclaimed Dick Dewy.

'If she'd been rale wexwork she couldn't ha' been comelier,' said Michael Mail.

'As near a thing to a spiritual vision as ever *I* wish to see!' said tranter Dewy.

'O, sich I never, never see!' said Leaf fervently.

All the rest, after clearing their throats and adjusting their hats, agreed that such a sight was worth singing for.

'Now to Farmer Shiner's, and then replenish our insides, father?' said the tranter.

'Wi' all my heart,' said old William, shouldering his bass-viol.

Farmer Shiner's was a queer lump of a house, standing at the corner of a lane that ran into the principal thoroughfare. The upper windows were much wider than they were high, and this feature, together with a broad bay-window where the door might have been expected, gave it by day the aspect of a human countenance turned askance, and wearing a sly and wicked leer. Tonight nothing was visible but the outline of the roof upon the sky.

The front of this building was reached, and the preliminaries arranged as usual.

'Four breaths, and number thirty-two, "Behold the Morning Star," ' said old William.

They had reached the end of the second verse, and the fiddlers were doing the up bow-stroke previously to pouring forth the opening chord of the third verse, when, without a light appearing or any signal being given a roaring voice exclaimed –

'Shut up, woll 'ee! Don't make your blaring row here! A feller wi' a headache enough to split his skull likes a quiet night!'

Slam went the window.

'Hullo, that's a' ugly blow for we!' said the tranter, in a keenly appreciative voice, and turning to his companions.

'Finish the carrel, all who be friends of harmony!' commanded old William; and they continued to the end.

'Four breaths, and number nineteen!' said William firmly. 'Give it him well; the quire can't be insulted in this manner!'

A light now flashed into existence, the window opened, and the farmer stood revealed as one in a terrific passion.

'Drown en! – drown en!' the tranter cried, fiddling frantically. 'Play fortissimy, and drown his spaking!'

'Fortissimy!' said Michael Mail, and the music and singing

waxed so loud that it was impossible to know what Mr Shiner had said, was saying, or was about to say; but wildly flinging his arms and body about in the forms of capital Xs and Ys, he appeared to utter enough invectives to consign the whole parish to perdition.

'Very onseemly – very!' said old William, as they retired. 'Never such a dreadful scene in the whole round o' my carrel practice – never! And he a churchwarden!'

'Only a drap o' drink got into his head,' said the tranter. 'Man's well enough when he's in his religious frame. He's in his worldly frame now. Must ask en to our bit of a party tomorrow night, I suppose, and so put en in humour again. We bear no mortal man ill-will.'

They now crossed Mellstock Bridge, and went along an embowered path beside the Froom towards the church and vicarage, meeting Voss with the hot mead and bread-and-cheese as they were approaching the churchyard. This determined them to eat and drink before proceeding further, and they entered the church and ascended to the gallery. The lanterns were opened, and the whole body sat round against the wall on benches and whatever else was available, and made a hearty meal. In the pauses of conversation there could be heard through the floor overhead a little world of undertones and creaks from the halting clockwork, which never spread further than the tower they were born in, and raised in the more meditative minds a fancy that here lay the direct pathway of Time.

Having done eating and drinking they again tuned the instruments, and once more the party emerged into the night air.

'Where's Dick?' said old Dewy.

Every man looked round upon every other man, as if Dick might have been transmuted into one or the other; and then they said they didn't know.

'Well now, that's what I call very nasty of Master Dicky, that I do,' said Michael Mail.

'He've clinked off home-along, depend upon't,' another suggested, though not quite believing that he had.

'Dick!' exclaimed the tranter, and his voice rolled sonorously forth among the yews.

He suspended his muscles rigid as stone whilst listening for an answer, and finding he listened in vain, turned to the assemblage.

'The treble man too! Now if he'd been a tenor or counter chap, we might ha' contrived the rest o't without en, you see. But for a quire to lose the treble, why, my sonnies, you may so well lose your...' The tranter paused, unable to mention an image vast enough for the occasion.

'Your head at once,' suggested Mr Penny.

The tranter moved a pace as if it were puerile of people to complete sentences when there were more pressing things to be done.

'Was ever heard such a thing as a young man leaving his work half done and turning tail like this!'

'Never,' replied Bowman, in a tone signifying that he was the last man in the world to wish to withhold the formal finish required of him.

'I hope no fatal tragedy has overtook the lad!' said his grandfather.

'O no,' replied tranter Dewy placidly. 'Wonder where he's put that there fiddle of his. Why that fiddle cost thirty shillings, and good words besides. Somewhere in the damp, without doubt; that instrument will be unglued and spoilt in ten minutes – ten! ay, two.'

'What in the name o' righteousness can have happened?' said old William, more uneasily. 'Perhaps he's drownded!'

Leaving their lanterns and instruments in the belfry they retraced their steps along the waterside track. 'A strapping lad like Dick d'know better than let anything happen onawares,' Reuben remarked. 'There's sure to be some poor little scram [23] reason for't staring us in the face all the while.' He lowered his voice to a mysterious tone: 'Neighbours, have ye noticed any sign of a scornful woman in his head, or suchlike?'

'Not a glimmer of such a body. He's as clear as water yet.'

'And Dicky said he should never marry,' cried Jimmy, 'but live at home always along wi' mother and we!'

'Ay, ay, my sonny; every lad has said that in his time.'

They had now again reached the precincts of Mr Shiner's, but hearing nobody in that direction, one or two went across to the schoolhouse. A light was still burning in the bedroom, and though the blind was down the window had been slightly opened, as if to admit the distant notes of the carollers to the ears of the occupant of the room.

Opposite the window, leaning motionless against a beech tree, was the lost man, his arms folded, his head thrown back, his eyes fixed upon the illuminated lattice.

'Why, Dick, is that thee? What b'st doing here?'

Dick's body instantly flew into a more rational attitude, and his head was seen to turn east and west in the gloom as if endeavouring to discern some proper answer to that question; and at last he said in rather feeble accents –

'Nothing, father.'

'Th'st take long enough time about it then, upon my body,' said the tranter as they all turned anew towards the vicarage.

'I thought you hadn't done having snap ²⁴ in the gallery,' said Dick.

'Why, we've been traypsing and rambling about, looking everywhere, and thinking you'd done fifty deathly things, and here have you been at nothing at all!'

'The stupidness lies in that point of it being nothing at all,' murmured Mr Spinks.

The vicarage front was their next field of operation, and Mr Maybold, the lately-arrived incumbent, duly received his share of the night's harmonies. It was hoped that by reason of his profession he would have been led to open the window, and an extra carol in quick time was added to draw him forth. But Mr Maybold made no stir.

'A bad sign!' said old William, shaking his head.

However, at that same instant a musical voice was heard exclaiming from inner depths of bedclothes –

'Thanks, villagers!'

'What did he say?' asked Bowman, who was rather dull of hearing. Bowman's voice, being therefore loud, had been heard by the vicar within.

'I said, "Thanks, villagers!"' cried the vicar again.

'Oh, we didn't hear 'ee the first time!' cried Bowman.

'Now don't for heaven's sake spoil the young man's temper by answering like that!' said the tranter.

'You won't do that, my friends!' the vicar shouted.

'Well to be sure, what ears!' said Mr Penny in a whisper. 'Beats any horse or dog in the parish, and depend upon't that's a sign he's a proper clever chap.'

'We shall see that in time,' said the tranter.

Old William, in his gratitude for such thanks from a comparatively new inhabitant, was anxious to play all the tunes over again; but renounced his desire on being reminded by Reuben that it would be best to leave well alone.

'Now putting two and two together,' the tranter continued, as they went their way over the hill, and across to the last remaining houses; 'that is, in the form of that young female vision we zeed just now, and this young tenor-voiced parson, my belief is she'll wind en round her finger, and twist the pore young feller about like the figure of 8 – that she will, my sonnies.'

* VI *

Christmas Morning

THE choir at last reached their beds, and slept like the rest of the parish. Dick's slumbers, through the three or four hours remaining for rest, were disturbed and slight; an exhaustive variation upon the incidents that had passed that night in connection with the school-window going on in his brain every moment of the time.

In the morning, do what he would – go upstairs, downstairs, out of doors, speak of the wind and weather, or what not – he could not refrain from an unceasing renewal, in imagination, of that interesting enactment. Tilted on the edge of one foot he stood beside the fireplace, watching his mother grilling rashers; but there was nothing in grilling, he thought, unless the Vision grilled. The limp rasher hung down between the bars of the gridiron like a cat in a child's arms; but there was nothing in similes unless She uttered them. He looked at the daylight shadows of a yellow hue, dancing with the firelight shadows in blue on the whitewashed chimney corner, but there was nothing in shadows. 'Perhaps the new young wom – sch – Miss Fancy Day will sing in church with us this morning,' he said.

The tranter looked a long time before he replied, 'I fancy she will; and yet I fancy she won't.'

Dick implied that such a remark was rather to be tolerated than admired; though deliberateness in speech was known to have, as a rule, more to do with the machinery of the tranter's throat than with the matter enunciated.

They made preparations for going to church as usual; Dick with extreme alacrity, though he would not definitely consider why he was so religious. His wonderful nicety in brushing and cleaning his best light boots had features which elevated it to the rank of an art. Every particle and speck of last week's mud was scraped and brushed from toe and heel; new blacking from the packet was carefully mixed and made use of, regardless of expense. A coat was laid on and polished; then another coat for increased blackness; and lastly a third, to give the perfect and mirror-like jet which the hoped-for rencounter demanded.

It being Christmas-day, the tranter prepared himself with Sunday particularity. Loud sousing and snorting noises were heard to proceed from a tub in the back quarters of the dwelling, proclaiming that he was there performing his great Sunday wash, lasting half-an-hour, to which his washings on working-day mornings were mere flashes in the pan. Vanishing into the outhouse with a large brown towel, and the above-named bubblings and snortings being carried on for about twenty minutes, the tranter would appear round the edge of the door, smelling like a summer fog, and looking as if he had just narrowly escaped a watery grave with the loss of much of his clothes, having since been weeping bitterly till his eyes were red; a crystal drop of water hanging ornamentally at the bottom of each ear, one at the tip of his nose, and others in the form of spangles about his hair.

After a great deal of crunching upon the sanded stone floor by the feet of father, son, and grandson as they moved to and fro in these preparations, the bass-viol and fiddles were taken from their nook, and the strings examined and screwed a little above concert-pitch that they might keep their tone when the service began, to obviate the awkward contingency of having to retune them at the back of the gallery during a cough, sneeze, or amen – an inconvenience which had been known to arise in damp wintry weather.

The three left the door and paced down Mellstock-lane and across the ewe-lease,[25] bearing under their arms the instruments in faded green-baize bags, and old brown music-books in their hands; Dick continually finding himself in advance of the other two, and the tranter moving on with toes turned outwards to an enormous angle.

At the foot of an incline the church became visible through the north gate, or 'church hatch', as it was called here. Seven agile figures in a clump were observable beyond, which proved to be the choristers waiting; sitting on an altar-tomb to pass the time, and letting their heels dangle against it. The musicians being now in sight the youthful party scampered off and rattled up the old wooden stairs of the gallery like a regiment of cavalry; the other boys of the parish waiting outside and observing birds, cats, and other creatures till the vicar entered, when they suddenly subsided into sober church-goers, and passed down the aisle with echoing heels.

The gallery of Mellstock Church had a status and sentiment of its own. A stranger there was regarded with a feeling altogether differing from that of the congregation below towards him. Banished from the nave as an intruder whom no originality could make interesting, he was received above as a curiosity that no unfitness could render dull. The gallery, too, looked down upon and knew the habits of the nave to its remotest peculiarity, and had an extensive stock of exclusive information about it; while the nave knew nothing of the gallery folk, as gallery folk, beyond their loud-sounding minims and chest notes. Such topics as that the clerk was always chewing tobacco except at the moment of crying amen; that he had a dust-hole in his pew; that during the sermon certain young daughters of the village had left off caring to read anything so mild as the marriage service for some years, and now regularly studied the one which chronologically follows it,[26] that a pair of lovers touched fingers through a knot-hole between their pews in the manner ordained by their great exemplars, Pyramus and Thisbe; that Mrs Ledlow, the farmer's wife, counted her money and reckoned her week's marketing expenses during the first lesson – all news to those below – were stale subjects here.

Old William sat in the centre of the front row, his violoncello between his knees and two singers on each hand. Behind him, on the left, came the treble singers and Dick; and on the right the tranter and the tenors. Further back was old Mail with the altos and supernumeraries.

But before they had taken their places, and whilst they were standing in a circle at the back of the gallery practising a psalm or two, Dick cast his eyes over his grandfather's shoulder, and saw the vision of the past night enter the porch-door as methodically as if she had never been a vision at all. A new atmosphere seemed suddenly to be puffed into the ancient edifice by her movement, which made Dick's body and soul tingle with novel sensations. Directed by Shiner, the churchwarden, she proceeded to the small aisle on the north side of the chancel, a spot now allotted to a throng of Sunday-school girls, and distinctly visible from the gallery-front by looking under the curve of the furthermost arch on that side.

Before this moment the church had seemed comparatively empty – now it was thronged; and as Miss Fancy rose from her knees and looked around her for a permanent place in which to deposit herself – finally choosing the remotest corner – Dick began to breathe more freely the warm new air she had brought with her; to feel rushings of blood, and to have impressions that there was a tie between her and himself visible to all the congregation.

Ever afterwards the young man could recollect individually each part of the service of that bright Christmas morning, and the trifling occurrences which took place as its minutes slowly drew along; the duties of that day dividing themselves by a complete line from the services of other times. The tunes they that morning essayed remained with him for years, apart from all others; also the text; also the appearance of the layer of dust upon the capitals of the piers; that the holly-bough in the chancel archway was hung a little out of the centre – all the ideas, in short, that creep into the mind when reason is only exercising its lowest activity through the eye.

By chance or by fate, another young man who attended Mellstock Church on that Christmas morning had towards the end of the service the same instinctive perception of an interesting presence, in the shape of the same bright maiden, though his emotion reached a far less developed stage. And there was this difference, too, that the person in question was surprised at his condition, and sedulously endeavoured to reduce himself to his normal state of mind. He was the young vicar, Mr Maybold.

The music on Christmas mornings was frequently below the standard of church-performances at other times. The boys were sleepy from the heavy exertions of the night; the men were slightly wearied; and now, in addition to these constant reasons, there was a dampness in the atmosphere that still further aggravated the evil. Their strings, from the recent long exposure to the night air, rose whole semitones, and snapped with a loud twang at the most silent moment; which necessitated more retiring than ever to the back of the gallery, and made the gallery throats quite husky with the quantity of coughing and hemming required for tuning in. The vicar looked cross.

When the singing was in progress there was suddenly discovered to be a strong and shrill reinforcement from some point, ultimately found to be the school-girls' aisle. At every attempt it grew bolder and more distinct. At the third time of singing, these intrusive feminine voices were as mighty as those of the regular singers; in fact, the flood of sound from this quarter assumed such an individuality, that it had a time, a key, almost a tune of its own, surging upwards when the gallery plunged downwards, and the reverse.

Now this had never happened before within the memory of man. The girls, like the rest of the congregation, had always been humble and respectful followers of the gallery; singing at sixes and sevens if without gallery leaders; never interfering with the ordinances of these practised artists – having no will, union, power, or proclivity except it was given them from the established choir enthroned above them.

A good deal of desperation became noticeable in the gallery throats and strings, which continued throughout the musical portion of the service. Directly the fiddles were laid down, Mr Penny's spectacles put in their sheath, and the text had been given out, an indignant whispering began.

'Did ye hear that, souls?' Mr Penny said, in a groaning breath.

'Brazen-faced hussies!' said Bowman.

'True; why, they were every note as loud as we, fiddles and all, if not louder!'

'Fiddles and all!' echoed Bowman bitterly.

'Shall anything saucier be found than united 'ooman?' Mr Spinks murmured.

'What I want to know is,' said the tranter (as if he knew already, but that civilization required the form of words), 'what business people have to tell maidens to sing like that when they don't sit in a gallery, and never have entered one in their lives? That's the question, my sonnies.'

' 'Tis the gallery have got to sing, all the world knows,' said Mr Penny. 'Why, souls, what's the use o' the ancients spending scores of pounds to build galleries if people down in the lowest depths of the church sing like that at a moment's notice?'

'Really, I think we useless ones had better march out of church, fiddles and all!' said Mr Spinks, with a laugh which, to a stranger, would have sounded mild and real. Only the initiated body of men he addressed could understand the horrible bitterness of irony that lurked under the quiet words 'useless ones', and the ghastliness of the laughter apparently so natural.

'Never mind! Let 'em sing too – 'twill make it all the louder – hee, hee!' said Leaf.

'Thomas Leaf, Thomas Leaf! Where have you lived all your life?' said grandfather William sternly.

The quailing Leaf tried to look as if he had lived nowhere at all.

'When all's said and done, my sonnies,' Reuben said, 'there'd have been no real harm in their singing if they had let nobody hear 'em, and only jined in now and then.'

'None at all,' said Mr Penny. 'But though I don't wish to accuse people wrongfully, I'd say before my lord judge that I could hear every note o' that last psalm come from 'em as much as from us – every note as if 'twas their own.'

'Know it! ah, I should think I did know it!' Mr Spinks was heard to observe at this moment without reference to his fellow-players – shaking his head at some idea he seemed to see floating before him, and smiling as if he were attending a funeral at the time. 'Ah, do I or don't I know it!'

No one said, 'Know what?' because all were aware from experience that what he knew would declare itself in process of time.

'I could fancy last night that we should have some trouble

wi' that young man,' said the tranter, pending the continuance of Spinks's speech, and looking towards the unconscious Mr Maybold in the pulpit.

'I fancy,' said old William, rather severely, 'I fancy there's too much whispering going on to be of any spiritual use to gentle or simple.' Then folding his lips and concentrating his glance on the vicar, he implied that none but the ignorant would speak again; and accordingly there was silence in the gallery, Mr Spinks's telling speech remaining for ever unspoken.

Dick had said nothing, and the tranter little, on this episode of the morning; for Mrs Dewy at breakfast expressed it as her intention to invite the youthful leader of the culprits to the small party it was customary with them to have on Christmas night – a piece of knowledge which had given a particular brightness to Dick's reflections since he had received it. And in the tranter's slightly-cynical nature, party feeling was weaker than in the other members of the choir, though friendliness and faithful partnership still sustained in him a hearty earnestness on their account.

VII

The Tranter's Party

DURING the afternoon unusual activity was seen to prevail about the precincts of tranter Dewy's house. The flagstone floor was swept of dust, and a sprinkling of the finest yellow sand from the innermost stratum of the adjoining sand-pit lightly scattered thereupon. Then were produced large knives and forks, which had been shrouded in darkness and grease since the last occasion of the kind, and bearing upon their sides, 'Shear-steel, warranted,' in such emphatic letters of assurance, that the warranter's name was not required as further proof, and not given. The key was left in the tap of the cider-barrel instead of being carried in a pocket. And finally the tranter had to stand up in the room and let his wife wheel him round like a turnstile, to see if anything discreditable was visible in his appearance.

'Stand still till I've been for the scissors,' said Mrs Dewy.

The tranter stood as still as a sentinel at the challenge.

The only repairs necessary were a trimming of one or two whiskers that had extended beyond the general contour of the mass; a like trimming of a slightly-frayed edge visible on his shirt-collar; and a final tug at a grey hair – to all of which operations he submitted in resigned silence, except the last, which produced a mild 'Come, come, Ann', by way of expostulation.

'Really, Reuben, 'tis quite a disgrace to see such a man,' said Mrs Dewy, with the severity justifiable in a long-tried companion, giving him another turn round, and picking several of Smiler's hairs from the shoulder of his coat. Reuben's thoughts seemed engaged elsewhere, and he yawned. 'And the collar of your coat is a shame to behold – so plastered with dirt, or dust, or grease, or something. Why, wherever could you have got it?'

' 'Tis my warm nater in summer-time, I suppose. I always did get in such a heat when I bustle about.'

'Ay, the Dewys always were such a coarse-skinned family. There's your brother Bob just as bad – as fat as a porpoise – wi' his low, mean, "How'st do, Ann?" whenever he meets me. I'd "How'st do" him indeed![27] If the sun only shines out a minute, there be you all streaming in the face – I never see!'

'If I be hot week-days, I must be hot Sundays.'

'If any of the girls should turn after their father 'twill be a bad look-out for 'em, poor things! None of my family was sich vulgar sweaters, not one of 'em. But, Lord-a-mercy, the Dewys! I don't know how ever I cam' into such a family!'

'Your woman's weakness when I asked ye to jine us. That's how it was, I suppose.' But the tranter appeared to have heard some such words from his wife before, and hence his answer had not the energy it might have shown if the inquiry had possessed the charm of novelty.

'You never did look so well in a pair o' trousers as in them,' she continued in the same unimpassioned voice, so that the unfriendly criticism of the Dewy family seemed to have been more normal than spontaneous. 'Such a cheap pair as 'twas too. As big as any man could wish to have, and lined inside, and double-lined in the lower parts, and an extra piece of stiffening at the bottom. And 'tis a nice high cut that comes up right under your armpits, and there's enough turned down inside the seams to make half a pair more, besides a piece of cloth left that will make an honest waistcoat – all by my contriving in buying the stuff at a bargain, and having it made up under my eye. It only shows what may be done by taking a little trouble, and not going straight to the rascally tailors.'

The discourse was cut short by the sudden appearance of Charley on the scene, with a face and hands of hideous blackness, and a nose like a guttering candle. Why, on that particularly cleanly afternoon, he should have discovered that the chimney-crook and chain from which the hams were suspended should have possessed more merits and general interest as playthings than any other articles in the house, is a question for nursing mothers to decide. However, the humour seemed to lie in the result being, as has been seen, that any given player with these articles was in the long-run daubed with soot. The last that was seen of Charley by daylight after this piece of in-genuity was when in the act of vanishing from his father's presence round the corner of the house – looking back over his shoulder with an expression of great sin on his face, like Cain as the Outcast in Bible pictures.

The guests had all assembled, and the tranter's party had reached that degree of development which accords with ten o'clock p.m. in rural assemblies. At that hour the sound of a fiddle in process of tuning was heard from the inner pantry.

'That's Dick,' said the tranter. 'That lad's crazy for a jig.'

'Dick! Now I cannot – really, I cannot have any dancing at all till Christmas-day is out,' said old William emphatically. 'When the clock ha' done striking twelve, dance as much as ye like.'

'Well, I must say there's reason in that, William,' said Mrs Penny. 'If you do have a party on Christmas-night, 'tis only fair and honourable to the sky-folk to have it a sit-still party. Jigging parties be all very well on the Devil's holidays; but a jigging party looks suspicious now. O yes; stop till the clock strikes, young folk – so say I.'

It happened that some warm mead accidentally got into Mr Spinks's head about this time.

'Dancing,' he said, 'is a most strengthening, livening, and courting movement, 'specially with a little beverage added! And dancing is good. But why disturb what is ordained, Richard and Reuben, and the company zhinerally? Why, I ask, as far as that do go?'

'Then nothing till after twelve,' said William.

Though Reuben and his wife ruled on social points, religious questions were mostly disposed of by the old man, whose firm-ness on this head quite counterbalanced a certain weakness in his handling of domestic matters. The hopes of the younger members of the household were therefore relegated to a dist-ance of one hour and three-quarters – a result that took visible shape in them by a remote and listless look about the eyes – the singing of songs being permitted in the interim.

At five minutes to twelve the soft tuning was again heard in the back quarters; and when at length the clock had whizzed forth the last stroke, Dick appeared ready primed, and the instruments were boldly handled; old William very readily taking the bass-viol from its accustomed nail, and touching the strings as irreligiously as could be desired.

The country-dance called the 'Triumph, or Follow my Lover', was the figure with which they opened.[28] The tranter took for his partner Mrs Penny, and Mrs Dewy was chosen by Mr Penny, who made so much of his limited height by a judicious carriage of the head, straightening of the back, and important flashes of his spectacle-glasses, that he seemed almost as tall as the tranter. Mr Shiner, age about thirty-five, farmer and church-warden, a character principally composed of a crimson stare, vigorous breath, and a watch-chain, with a mouth hanging on a dark smile but never smiling, had come quite willingly to the party, and showed a wondrous obliviousness of all his antics on the previous night. But the comely, slender, prettily-dressed prize Fancy Day fell to Dick's lot, in spite of some private machinations of the farmer, for the reason that Mr Shiner, as a richer man, had shown too much assurance in asking the favour, whilst Dick had been duly courteous.

We gain a good view of our heroine as she advances to her place in the ladies' line. She belonged to the taller division of middle height. Flexibility was her first characteristic, by which she appeared to enjoy the most easeful rest when she was in gliding motion. Her dark eyes – arched by brows of so keen, slender, and soft a curve that they resembled nothing so much as two slurs in music – showed primarily a bright sparkle each. This was softened by a frequent thoughtfulness, yet not so frequent as to do away, for more than a few minutes at a time, with a certain coquettishness; which in its turn was never so decided as to banish honesty. Her lips imitated her brows in their clearly-cut outline and softness of bend; and her nose was well shaped – which is saying a great deal, when it is remembered that there are a hundred pretty mouths and eyes for one pretty nose. Add to this, plentiful knots of dark-brown hair, a gauzy dress of white with blue facings; and the slightest idea may be gained of the young maiden who showed, amidst the rest of the dancing-ladies, like a flower among vegetables. And so the dance proceeded. Mr Shiner, according to the interesting rule laid down, deserted his own partner and made off down the middle with this fair one of Dick's – the pair appearing from the top of the room like two persons tripping down a lane to be married. Dick trotted behind with what was intended to be a look of composure, but which was, in fact, a rather silly expression of feature – implying, with too much earnestness, that such an elopement could not be tolerated. Then they turned and came back, when Dick grew more rigid around his mouth, and blushed with ingenuous ardour as he joined hands with the rival and formed the arch over his lady's head, which presumably gave the figure its name; relinquishing her again at setting to partners, when Mr Shiner's new chain quivered in every link, and all the loose flesh upon the tranter – who here came into action again – shook like jelly. Mrs Penny, being always rather concerned for her personal safety when she danced with the tranter, fixed her face to a chronic smile of timidity the whole time it lasted – a peculiarity which filled her features with wrinkles, and reduced her eyes to little straight lines like hyphens, as she jigged up and down opposite him; repeating in her own person not only his proper movements, but also the minor flourishes which the richness of the tranter's imagination led him to introduce from time to time – an imitation which had about it something of slavish obedience, not unmixed with fear.

The ear-rings of the ladies now flung themselves wildly about, turning violent summersaults, banging this way and that, and then swinging quietly against the ears sustaining them. Mrs Crumpler – a heavy woman, who, for some reason which nobody ever thought worth inquiry, danced in a clean apron – moved so smoothly through the figure that her feet were never seen; conveying to imaginative minds the idea that she rolled on castors.

Minute after minute glided by, and the party reached the period when ladies' back-hair begins to look forgotten and dissipated; when a perceptible dampness makes itself apparent upon the faces even of delicate girls – a ghastly dew having for some time rained from the features of their masculine partners; when skirts begin to be torn out of their gathers; when elderly people, who have stood up to please their juniors, begin to feel sundry small tremblings in the region of the knees, and to wish the interminable dance was at Jericho; when (at country parties of the thorough sort) waistcoats begin to be unbuttoned, and when the fiddlers' chairs have been wriggled, by the frantic bowing of their occupiers, to a distance of about two feet from where they originally stood.

Fancy was dancing with Mr Shiner. Dick knew that Fancy, by the law of good manners, was bound to dance as pleasantly with one partner as with another; yet he could not help suggesting to himself that she need not have put *quite* so much spirit into her steps, nor smiled *quite* so frequently whilst in the farmer's hands.

'I'm afraid you didn't cast off,' said Dick mildly to Mr Shiner, before the latter man's watch-chain had done vibrating from a recent whirl.

Fancy made a motion of accepting the correction; but her partner took no notice, and proceeded with the next movement with an affectionate bend towards her.

'That Shiner's too fond of her,' the young man said to himself as he watched them. They came to the top again, Fancy smiling warmly towards her partner, and went to their places.

'Mr Shiner, you didn't cast off,' said Dick, for want of something else to demolish him with; casting off himself, and being put out at the farmer's irregularity.

'Perhaps I shan't cast off for any man,' said Mr Shiner.

'I think you ought to, sir.'

Dick's partner, a young lady of the name of Lizzy – called Lizz for short – tried to mollify.

'I can't say that I myself have much feeling for casting off,' she said.

'Nor I,' said Mrs Penny, following up the argument; 'especially if a friend and neighbour is set against it. Not but that 'tis a terrible tasty thing in good hands and well done; yes, indeed, so say I.'

'All I meant was,' said Dick, rather sorry that he had spoken correctly to a guest, 'that 'tis in the dance; and a man has hardly any right to hack and mangle what was ordained by the regular dance-maker, who, I daresay, got his living by making 'em, and thought of nothing else all his life.'

'I don't like casting off: then very well; I cast off for no dance-maker that ever lived.'

Dick now appeared to be doing mental arithmetic, the act being really an effort to present to himself, in an abstract form, how far an argument with a formidable rival ought to be carried when that rival was his mother's guest. The dead-lock was put an end to by the stamping arrival up the middle of the tranter, who, despising minutiæ on principle, started a theme of his own.

'I assure you, neighbours,' he said, 'the heat of my frame no tongue can tell!' He looked around and endeavoured to give, by a forcible gaze of self-sympathy, some faint idea of the truth.

Mrs Dewy formed one of the next couple.

'Yes,' she said in an auxiliary tone, 'Reuben always was such a hot man.'

Mrs Penny implied the species of sympathy that such a class of affliction required by trying to smile and to look grieved at the same time.

'If he only walk round the garden of a Sunday morning his shirt-collar is as limp as no starch at all,' continued Mrs Dewy, her countenance lapsing parenthetically into a housewifely expression of concern at the reminiscence.

'Come, come, you women-folk; 'tis hands-across — come, come!' said the tranter; and the conversation ceased for the present.

* VIII *

They Dance more Wildly

DICK had at length secured Fancy for that most delightful of country-dances, opening with six-hands-round.[29]

'Before we begin,' said the tranter, 'my proposal is, that 'twould be a right and proper plan for every mortal man in the dance to pull off his jacket, considering the heat.'

'Such low notions as you have, Reuben! Nothing but strip will go down with you when you are a-dancing. Such a hot man as he is!'

'Well, now, look here, my sonnies,' he argued to his wife, whom he often addressed in the plural masculine for economy of epithet merely; 'I don't see that. You dance and get hot as fire; therefore you lighten your clothes. Isn't that nature and reason for gentle and simple? If I strip by myself and not necessary, 'tis rather pot-housey I own; but if we stout chaps strip one and all, why, 'tis the native manners of the country, which no man can gainsay? Hey – what did you say, my sonnies?'

'Strip we will!' said the three other heavy men who were in the dance; and their coats were accordingly taken off and hung in the passage, whence the four sufferers from heat soon reappeared marching in close column, with flapping shirt-sleeves, and having as common to them all a general glance of being now a match for any man or dancer in England or Ireland. Dick, fearing to lose ground in Fancy's good opinion, retained his coat like the rest of the thinner men; and Mr Shiner did the same from superior knowledge.

And now a further phase of revelry had disclosed itself. It was the time of night when a guest may write his name in the dust upon the tables and chairs, and a bluish mist pervades the atmosphere, becoming a distinct halo round the candles; when people's nostrils, wrinkles, and crevices in general seem to be getting gradually plastered up; when the very fiddlers as well as the dancers get red in the face, the dancers having advanced further still towards incandescence, and entered the cadaverous phase; the fiddlers no longer sit down, but kick back their chairs and saw madly at the strings with legs firmly spread and eyes closed, regardless of the visible world. Again and again did Dick share his Love's hand with another man, and wheel round; then, more delightfully, promenade in a circle with her all to himself, his arm holding her waist more firmly each time, and his elbow getting further and further behind her back, till the distance reached was rather noticeable; and, most blissful, swinging to places shoulder to shoulder, her breath curling round his neck like a summer zephyr that had strayed from its proper date. Threading the couples one by one they reached the bottom, when there arose in Dick's mind a minor misery lest the tune should end before they could work their way to the top again, and have anew the same exciting run down through. Dick's feelings on actually reaching the top in spite of his doubts were supplemented by a mortal fear that the fiddling might even stop at this supreme moment; which prompted him to convey a stealthy whisper to the far-gone musicians to the effect that they were not to leave off till he and his partner had reached the bottom of the dance once more, which remark was replied to by the nearest of those convulsed and quivering men by a private nod to the anxious young man between two semiquavers of the tune, and a simultaneous 'All right, ay, ay', without opening the eyes. Fancy was now held so closely that Dick and she were practically one person. The room became to Dick like a picture in a dream; all that he could remember of it afterwards being the look of the fiddlers going to sleep as humming-tops sleep, by increasing their motion and hum, together with the figures of grandfather James and old Simon Crumpler sitting by the chimney-corner talking and nodding in dumb-show, and beating the air to their emphatic sentences like people near a threshing machine.

The dance ended. 'Piph-h-h-h!' said tranter Dewy, blowing out his breath in the very finest stream of vapour that a man's lips could form. 'A regular tightener, that one, sonnies!' He wiped his forehead, and went to the cider and ale mugs on the table.

'Well!' said Mrs Penny, flopping into a chair, 'my heart haven't been in such a thumping state of uproar since I used to sit up on old Midsummer-eves to see who my husband was going to be.'

'And that's getting on for a good few years ago now, from what I've heard you tell,' said the tranter without lifting his eyes from the cup he was filling. Being now engaged in the business of handing round refreshments he was warranted in keeping his coat off still, though the other heavy men had resumed theirs.

'And a thing I never expected would come to pass, if you'll believe me, came to pass then,' continued Mrs Penny. 'Ah, the first spirit ever I see on a Midsummer-eve was a puzzle to me when he appeared, a hard puzzle, so say I!'

'So I should have fancied,' said Elias Spinks.

'Yes,' said Mrs Penny, throwing her glance into past times and talking on in a running tone of complacent abstraction, as if a listener were not a necessity. 'Yes; never was I in such a taking as on that Midsummer-eve! I sat up, quite determined to see if John Wildway was going to marry me or no. I put the bread-and-cheese and beer quite ready, as the witch's book ordered, and I opened the door, and I waited till the clock struck twelve, my nerves all alive and so strained that I could feel every one of 'em twitching like bell-wires. Yes, sure! and when the clock had struck, lo and behold I could see through the door a *little small* man in the lane wi' a shoemaker's apron on.'

Here Mr Penny stealthily enlarged himself half an inch.

'Now, John Wildway,' Mrs Penny continued, 'who courted me at that time, was a shoemaker, you see, but he was a very fair-sized man, and I couldn't believe that any such a little small man had anything to do wi' me, as anybody might. But on he came, and crossed the threshold – not John, but actually the same little man in the shoemaker's apron –'

'You needn't be so mighty particular about little and small!' said her husband.

'In he walks, and down he sits, and O my goodness me, didn't I flee upstairs, body and soul hardly hanging together! Well, to cut a long story short, by-long and by-late John Wild-way and I had a miff and parted; and lo and behold, the coming man came! Penny asked me if I'd go snacks with him, and afore I knew what I was about a'most, the thing was done.'

'I've fancied you never knew better in your life; but I mid be mistaken,' said Mr Penny in a murmur.

After Mrs Penny had spoken, there being no new occupation for her eyes she still let them stay idling on the past scenes just related, which were apparently visible to her in the centre of the room. Mr Penny's remark received no reply.

During this discourse the tranter and his wife might have been observed standing in an unobtrusive corner in mysterious closeness to each other, a just perceptible current of intelligence passing from each to each, which had apparently no relation whatever to the conversation of their guests, but much to their sustenance. A conclusion of some kind having at length been drawn, the palpable confederacy of man and wife was once more obliterated, the tranter marching off into the pantry humming a tune that he couldn't quite recollect, and then breaking into the words of a song of which he could remember about one line and a quarter. Mrs Dewy spoke a few words about preparations for a bit of supper.

That elder portion of the company which loved eating and drinking put on a look to signify that till this moment they had quite forgotten that it was customary to expect suppers on these occasions; going even further than this politeness of feature, and starting irrelevant subjects, the exceeding flatness and forced tone of which rather betrayed their object. The younger members said they were quite hungry, and that supper would be delightful though it was so late.

Good luck attended Dick's love-passes during the meal. He sat next Fancy, and had the thrilling pleasure of using permanently a glass which had been taken by Fancy in mistake; of letting the outer edge of the sole of his boot touch the lower verge of her skirt; and to add to these delights the cat, which had lain unobserved in her lap for several minutes, crept across into his own, touching him with fur that had touched her hand a moment before. There were, besides, some little pleasures in the shape of helping her to vegetable she didn't want, and when it had nearly alighted on her plate taking it across for his own use, on the plea of waste not, want not. He also, from time to time, sipped sweet sly glances at her profile; noticing the set of her head, the curve of her throat, and other artistic pro- perties of the lively goddess, who the while kept up a rather free, not to say too free, conversation with Mr Shiner sitting opposite; which, after some uneasy criticism, and much shifting of argument backwards and forwards in Dick's mind, he de- cided not to consider of alarming significance.

'A new music greets our ears now,' said Miss Fancy, alluding, with the sharpness that her position as village sharpener de- manded, to the contrast between the rattle of knives and forks and the late notes of the fiddlers.

'Ay; and I don't know but what 'tis sweeter in tone when you get above forty,' said the tranter; 'except, in faith, as regards father there. Never such a mortal man as he for tunes. They do move his soul; don't 'em, father?'

The eldest Dewy smiled across from his distant chair an assent to Reuben's remark.

'Spaking of being moved in soul,' said Mr Penny, 'I shall never forget the first time I heard the "Dead March". 'Twas at poor Corp'l Nineman's funeral at Casterbridge. It fairly made my hair creep and fidget about like a vlock of sheep – ah, it did, souls! And when they had done, and the last trump had sounded, and the guns was fired over the dead hero's grave, a' icy-cold drop o' moist sweat hung upon my forehead, and another upon my jawbone. Ah, 'tis a very solemn thing!'

'Well, as to father in the corner there,' the tranter said, pointing to old William, who was in the act of filling his mouth; 'he'd starve to death for music's sake now, as much as when he was a boy-chap of fifteen.'

'Truly, now,' said Michael Mail, clearing the corner of his throat in the manner of a man who meant to be convincing; 'there's a friendly tie of some sort between music and eating.' He lifted the cup to his mouth, and drank himself gradually backwards from a perpendicular position to a slanting one, during which time his looks performed a circuit from the wall opposite him to the ceiling overhead. Then clearing the other corner of his throat: 'Once I was a-setting in the little kitchen of the Dree Mariners at Casterbridge,[30] having a bit of dinner, and a brass band struck up in the street. Such a beautiful band as that were! I was setting eating fried liver and lights, I well can mind – ah, I was! and to save my life, I couldn't help chawing to the tune. Band played six-eight time; six-eight chaws I, willynilly. Band plays common; common time went my teeth among the liver and lights as true as a hair. Beautiful 'twere! Ah, I shall never forget that there band!'

'That's as tuneful a thing as ever I heard of,' said grandfather James, with the absent gaze which accompanies profound criticism.

'I don't like Michael's tuneful stories then,' said Mrs Dewy. 'They are quite coarse to a person o' decent taste.'

Old Michael's mouth twitched here and there, as if he wanted to smile but didn't know where to begin, which gradually settled to an expression that it was not displeasing for a nice woman like the tranter's wife to correct him.

'Well, now,' said Reuben, with decisive earnestness, 'that sort o' coarse touch that's so upsetting to Ann's feelings is to my mind a recommendation; for it do always prove a story to be true. And for the same reason, I like a story with a bad moral. My sonnies, all true stories have a coarse touch or a bad moral, depend upon't. If the story-tellers could ha' got decency and good morals from true stories, who'd have troubled to invent parables?' Saying this the tranter arose to fetch a new stock of cider, ale, mead, and home-made wines.

Mrs Dewy sighed and appended a remark (ostensibly behind her husband's back, though that the words should reach his ears distinctly was understood by both): 'Such a man as Dewy is! Nobody do know the trouble I have to keep that man barely respectable. And did you ever hear too – just now at supper-time – talking about "taties" with Michael in such a work-folk way. Well, 'tis what I was never brought up to! With our family 'twas never less than "taters", and very often "pertatoes" outright; mother was so particular and nice with us girls: there was no family in the parish that kept themselves up more than we.'

The hour of parting came. Fancy could not remain for the night because she had engaged a woman to wait up for her. She disappeared temporarily from the flagging party of dancers, and then came downstairs wrapped up and looking altogether a different person from whom she had been hitherto, in fact (to Dick's sadness and disappointment), a woman somewhat reserved and of a phlegmatic temperament – nothing left in her of the romping girl that she had seemed but a short quarter-hour before, who had not minded the weight of Dick's hand upon her waist, nor shirked the purlieus of the mistletoe.

'What a difference!' thought the young man – hoary cynic *pro tem*. 'What a miserable deceiving difference between the manners of a maid's life at dancing times and at others! Look at this lovely Fancy! Through the whole past evening touchable, squeezable – even kissable! For whole half-hours I held her so close to me that not a sheet of paper could have been slipped between us; and I could feel her heart only just outside my own, her life beating on so close to mine, that I was aware of every breath in it. A flit is made upstairs – a hat and a cloak put on – and I no more dare to touch her than –' Thought failed him, and he returned to realities.

But this was an endurable misery in comparison with what followed. Mr Shiner and his watch-chain, taking the intrusive advantage that ardent bachelors who are going homeward along the same road as a pretty young woman always do take of that circumstance, came forward to assure Fancy – with a total disregard of Dick's emotions, and in tones which were certainly not frigid – that he (Shiner) was not the man to go to bed before seeing his Lady Fair safe within her own door – not he, nobody should say he was that; – and that he would not leave her side an inch till the thing was done – drown him if he would. The proposal was assented to by Miss Day, in Dick's foreboding judgement, with one degree – or at any rate, an appreciable fraction of a degree – of warmth beyond that required by a disinterested desire for protection from the dangers of the night.

All was over; and Dick surveyed the chair she had last occupied, looking now like a setting from which the gem has been torn. There stood her glass, and the romantic teaspoonful of elder wine at the bottom that she couldn't drink by trying ever so hard, in obedience to the mighty arguments of the tranter (his hand coming down upon her shoulder the while like a Nasmyth hammer),[31] but the drinker was there no longer. There were the nine or ten pretty little crumbs she had left on her plate; but the eater was no more seen.

There seemed a disagreeable closeness of relationship between himself and the members of his family now that they were left alone again face to face. His father seemed quite offensive for appearing to be in just as high spirits as when the guests were there; and as for grandfather James (who had not yet left), he was quite fiendish in being rather glad they were gone.

'Really,' said the tranter, in a tone of placid satisfaction, 'I've had so little time to attend to myself all the evenen that I mean to enjoy a quiet meal now! A slice of this here ham – neither too fat nor too lean – so; and then a drop of this vinegar and pickles – there, that's it – and I shall be as fresh as a lark again! And to tell the truth, my sonny, my inside has been as dry as a lime-basket all night.'

'I like a party very well once in a while,' said Mrs Dewy, leaving off the adorned tones she had been bound to use throughout the evening and returning to the natural marriage voice; 'but, Lord, 'tis such a sight of heavy work next day! What with the dirty plates, and knives and forks, and dust and smother, and bits kicked off your furniture, and I don't know what all, why a body could a'most wish there were no such things as Christmases. . . Ah'h dear!' she yawned, till the clock in the corner had ticked several beats. She cast her eyes round upon the displaced, dust-laden furniture, and sat down overpowered at the sight.

'Well, I be getting all right by degrees, thank the Lord for't!' said the tranter cheerfully through a mangled mass of ham and bread, without lifting his eyes from his plate, and chopping away with his knife and fork as if he were felling trees. 'Ann, you may as well go on to bed at once, and not bide there making such sleepy faces; you look as long-favoured as a fiddle, upon my life, Ann. There, you must be wearied out, 'tis true. I'll do the doors and draw up the clock; and you go on, or you'll be as white as a sheet tomorrow.'

'Ay; I don't know whether I shan't or no.' The matron passed her hand across her eyes to brush away the film of sleep till she got upstairs.

Dick wondered how it was that when people were married they could be so blind to romance; and was quite certain that if he ever took to wife that dear impossible Fancy, he and she would never be so dreadfully practical and undemonstrative of the Passion as his father and mother were. The most extraordinary thing was that all the fathers and mothers he knew were just as undemonstrative as his own.

* IX *

Dick calls at the School

THE early days of the year drew on, and Fancy, having spent the holiday weeks at home, returned again to Mellstock.

Every spare minute of the week following her return was used by Dick in accidentally passing the schoolhouse in his journeys about the neighbourhood; but not once did she make herself visible. A handkerchief belonging to her had been providentially found by his mother in clearing the rooms the day after that of the dance; and by much contrivance Dick got it handed over to him, to leave with her at any time he should be near the school after her return. But he delayed taking the extreme measure of calling with it lest, had she really no sentiment of interest in him, it might be regarded as a slightly absurd errand, the reason guessed, and the sense of the ludicrous, which was rather keen in her, do his dignity considerable injury in her eyes; and what she thought of him, even apart from the question of her loving, was all the world to him now.

But the hour came when the patience of love at twenty-one could endure no longer. One Saturday he approached the school with a mild air of indifference, and had the satisfaction of seeing the object of his quest at the further end of her garden, trying, by the aid of a spade and gloves, to root a bramble that had intruded itself there.

He disguised his feelings from some suspicious-looking cottage-windows opposite by endeavouring to appear like a man in a great hurry of business, who wished to leave the handkerchief and have done with such trifling errands.

This endeavour signally failed; for on approaching the gate he found it locked to keep the children, who were playing 'cross-dadder'[32] in the front, from running into her private grounds.

She did not see him; and he could only think of one thing to be done, which was to shout her name.

'Miss Day!'

The words were uttered with a jerk and a look meant to imply to the cottages opposite that he was now simply one who liked shouting as a pleasant way of passing his time, without any reference to persons in gardens. The name died away, and the unconscious Miss Day continued digging and pulling as before.

He screwed himself up to enduring the cottage-windows yet more stoically, and shouted again. Fancy took no notice whatever.

He shouted the third time, with desperate vehemence, turning suddenly about and retiring a little distance as if it were by no means for his own pleasure that he had come.

This time she heard him, came down the garden, and entered the school at the back. Footsteps echoed across the interior, the door opened, and three-quarters of the blooming young schoolmistress's face and figure stood revealed before him; a slice on her left-hand side being cut off by the edge of the door. Having surveyed and recognized him she came to the gate.

At sight of him had the pink of her cheeks increased, lessened, or did it continue to cover its normal area of ground? It was a question meditated several hundreds of times by her visitor in after-hours – the meditation, after wearying involutions, always ending in one way, that it was impossible to say.

'Your handkerchief: Miss Day: I called with.' He held it out spasmodically and awkwardly. 'Mother found it: under a chair.'

'O, thank you very much for bringing it, Mr Dewy. I couldn't think where I had dropped it.'

Now Dick, not being an experienced lover – indeed, never before having been engaged in the practice of love-making at all, except in a small schoolboy way – could not take advantage of the situation; and out came the blunder which afterwards cost him so many bitter moments and a sleepless night: –

'Good-morning, Miss Day.'

'Good-morning, Mr Dewy.'

The gate was closed; she was gone; and Dick was standing

outside, unchanged in his condition from what he had been before he called. Of course the Angel was not to blame – a young woman living alone in a house could not ask him indoors unless she had known him better – he should have kept her outside before floundering into that fatal farewell. He wished that before he called he had realized more fully than he did the pleasure of being about to call; and turned away.

PART THE SECOND

SPRING

Passing by the School

IT followed that as the spring advanced Dick walked abroad much more frequently than had hitherto been usual with him, and was continually finding that his nearest way to or from home lay by the road which skirted the garden of the school. The first-fruits of his perseverance were that, on turning the angle on the nineteenth journey by that track, he saw Miss Fancy's figure, clothed in a dark-grey dress, looking from a high open window upon the crown of his hat. The friendly greeting resulting from this rencounter was considered so valuable an elixir that Dick passed still oftener; and by the time he had almost trodden a little path under the fence where never a path was before, he was rewarded with an actual meeting face to face on the open road before her gate. This brought another meeting, and another, Fancy faintly showing by her bearing that it was a pleasure to her of some kind to see him there; but the sort of pleasure she derived, whether exultation at the hope her exceeding fairness inspired, or the true feeling which was alone Dick's concern, he could not anyhow decide, although he meditated on her every little movement for hours after it was made.

A Meeting of the Quire

IT was the evening of a fine spring day. The descending sun appeared as a nebulous blaze of amber light, its outline being lost in cloudy masses hanging round it like wild locks of hair.

The chief members of Mellstock parish choir were standing in a group in front of Mr Penny's workshop in the lower village. They were all brightly illuminated, and each was backed up by a shadow as long as a steeple; the lowness of the source of light rendering the brims of their hats of no use at all as a protection to the eyes.

Mr Penny's was the last house in that part of the parish, and stood in a hollow by the roadside; so that cart-wheels and horses' legs were about level with the sill of his shop-window. This was low and wide, and was open from morning till evening, Mr Penny himself being invariably seen working inside like a framed portrait of a shoemaker by some modern Moroni.[33] He sat facing the road, with a boot on his knees and the awl in his hand, only looking up for a moment as he stretched out his arms and bent forward at the pull, when his spectacles flashed in the passer's face with a shine of flat whiteness, and then returned again to the boot as usual. Rows of lasts, small and large, stout and slender, covered the wall which formed the background, in the extreme shadow of which a kind of dummy was seen sitting, in the shape of an apprentice with a string tied round his hair (probably to keep it out of his eyes). He smiled at remarks that floated in from without, but was never known to answer them in Mr Penny's presence. Outside the window the upper-leather of a Wellington-boot was usually hung, pegged to a board as if to dry. No sign was over his door; in fact – as with old banks and mercantile houses – advertising in any shape was scorned, and it would have been felt as beneath his dignity to paint up, for the benefit of strangers, the name of an establishment whose trade came solely by connection based on personal respect.

His visitors now came and stood on the outside of his window, sometimes leaning against the sill, sometimes moving a pace or two backwards and forwards in front of it. They talked with deliberate gesticulations to Mr Penny, enthroned in the shadow of the interior.

'I do like a man to stick to men who be in the same line o' life – o' Sundays, anyway – that I do so.'

' 'Tis like all the doings of folk who don't know what a day's work is, that's what I say.'

'My belief is the man's not to blame; 'tis *she* – she's the bitter weed!'

'No, not altogether. He's a poor gawk-hammer.[34] Look at his sermon yesterday.'

'His sermon was well enough, a very good guessable sermon, only he couldn't put it into words and speak it. That's all was the matter wi' the sermon. He hadn't been able to get it past his pen.'

'Well – ay, the sermon might have been good; for, 'tis true, the sermon of Old Eccl'iastes himself lay in Eccl'iastes's ink-bottle afore he got it out.'

Mr Penny, being in the act of drawing the last stitch tight, could afford time to look up and throw in a word at this point.

'He's no spouter – that must be said, 'a b'lieve.'

' 'Tis a terrible muddle sometimes with the man, as far as spout do go,' said Spinks.

'Well, we'll say nothing about that,' the tranter answered; 'for I don't believe 'twill make a penneth o' difference to we poor martels here or hereafter whether his sermons be good or bad, my sonnies.'

Mr Penny made another hole with his awl, pushed in the thread, and looked up and spoke again at the extension of arms.

' 'Tis his goings-on, souls, that's what it is.' He clenched his features for an Herculean addition to the ordinary pull, and continued, 'The first thing he done when he came here was to be hot and strong about church business.'

'True,' said Spinks; 'that was the very first thing he done.'

Mr Penny, having now been offered the ear of the assembly, accepted it, ceased stitching, swallowed an unimportant quantity of air as if it were a pill, and continued:

'The next thing he do do is to think about altering the church, until he found 'twould be a matter o' cost and what not, and then not to think no more about it.'

'True: that was the next thing he done.'

'And the next thing was to tell the young chaps that they were not on no account to put their hats in the christening font during service.'

'True.'

'And then 'twas this, and then 'twas that, and now 'tis –'

Words were not forcible enough to conclude the sentence, and Mr Penny gave a huge pull to signify the concluding word.

'Now 'tis to turn us out of the quire neck and crop,' said the tranter after an interval of half a minute, not by way of explaining the pause and pull, which had been quite understood, but as a means of keeping the subject well before the meeting.

Mrs Penny came to the door at this point in the discussion. Like all good wives, however much she was inclined to play the Tory to her husband's Whiggism, and *vice versâ*, in times of peace, she coalesced with him heartily enough in time of war.

'It must be owned he's not all there,' she replied in a general way to the fragments of talk she had heard from indoors. 'Far below poor Mr Grinham' (the late vicar).

'Ay, there was this to be said for he, that you were quite sure he'd never come mumbudgeting[35] to see ye, just as you were in the middle of your work, and put you out with his fuss and trouble about ye.'

'Never. But as for this new Mr Maybold, though he mid be a very well-intending party in that respect, he's unbearable; for as to sifting your cinders, scrubbing your floors, or emptying your slops, why, you can't do it. I assure you I've not been able to empt them for several days, unless I throw 'em up the chimley or out of winder; for as sure as the sun you meet him at the door, coming to ask how you are, and 'tis such a confusing thing to meet a gentleman at the door when ye are in the mess o' washing.'

' 'Tis only for want of knowing better, poor gentleman,' said the tranter. 'His meaning's good enough. Ay, your pa'son comes by fate: 'tis heads or tails, like pitch-halfpenny, and no choosing; so we must take en as he is, my sonnies, and thank God he's no worse, I suppose.'

'I fancy I've seen him look across at Miss Day in a warmer way than Christianity asked for,' said Mrs Penny musingly; 'but I don't quite like to say it.'

'O no; there's nothing in that,' said grandfather William.

'If there's nothing, we shall see nothing,' Mrs Penny replied in the tone of a woman who might possibly have private opinions still.

'Ah, Mr Grinham was the man!' said Bowman. 'Why, he never troubled us wi' a visit from year's end to year's end. You might go anywhere, do anything: you'd be sure never to see him.'

'Yes; he was a right sensible pa'son,' said Michael. 'He never entered our door but once in his life, and that was to tell my poor wife – ay, poor soul, dead and gone now, as we all shall! – that as she was such a' old aged person, and lived so far from the church, he didn't at all expect her to come any more to the service.'

'And 'a was a very jinerous gentleman about choosing the psalms and hymns o' Sundays. "Confound ye," says he, "blare and scrape what ye will, but don't bother me!"'

'And he was a very honourable man in not wanting any of us to come and hear him if we were all on-end for a jaunt or spree, or to bring the babies to be christened if they were inclined to squalling. There's good in a man's not putting a parish to unnecessary trouble.'

'And there's this here man never letting us have a bit o' peace; but keeping on about being good and upright till 'tis carried to such a pitch as I never see the like afore nor since!'

'No sooner had he got here than he found the font wouldn't hold water, as it hadn't for years off and on; and when I told him that Mr Grinham never minded it, but used to spet upon his vinger and christen 'em just as well, 'a said, "Good Heavens! Send for a workman immediate. What place have I come to!" Which was no compliment to us, come to that.'[36]

'Still, for my part,' said old William, 'though he's arrayed against us, I like the hearty borus-snorus[37] ways of the new pa'son.'

'You, ready to die for the quire,' said Bowman reproachfully, 'to stick up for the quire's enemy, William!'

'Nobody will feel the loss of our church-work so much as I,' said the old man firmly: 'that you d'all know. I've a-been in the quire man and boy ever since I was a chiel of eleven. But for all that 'tisn't in me to call the man a bad man, because I truly and sincerely believe en to be a good young feller.'

Some of the youthful sparkle that used to reside there animated William's eye as he uttered the words, and a certain nobility of aspect was also imparted to him by the setting sun, which gave him a Titanic shadow at least thirty feet in length, stretching away to the east in outlines of imposing magnitude, his head finally terminating upon the trunk of a grand old oak-tree.

'Mayble's a hearty feller enough,' the tranter replied, 'and will spak to you be you dirty or be you clane. The first time I met en was in a drong,[38] and though 'a didn't know me no more than the dead 'a passed the time of day. "D'ye do!" he said says he, nodding his head. "A fine day." Then the second time I met en was full-buff[39] in town street, when my breeches were tore into a long strent[40] by getting through a copse of thorns and brimbles for a short cut home-along; and not wanting to disgrace the man by spaking in that state, I fixed my eye on the weathercock to let en pass me as a stranger. But no: "How d'ye do, Reuben?" says he, right hearty, and shook my hand. If I'd been dressed in silver spangles from top to toe the man couldn't have been civiller.'

At this moment Dick was seen coming up the village-street, and they turned and watched him.

III

A Turn in the Discussion

'I'M afraid Dick's a lost man,' said the tranter.

'What? – no!' said Mail, implying by his manner that it was a far commoner thing for his ears to report what was not said than that his judgement should be at fault.

'Ay,' said the tranter, still gazing at Dick's unconscious advance. 'I don't at all like what I see! There's too many o' them looks out of the winder without noticing anything; too much shining of boots; too much peeping round corners; too much looking at the clock; telling about clever things *she* did till you be sick of it, and then upon a hint to that effect a horrible silence about her. I've walked the path once in my life and know the country, neighbours; and Dick's a lost man!' The tranter turned a quarter round and smiled a smile of miserable satire at the setting new moon, which happened to catch his eye.

The others became far too serious at this announcement to allow them to speak; and they still regarded Dick in the distance.

' 'Twas his mother's fault,' the tranter continued, 'in asking the young woman to our party last Christmas. When I eyed the blue frock and light heels o' the maid, I had my thoughts directly. "God bless thee, Dicky my sonny," I said to myself, "there's a delusion for thee!" '

'They seemed to be rather distant in manner last Sunday, I thought?' Mail tentatively observed, as became one who was not a member of the family.

'Ay, that's a part of the zickness. Distance belongs to it, slyness belongs to it, queerest things on earth belongs to it! There, 'tmay as well come early as late s'far as I know. The sooner begun, the sooner over; for come it will.'

'The question I ask is,' said Mr Spinks, connecting into one thread the two subjects of discourse, as became a man learned in rhetoric, and beating with his hand in a way which signified that the manner rather than the matter of his speech was to be observed, 'how did Mr Maybold know she could play the organ? You know we had it from her own lips, as far as lips go, that she has never, first or last, breathed such a thing to him; much less that she ever would play.'

In the midst of this puzzle Dick joined the party, and the news which had caused such a convulsion among the ancient musicians was unfolded to him. 'Well,' he said, blushing at the allusion to Miss Day, 'I know by some words of hers that she has a particular wish not to play, because she is a friend of ours; and how the alteration comes I don't know.'

'Now, this is my plan,' said the tranter, reviving the spirit of the discussion by the infusion of new ideas, as was his custom – 'this is my plan; if you don't like it, no harm's done. We all know one another very well, don't we, neighbours?'

That they knew one another very well was received as a statement which, though familiar, should not be omitted in introductory speeches.

'Then I say this' – and the tranter in his emphasis slapped down his hand on Mr Spinks's shoulder with a momentum of several pounds, upon which Mr Spinks tried to look not in the least startled – 'I say that we all move down-along straight as a line to Pa'son Mayble's when the clock has gone six tomorrow night. There we one and all stand in the passage; then one or two of us go in and spak to en, man and man, and say, "Pa'son Mayble, every tradesman d'like to have his own way in his workshop, and Mellstock Church is yours. Instead of turning us out neck and crop, let us stay on till Christmas, and we'll gie way to the young woman, Mr Mayble, and make no more ado about it. And we shall always be quite willing to touch our hats when we meet ye, Mr Mayble, just as before." That sounds very well? Hey?'

'Proper well, in faith, Reuben Dewy.'

'And we won't sit down in his house; 'twould be looking too familiar when only just reconciled?'

'No need at all to sit down. Just do our duty man and man,

turn round, and march out – he'll think all the more of us for it.'

'I hardly think Leaf had better go wi' us?' said Michael, turning to Leaf and taking his measure from top to bottom by the eye. 'He's so terrible silly that he might ruin the concern.'

'He don't want to go much; do ye, Thomas Leaf?' said William.

'Hee-hee! no; I don't want to. Only a teeny bit!'

'I be mortal afeard, Leaf, that you'll never be able to tell how many cuts d'take to sharpen a spar,' said Mail.

'I never had no head, never! that's how it happened to happen, hee-hee!'

They all assented to this, not with any sense of humiliating Leaf by disparaging him after an open confession, but because it was an accepted thing that Leaf didn't in the least mind having no head, that deficiency of his being an unimpassioned matter of parish history.

'But I can sing my treble!' continued Thomas Leaf, quite delighted at being called a fool in such a friendly way; 'I can sing my treble well as any maid, or married woman either, and better! And if Jim had lived, I should have had a clever brother! Tomorrow is poor Jim's birthday. He'd ha' been twenty-six if he'd lived till tomorrow.'

'You always seem very sorry for Jim,' said old William musingly.

'Ah! I do. Such a stay to mother as he'd always have been! She'd never have had to work in her old age if he had continued strong, poor Jim!'

'What was his age when 'a died?'

'Four hours and twenty minutes, poor Jim. 'A was born as might be at night; and 'a didn't last as might be till the morning. No, 'a didn't last. Mother called en Jim on the day that would ha' been his christening-day if he had lived; and she's always thinking about en. You see he died so very young.'

'Well, 'twas rather youthful,' said Michael.

'Now to my mind that woman is very romantical on the matter o' children?' said the tranter, his eye sweeping his audience.

'Ah, well she mid be,' said Leaf. 'She had twelve regular one after another, and they all, except myself, died very young; either before they was born or just afterwards.'

'Pore feller, too. I suppose th'st want to come wi' us?' the tranter murmured.

'Well, Leaf, you shall come wi' us as yours is such a melancholy family,' said old William rather sadly.

'I never see such a melancholy family as that afore in my life,' said Reuben. 'There's Leaf's mother, poor woman! Every morning I see her eyes mooning out through the panes of glass like a pot-sick winder-flower; and as Leaf sings a very high treble, and we don't know what we should do without en for upper G, we'll let en come as a trate, poor feller.'

'Ay, we'll let en come, 'a b'lieve,' said Mr Penny, looking up, as the pull happened to be at that moment.

'Now,' continued the tranter, dispersing by a new tone of voice these digressions about Leaf; 'as to going to see the pa'son, one of us might call and ask en his meaning, and 'twould be just as well done; but it will add a bit of a flourish to the cause if the quire waits on him as a body. Then the great thing to mind is, not for any of our fellers to be nervous; so before starting we'll one and all come to my house and have a rasher of bacon; then every man-jack het[41] a pint of cider into his inside; then we'll warm up an extra drop wi' some mead and a bit of ginger; every one take a thimbleful – just a glimmer of a drop, mind ye, no more, to finish off his inner man – and march off to Pa'son Mayble. Why, sonnies, a man's not himself till he is fortified wi' a bit and a drop? We shall be able to look any gentleman in the face then without shrink or shame.'

Mail recovered from a deep meditation and downward glance into the earth in time to give a cordial approval to this line of action, and the meeting adjourned.

IV

The Interview with the Vicar

AT six o'clock next day the whole body of men in the choir emerged from the tranter's door, and advanced with a firm step down the lane. This dignity of march gradually became obliterated as they went on, and by the time they reached the hill behind the vicarage a faint resemblance to a flock of sheep might have been discerned in the venerable party. A word from the tranter, however, set them right again; and as they descended the hill, the regular tramp, tramp, tramp of the united feet was clearly audible from the vicarage garden. At the opening of the gate there was another short interval of irregular shuffling, caused by a rather peculiar habit the gate had, when swung open quickly, of striking against the bank and slamming back into the opener's face.

'Now keep step again, will ye?' said the tranter. 'It looks better, and more becomes the high class of arrant which has brought us here.' Thus they advanced to the door.

At Reuben's ring the more modest of the group turned aside, adjusted their hats, and looked critically at any shrub that happened to lie in the line of vision; endeavouring thus to give a person who chanced to look out of the windows the impression that their request, whatever it was going to be, was rather a casual thought occurring whilst they were inspecting the vicar's shrubbery and grass-plot than a predetermined thing. The tranter who, coming frequently to the vicarage with luggage, coals, firewood, etc., had none of the awe for its precincts that filled the breasts of most of the others, fixed his eyes firmly on the knocker during this interval of waiting. The knocker having no characteristic worthy of notice he relinquished it for a knot in one of the door-panels, and studied the winding lines of the grain.

'O, sir, please, here's Tranter Dewy, and old William Dewy,

and young Richard Dewy, O, and all the quire too, sir, except the boys, a-come to see you!' said Mr Maybold's maid-servant to Mr Maybold, the pupils of her eyes dilating like circles in a pond.

'All the choir?' said the astonished vicar (who may be shortly described as a good-looking young man with courageous eyes, timid mouth, and neutral nose), abandoning his writing and looking at his parlourmaid after speaking, like a man who fancied he had seen her face before but couldn't recollect where.

'And they looks very firm, and Tranter Dewy do turn neither to the right hand nor to the left, but stares quite straight and solemn with his mind made up!'

'O, all the choir,' repeated the vicar to himself, trying by that simple device to trot out his thoughts on what the choir could come for.

'Yes; every man-jack of 'em, as I be alive!' (The parlour-maid was rather local in manner, having in fact been raised in the same village.) 'Really, sir, 'tis thoughted by many in town and country that –'

'Town and country! – Heavens, I had no idea that I was public property in this way!' said the vicar, his face acquiring a hue somewhere between that of the rose and the peony. 'Well, "It is thought in town and country that –"'

'It is thought that you be going to get it hot and strong! – excusen my incivility, sir.'

The vicar suddenly recalled to his recollection that he had long ago settled it to be decidedly a mistake to encourage his servant Jane in giving personal opinions. The servant Jane saw by the vicar's face that he recalled this fact to his mind; and removing her forehead from the edge of the door, and rubbing away the indent that edge had made, vanished into the passage as Mr Maybold remarked, 'Show them in, Jane.'

A few minutes later a shuffling and jostling (reduced to as refined a form as was compatible with the nature of shuffles and jostles) was heard in the passage; then an earnest and prolonged wiping of shoes, conveying the notion that volumes of mud had to be removed; but the roads being so clean that not a particle of dirt appeared on the choir's boots (those of all the elder members being newly oiled, and Dick's brightly polished), this wiping might have been set down simply as a desire to show that respectable men had no wish to take a mean advantage of clean roads for curtailing proper ceremonies. Next there came a powerful whisper from the same quarter: —

'Now stand stock-still there, my sonnies, one and all! And don't make no noise; and keep your backs close to the wall, that company may pass in and out easy if they want to without squeezing through ye: and we two are enough to go in.' . . . The voice was the tranter's.

'I wish I could go in too and see the sight!' said a reedy voice — that of Leaf.

' 'Tis a pity Leaf is so terrible silly, or else he might,' another said.

'I never in my life seed a quire go into a study to have it out about the playing and singing,' pleaded Leaf; 'and I should like to see it just once!'

'Very well; we'll let en come in,' said the tranter. 'You'll be like chips in porridge.* Leaf — neither good nor hurt. All right, my sonny, come along;' and immediately himself, old William, and Leaf appeared in the room.

'We took the liberty to come and see 'ee, sir,' said Reuben, letting his hat hang in his left hand, and touching with his right the brim of an imaginary one on his head. 'We've come to see 'ee, sir, man and man, and no offence, I hope?'

'None at all,' said Mr Maybold.

'This old aged man standing by my side is father; William Dewy by name, sir.'

'Yes; I see it is,' said the vicar, nodding aside to old William, who smiled.

'I thought ye mightn't know en without his bass-viol,' the tranter apologized. 'You see, he always wears his best clothes and his bass-viol a-Sundays, and it do make such a difference in a' old man's look.'

'And who's that young man?' the vicar said.

* This, a local expression, must be a corruption of something less questionable.

'Tell the pa'son yer name,' said the tranter, turning to Leaf, who stood with his elbows nailed back to a bookcase.

'Please, Thomas Leaf, your holiness!' said Leaf, trembling.

'I hope you'll excuse his looks being so very thin,' continued the tranter deprecatingly, turning to the vicar again. 'But 'tisn't his fault, poor feller. He's rather silly by nature, and could never get fat; though he's a' excellent treble, and so we keep him on.'

'I never had no head, sir,' said Leaf, eagerly grasping at this opportunity for being forgiven his existence.

'Ah, poor young man!' said Mr Maybold.

'Bless you, he don't mind it a bit, if you don't, sir,' said the tranter assuringly. 'Do ye, Leaf?'

'Not I – not a morsel – hee, hee! I was afeard it mightn't please your holiness, sir, that's all.'

The tranter, finding Leaf get on so very well through his negative qualities, was tempted in a fit of generosity to advance him still higher, by giving him credit for positive ones. 'He's very clever for a silly chap, good-now, sir.[42] You never knowed a young feller keep his smock-frocks so clane; very honest too. His ghastly looks is all there is against en, poor feller; but we can't help our looks, you know, sir.'

'True: we cannot. You live with your mother, I think, Leaf?'

The tranter looked at Leaf to express that the most friendly assistant to his tongue could do no more for him now, and that he must be left to his own resources.

'Yes, sir: a widder, sir. Ah, if brother Jim had lived she'd have had a clever son to keep her without work!'

'Indeed! poor woman. Give her this half-crown. I'll call and see your mother.'

'Say, "Thank you, sir,"' the tranter whispered imperatively towards Leaf.

'Thank you, sir!' said Leaf.

'That's it, then; sit down, Leaf,' said Mr Maybold.

'Y-yes, sir!'

The tranter cleared his throat after this accidental parenthesis about Leaf, rectified his bodily position, and began his speech.

'Mr Mayble,' he said, 'I hope you'll excuse my common way, but I always like to look things in the face.'

Reuben made a point of fixing this sentence in the vicar's mind by gazing hard at him at the conclusion of it, and then out of the window.

Mr Maybold and old William looked in the same direction, apparently under the impression that the things' faces alluded to were there visible.

'What I have been thinking' – the tranter implied by this use of the past tense that he was hardly so discourteous as to be positively thinking it then – 'is that the quire ought to be gie'd a little time, and not done away wi' till Christmas, as a fair thing between man and man. And, Mr Mayble, I hope you'll excuse my common way?'

'I will, I will. Till Christmas,' the vicar murmured, stretching the two words to a great length, as if the distance to Christmas might be measured in that way. 'Well, I want you all to under-stand that I have no personal fault to find, and that I don't wish to change the church music by forcible means, or in a way which should hurt the feelings of any parishioners. Why I have at last spoken definitely on the subject is that a player has been brought under – I may say pressed upon – my notice several times by one of the churchwardens. And as the organ I brought with me is here waiting' (pointing to a cabinet-organ standing in the study), 'there is no reason for longer delay.'

'We made a mistake I suppose then, sir? But we understood the young woman didn't want to play particularly?' The tran-ter arranged his countenance to signify that he did not want to be inquisitive in the least.

'No, nor did she. Nor did I definitely wish her to just yet; for your playing is very good. But, as I said, one of the church-wardens has been so anxious for a change that, as matters stand, I couldn't consistently refuse my consent.'

Now for some reason or other the vicar at this point seemed to have an idea that he had prevaricated; and as an honest vicar it was a thing he determined not to do. He corrected himself, blushing as he did so, though why he should blush was not known to Reuben.

'Understand me rightly,' he said: 'the churchwarden proposed it to me, but I had thought myself of getting – Miss Day to play.'

'Which churchwarden might that be who proposed her, sir? – excusing my common way.' The tranter intimated by his tone that so far from being inquisitive he did not even wish to ask a single question.

'Mr Shiner, I believe.'

'Clk, my sonny! – beg your pardon, sir, that's only a form of words of mine, and slipped out accidental – he nourishes enmity against us for some reason or another; perhaps because we played rather hard upon en Christmas night. Anyhow 'tis certain sure that Mr Shiner's real love for music of a particular kind isn't his reason. He've no more ear than that chair. But let that be.'

'I don't think you should conclude that, because Mr Shiner wants a different music, he has any ill-feeling for you. I myself, I must own, prefer organ-music to any other. I consider it most proper, and feel justified in endeavouring to introduce it; but then, although other music is better, I don't say yours is not good.'

'Well then, Mr Mayble, since death's to be, we'll die like men any day you name (excusing my common way).'

Mr Maybold bowed his head.

'All we thought was, that for us old ancient singers to be choked off quiet at no time in particular, as now, in the Sundays after Easter, would seem rather mean in the eyes of other parishes, sir. But if we fell glorious with a bit of a flourish at Christmas, we should have a respectable end, and not dwindle away at some nameless paltry second-Sunday-after or Sunday-next-before something, that's got no name of his own.'

'Yes, yes, that's reasonable; I own it's reasonable.'

'You see, Mr Mayble, we've got – do I keep you inconvenient long sir?'

'No, no.'

'We've got our feelings – father there especially.'

The tranter, in his earnestness, had advanced his person to within six inches of the vicar's.

'Certainly, certainly!' said Mr Maybold, retreating a little for convenience of seeing. 'You are all enthusiastic on the subject, and I am all the more gratified to find you so. A Laodicean luke-warmness is worse than wrongheadedness itself.'[43]

'Exactly, sir. In fact now, Mr Mayble,' Reuben continued more impressively, and advancing a little closer still to the vicar, 'father there is a perfect figure o' wonder, in the way of being fond of music!'

The vicar drew back a little further, the tranter suddenly also standing back a foot or two to throw open the view of his father, and pointing to him at the same time.

Old William moved uneasily in the large chair, and with a minute smile on the mere edge of his lips for good-manners, said he was indeed very fond of tunes.

'Now, you see exactly how it is,' Reuben continued, appealing to Mr Maybold's sense of justice by looking sideways into his eyes. The vicar seemed to see how it was so well that the gratified tranter walked up to him again with even vehement eagerness, so that his waistcoat-buttons almost rubbed against the vicar's as he continued: 'As to father, if you or I, or any man or woman of the present generation, at the time music is a-playing, was to shake your fist in father's face, as may be this way, and say, "Don't you be delighted with that music!"'
— the tranter went back to where Leaf was sitting, and held his fist so close to Leaf's face that the latter pressed his head back against the wall: 'All right, Leaf, my sonny, I won't hurt you; 'tis just to show my meaning to Mr Mayble. — As I was saying, if you or I, or any man, was to shake your fist in father's face this way, and say, "William, your life or your music!" he'd say, "My life!" Now that's father's nature all over; and you see, sir, it must hurt the feelings of a man of that kind for him and his bass-viol to be done away wi' neck and crop.'

The tranter went back to the vicar's front and again looked earnestly at his face.

'True, true, Dewy,' Mr Maybold answered, trying to with-draw his head and shoulders without moving his feet; but find-ing this impracticable edging back another inch. These frequent retreats had at last jammed Mr Maybold between his easy-chair and the edge of the table.

And at the moment of the announcement of the choir Mr Maybold had just re-dipped the pen he was using; at their entry, instead of wiping it, he had laid it on the table with the nib overhanging. At the last retreat his coat-tails came in contact with the pen, and down it rolled, first against the back of the chair, thence turning a summersault into the seat, thence falling to the floor with a rattle.

The vicar stooped for his pen, and the tranter, wishing to show that, however great their ecclesiastical differences, his mind was not so small as to let this affect his social feelings, stooped also.

'And have you anything else you want to explain to me, Dewy?' said Mr Maybold from under the table.

'Nothing, sir. And, Mr Mayble, you be not offended? I hope you see our desire is reason?' said the tranter from under the chair.

'Quite, quite; and I shouldn't think of refusing to listen to such a reasonable request,' the vicar replied. Seeing that Reuben had secured the pen he resumed his vertical position, and added, 'You know, Dewy, it is often said how difficult a matter it is to act up to our convictions and please all parties. It may be said with equal truth, that it is difficult for a man of any appreciativeness to have convictions at all. Now in my case, I see right in you, and right in Shiner. I see that violins are good, and that an organ is good; and when we introduce the organ it will not be that fiddles were bad, but that an organ was better. That you'll clearly understand, Dewy?'

'I will; and thank you very much for such feelings, sir. Piph-h-h-h! How the blood do get into my head, to be sure, whenever I quat down like that!' said Reuben, who having also risen to his feet stuck the pen vertically in the inkstand and almost through the bottom, that it might not roll down again under any circumstances whatever.

Now the ancient body of minstrels in the passage felt their curiosity surging higher and higher as the minutes passed. Dick, not having much affection for this errand, soon grew tired, and went away in the direction of the school. Yet their sense of propriety would probably have restrained them from any attempt to discover what was going on in the study had not the vicar's pen fallen to the floor. The conviction that the movement of chairs, &c., necessitated by the search, could only have been caused by the catastrophe of a bloody fight beginning, overpowered all other considerations; and they advanced to the door, which had only just fallen to. Thus, when Mr Maybold raised his eyes after the stooping he beheld glaring through the door Mr Penny in full-length portraiture, Mail's face and shoulders above Mr Penny's head, Spinks's forehead and eyes over Mail's crown, and a fractional part of Bowman's countenance under Spinks's arm – crescent-shaped portions of other heads and faces being visible behind these – the whole dozen and odd eyes bristling with eager inquiry.

Mr Penny, as is the case with excitable bootmakers and men, seeing the vicar look at him and hearing no word spoken, thought it incumbent upon himself to say something of any kind. Nothing suggested itself till he had looked for about half a minute at the vicar.

'You'll excuse my naming of it, sir,' he said, regarding with much commiseration the mere surface of the vicar's face; 'but perhaps you don't know that your chin have bust out a-bleeding where you cut yourself a-shaving this morning, sir.'

'Now, that was the stooping, depend upon't,' the tranter suggested, also looking with much interest at the vicar's chin. 'Blood always will bust out again if you hang down the member that's been bleeding.'

Old William raised his eyes and watched the vicar's bleeding chin likewise; and Leaf advanced two or three paces from the bookcase, absorbed in the contemplation of the same phenomenon with parted lips and delighted eyes.

'Dear me, dear me!' said Mr Maybold hastily, looking very red and brushing his chin with his hand, then taking out his handkerchief and wiping the place.

'That's it, sir; all right again now, 'a b'lieve – a mere nothing,' said Mr Penny. 'A little bit of fur off your hat will stop it in a minute if it should bust out again.'

'I'll let 'ee have a bit off mine,' said Reuben, to show his good feeling; 'my hat isn't so new as yours, sir, and 'twon't hurt mine a bit.'

'No, no; thank you, thank you,' Mr Maybold again nervously replied.

' 'Twas rather a deep cut seemingly?' said Reuben, feeling these to be the kindest and best remarks he could make.

'O, no; not particularly.'

'Well, sir, your hand will shake sometimes a-shaving, and just when it comes into your head that you may cut yourself, there's the blood.'

'I have been revolving in my mind that question of the time at which we make the change,' said Mr Maybold, 'and I know you'll meet me half-way. I think Christmas-day as much too late for me as the present time is too early for you. I suggest Michaelmas or thereabout as a convenient time for both parties; for I think your objection to a Sunday which has no name is not one of any real weight.'

'Very good, sir. I suppose mortal men mustn't expect their own way entirely; and I express in all our names that we'll make shift and be satisfied with what you say.' The tranter touched the brim of his imaginary hat again, and all the choir did the same. 'About Michaelmas, then, as far as you are concerned, sir, and then we make room for the next generation.'

'About Michaelmas,' said the vicar.

V

Returning Homeward

' 'A took it very well, then?' said Mail, as they all walked up the hill.

'He behaved like a man; 'a did so,' said the tranter. 'And I'm glad we've let en know our minds. And though, beyond that, we ha'n't got much by going, 'twas worth while. He won't forget it. Yes, he took it very well. Supposing this tree here was Pa'son Mayble, and I standing here, and thik gr't stone is father sitting in the easy-chair. "Dewy," says he, "I don't wish to change the church music in a forcible way." '

'That was very nice o' the man, even though words be wind.'

'Proper nice – out and out nice. The fact is,' said Reuben confidentially, ' 'tis how you take a man. Everybody must be managed. Queens must be managed: kings must be managed; for men want managing almost as much as women, and that's saying a good deal.'

' 'Tis truly!' murmured the husbands.

'Pa'son Mayble and I were as good friends all through it as if we'd been sworn brothers. Ay, the man's well enough; 'tis what's put in his head that spoils him, and that's why we've got to go.'

'There's really no believing half you hear about people nowadays.'

'Bless ye, my sonnies, 'tisn't the pa'son's move at all. That gentleman over there' (the tranter nodded in the direction of Shiner's farm) 'is at the root of the mischty.'[44]

'What! Shiner?'

'Ay; and I see what the pa'son don't see. Why, Shiner is for putting forward that young woman that only last night I was saying was our Dick's sweetheart, but I suppose can't be, and making much of her in the sight of the congregation, and thinking he'll win her by showing her off. Well, perhaps 'a woll.'

'Then the music is second to the woman, the other church-warden is second to Shiner, the pa'son is second to the church-wardens, and God A'mighty is nowhere at all.'

'That's true; and you see,' continued Reuben, 'at the very beginning it put me in a stud[45] as to how to quarrel wi' en. In short, to save my soul, I couldn't quarrel wi' such a civil man without belying my conscience. Says he to father there, in a voice as quiet as a lamb's, "William, you are a' old aged man, as all shall be, so sit down in my easy-chair, and rest yourself." And down father zot. I could fain ha' laughed at thee, father; for thou'st take it so unconcerned at first, and then looked so frightened when the chair-bottom sunk in.'

'You see,' said old William, hastening to explain, 'I was scared to find the bottom gie way — what should I know o' spring bottoms? — and thought I had broke it down: and of course as to breaking down a man's chair, I didn't wish any such thing.'

'And, neighbours, when a feller, ever so much up for a miff, d'see his own father sitting in his enemy's easy-chair, and a poor chap like Leaf made the best of, as if he almost had brains — why, it knocks all the wind out of his sail at once: it did out of mine.'

'If that young figure of fun — Fance Day, I mean,' said Bowman, 'hadn't been so mighty forward wi' showing herself off to Shiner and Dick and the rest, 'tis my belief we should never ha' left the gallery.'

' 'Tis my belief that though Shiner fired the bullets, the parson made 'em,' said Mr Penny. 'My wife sticks to it that he's in love wi' her.'

'That's a thing we shall never know. I can't onriddle her, nohow.'

'Thou'st ought to be able to onriddle such a little chiel as she,' the tranter observed.

'The littler the maid, the bigger the riddle, to my mind. And coming of such a stock, too, she may well be a twister.'

'Yes; Geoffrey Day is a clever man if ever there was one. Never says anything: not he.'

'Never.'

'You might live wi' that man, my sonnies, a hundred years, and never know there was anything in him.'

'Ay; one o' these up-country London ink-bottle chaps would call Geoffrey a fool.'[46]

'Ye never find out what's in that man: never,' said Spinks. 'Close? ah, he is close! He can hold his tongue well. That man's dumbness is wonderful to listen to.'

'There's so much sense in it. Every moment of it is brimmen over wi' sound understanding.'

' 'A can hold his tongue very clever – very clever truly,' echoed Leaf. ' 'A do look at me if 'a could see my thoughts running round like the works of a clock.'

'Well, all will agree that the man can halt well in his talk, be it a long time or be it a short time. And though we can't expect his daughter to inherit his closeness, she may have a few dribblets from his sense.'

'And his pocket, perhaps.'

'Yes; the nine hundred pound that everybody says he's worth; but I call it four hundred and fifty; for I never believe more than half I hear.'

'Well, he've made a pound or two, and I suppose the maid will have it, since there's nobody else. But 'tis rather sharp upon her, if she's born to fortune, to bring her up as if not born for it, and letting her work so hard.'

' 'Tis all upon his principle. A long-headed feller!'

'Ah,' murmured Spinks, ' 'twould be sharper upon her if she were born for fortune, and not to it! I suffer from that affliction.'

* VI *

Yalbury Wood and the Keeper's House

A MOOD of blitheness rarely experienced even by young men
was Dick's on the following Monday morning. It was the week
after the Easter holidays, and he was journeying along with
Smart the mare and the light spring-cart, watching the damp
slopes of the hill-sides as they streamed in the warmth of the
sun, which at this unsettled season shone on the grass with the
freshness of an occasional inspector rather than as an accustomed proprietor. His errand was to fetch Fancy, and some
additional household goods, from her father's house in the
neighbouring parish to her dwelling at Mellstock. The distant
view was darkly shaded with clouds; but the nearer parts of the
landscape were whitely illumined by the visible rays of the sun
streaming down across the heavy grey shade behind.

The tranter had not yet told his son of the state of Shiner's
heart that had been suggested to him by Shiner's movements.
He preferred to let such delicate affairs right themselves; experience having taught him that the uncertain phenomenon of
love, as it existed in other people, was not a groundwork upon
which a single action of his own life could be founded.

Geoffrey Day lived in the depths of Yalbury Wood,[47] which
formed portion of one of the outlying estates of the Earl of
Wessex, to whom Day was head gamekeeper, timber-steward,
and general overlooker for this district. The wood was inter-
sected by the highway from Casterbridge to London at a place
not far from the house, and some trees had of late years been
felled between its windows and the ascent of Yalbury Hill, to
give the solitary cottager a glimpse of the passers-by.

It was a satisfaction to walk into the keeper's house, even as
a stranger, on a fine spring morning like the present. A curl of
wood-smoke came from the chimney and drooped over the
roof like a blue feather in a lady's hat; and the sun shone

obliquely upon the patch of grass in front, which reflected its brightness through the open doorway and up the staircase opposite, lighting up each riser with a shiny green radiance and leaving the top of each step in shade.

The window-sill of the front room was between four and five feet from the floor, dropping inwardly to a broad low bench, over which, as well as over the whole surface of the wall beneath, there always hung a deep shade, which was considered objectionable on every ground save one, namely, that the perpetual sprinkling of seeds and water by the caged canary above was not noticed as an eyesore by visitors. The window was set with thickly-leaded diamond glazing, formed, especially in the lower panes, of knotty glass of various shades of green. Nothing was better known to Fancy than the extravagant manner in which these circular knots or eyes distorted everything seen through them from the outside – lifting hats from heads, shoulders from bodies; scattering the spokes of cart-wheels, and bending the straight fir-trunks into semicircles. The ceiling was carried by a beam traversing its midst, from the side of which projected a large nail, used solely and constantly as a peg for Geoffrey's hat; the nail was arched by a rainbow-shaped stain, imprinted by the brim of the said hat when it was hung there dripping wet.

The most striking point about the room was the furniture. This was a repetition upon inanimate objects of the old principle introduced by Noah, consisting for the most part of two articles of every sort. The duplicate system of furnishing owed its existence to the forethought of Fancy's mother, exercised from the date of Fancy's birthday onwards. The arrangement spoke for itself: nobody who knew the tone of the household could look at the goods without being aware that the second set was a provision for Fancy when she should marry and have a house of her own. The most noticeable instance was a pair of green-faced eight-day clocks ticking alternately, which were severally two-and-a-half minutes and three minutes striking the hour of twelve, one proclaiming, in Italian flourishes, Thomas Wood as the name of its maker, and the other – arched at the top, and altogether of more cynical appearance –

that of Ezekiel Saunders. They were two departed clockmakers of Casterbridge, whose desperate rivalry throughout their lives was nowhere more emphatically perpetuated than here at Geoffrey's. These chief specimens of the marriage provision were supported on the right by a couple of kitchen dressers, each fitted complete with their cups, dishes, and plates, in their turn followed by two dumb-waiters, two family Bibles, two warming-pans, and two intermixed sets of chairs.

But the position last reached – the chimney-corner – was, after all, the most attractive side of the parallelogram. It was large enough to admit, in addition to Geoffrey himself, Geoffrey's wife, her chair, and her work-table, entirely within the line of the mantel, without danger or even inconvenience from the heat of the fire; and was spacious enough overhead to allow of the insertion of wood poles for the hanging of bacon, which were cloaked with long shreds of soot floating on the draught like the tattered banners on the walls of ancient aisles.

These points were common to most chimney-corners of the neighbourhood; but one feature there was which made Geoffrey's fireside not only an object of interest to casual aristocratic visitors – to whom every cottage fireside was more or less a curiosity – but the admiration of friends who were accustomed to fireplaces of the ordinary hamlet model. This peculiarity was a little window in the chimney-back, almost over the fire, around which the smoke crept caressingly when it left the perpendicular course. The window-board was curiously stamped with black circles, burnt thereon by the heated bottoms of drinking-cups which had rested there after previously standing on the hot ashes of the hearth for the purpose of warming their contents, the result giving to the ledge the look of an envelope which has passed through innumerable post-offices.

Fancy was gliding about the room preparing dinner, her head inclining now to the right, now to the left, and singing the tips and ends of tunes that sprang up in her mind like mushrooms. The footsteps of Mrs Day could be heard in the room overhead. Fancy went finally to the door.

'Father! Dinner.'

A tall spare figure was seen advancing by the window with periodical steps, and the keeper entered from the garden. He appeared to be a man who was always looking down as if trying to recollect something he said yesterday. The surface of his face was fissured rather than wrinkled, and over and under his eyes were folds which seemed as a kind of exterior eyelids. His nose had been thrown backwards by a blow in a poaching fray, so that when the sun was low and shining in his face people could see far into his head. There was in him a quiet grimness which would in his moments of displeasure have become surliness, had it not been tempered by honesty of soul, and which was often wrongheadedness because not allied with subtlety.

Although not an extraordinarily taciturn man among friends slightly richer than himself, he never wasted words upon outsiders, and to his trapper Enoch his ideas were seldom conveyed by any other means than nods and shakes of the head. Their long acquaintance with each other's ways, and the nature of their labours, rendered words between them almost superfluous as vehicles of thought, whilst the coincidence of their horizons, and the astonishing equality of their social views, by startling the keeper from time to time as very damaging to the theory of master and man, strictly forbade any indulgence in words as courtesies.

Behind the keeper came Enoch (who had been assisting in the garden) at the well-considered chronological distance of three minutes – an interval of non-appearance on the trapper's part not arrived at without some reflection. Four minutes had been found to express indifference to indoor arrangements, and simultaneousness had implied too great an anxiety about meals.

'A little earlier than usual, Fancy,' the keeper said, as he sat down and looked at the clocks. 'That Ezekiel Saunders o' thine is tearing on afore Thomas Wood again.'

'I kept in the middle between them,' said Fancy, also looking at the two clocks.

'Better stick to Thomas,' said her father. 'There's a healthy beat in Thomas that would lead a man to swear by en offhand.

123

He is as true as the town time.[48] How is it your stap-mother isn't here?'

As Fancy was about to reply the rattle of wheels was heard, and 'Weh-hey, Smart!' in Mr Richard Dewy's voice rolled into the cottage from round the corner of the house.

'Hullo! there's Dewy's cart come for thee, Fancy – Dick driving – afore time, too. Well, ask the lad to have pot-luck with us.'

Dick on entering made a point of implying by his general bearing that he took an interest in Fancy simply as in one of the same race and country as himself; and they all sat down. Dick could have wished her manner had not been so entirely free from all apparent consciousness of those accidental meetings of theirs; but he let the thought pass. Enoch sat diagonally at a table afar off under the corner cupboard, and drank his cider from a long perpendicular pint cup having tall fir-trees done in brown on its sides. He threw occasional remarks into the general tide of conversation, and with this advantage to himself, that he participated in the pleasures of a talk (slight as it was) at meal-times, without saddling himself with the responsibility of sustaining it.

'Why don't your stap-mother come down, Fancy?' said Geoffrey. 'You'll excuse her, Mister Dick, she's a little queer sometimes.'

'O yes, – quite,' said Richard, as if he were in the habit of excusing people every day.

'She d'belong to that class of womankind that become second wives: a rum class rather.'

'Indeed,' said Dick, with sympathy for an indefinite something.

'Yes; and 'tis trying to a female, especially if you've been a first wife, as she have.'

'Very trying it must be.'

'Yes: you see her first husband was a young man who let her go too far; in fact, she used to kick up Bob's-a-dying at the least thing in the world. And when I'd married her and found it out, I thought, thinks I, " 'Tis too late now to being to cure 'ee;" and so I let her bide. But she's queer, – very queer, at times!'

'I'm sorry to hear that.'

'Yes: there; wives be such a provoking class of society because, though they be never right, they be never more than half wrong.'

Fancy seemed uneasy under the infliction of this household moralizing, which might tend to damage the airy-fairy nature that Dick, as maiden shrewdness told her, had accredited her with. Her dead silence impressed Geoffrey with the notion that something in his words did not agree with her educated ideas, and he changed the conversation.

'Did Fred Shiner send the cask 'o drink, Fancy?'

'I think he did: O yes, he did.'

'Nice solid feller, Fred Shiner!' said Geoffrey to Dick as he helped himself to gravy, bringing the spoon round to his plate by way of the potato-dish, to obviate a stain on the cloth in the event of a spill.

Now Geoffrey's eyes had been fixed upon his plate for the previous four or five minutes, and in removing them he had only carried them to the spoon, which, from its fulness and the distance of its transit, necessitated a steady watching through the whole of the route. Just as intently as the keeper's eyes had been fixed on the spoon Fancy's had been fixed on her father's, without premeditation or the slightest phase of furtiveness; but there they were fastened. This was the reason why:

Dick was sitting next to her on the right side, and on the side of the table opposite to her father. Fancy had laid her right hand lightly down upon the tablecloth for an instant, and to her alarm Dick, after dropping his fork and brushing his forehead as a reason, flung down his own left hand, overlapping a third of Fancy's with it, and keeping it there. So the innocent Fancy, instead of pulling her hand from the trap, settled her eyes on her father's, to guard against his discovery of this perilous game of Dick's. Dick finished his mouthful; Fancy finished her crumb, and nothing was done beyond watching Geoffrey's eyes. Then the hands slid apart; Fancy's going over six inches of cloth, Dick's over one. Geoffrey's eye had risen.

'I said Fred Shiner is a nice solid feller,' he repeated more emphatically.

'He is; yes, he is,' stammered Dick; 'but to me he is little more than a stranger.'

'O, sure. Now I know en as well as any man can be known. And you know en very well too, don't ye, Fancy?'

Geoffrey put on a tone expressing that these words signified at present about one hundred times the amount of meaning they conveyed literally.

Dick looked anxious.

'Will you pass me some bread?' said Fancy in a flurry, the red of her face becoming slightly disordered, and looking as solicitous as a human being could look about a piece of bread.

'Ay, that I will,' replied the unconscious Geoffrey. 'Ay,' he continued, returning to the displaced idea, 'we are likely to remain friendly wi' Mr Shiner if the wheels d'run smooth.'

'An excellent thing – a very capital thing, as I should say,' the youth answered with exceeding relevance, considering that his thoughts, instead of following Geoffrey's remark, were nestling at a distance of about two feet on his left the whole time.

'A young woman's face will turn the north wind, Master Richard: my heart if 'twon't.' Dick looked more anxious and was attentive in earnest at these words. 'Yes; turn the north wind,' added Geoffrey after an impressive pause. 'And though she's one of my own flesh and blood. . .'

'Will you fetch down a bit of raw-mil' cheese from pantry-shelf?' Fancy interrupted as if she were famishing.

'Ay, that I will, chiel; chiel, says I, and Mr Shiner only asking last Saturday night . . . cheese you said, Fancy?'

Dick controlled his emotion at these mysterious allusions to Mr Shiner – the better enabled to do so by perceiving that Fancy's heart went not with her father's – and spoke like a stranger to the affairs of the neighbourhood. 'Yes, there's a great deal to be said upon the power of maiden faces in settling your courses,' he ventured, as the keeper retreated for the cheese.

'The conversation is taking a very strange turn: nothing that *I* have ever done warrants such things being said!' murmured Fancy with emphasis just loud enough to reach Dick's ears.

'You think to yourself, 'twas to be,' cried Enoch from his dis-

tant corner, by way of filling up the vacancy caused by Geoffrey's momentary absence. 'And so you marry her, Master
Dewy, and there's an end o't.'

'Pray don't say such things, Enoch,' came from Fancy
severely, upon which Enoch relapsed into servitude.

'If we be doomed to marry, we marry; if we be doomed to
remain single, we do,' replied Dick.

Geoffrey had by this time sat down again, and he now made
his lips thin by severely straining them across his gums, and
looked out of the window along the vista to the distant highway up Yalbury Hill. 'That's not the case with some folk,' he
said at length, as if he read the words on a board at the further
end of the vista.

Fancy looked interested, and Dick said, 'No?'

'There's that wife o' mine. It was her doom to be nobody's
wife at all in the wide universe. But she made up her mind that
she would, and did it twice over. Doom? Doom is nothing
beside a elderly woman – quite a chiel in her hands!'

A movement was now heard along the upstairs passage, and
footsteps descending. The door at the foot of the stairs opened
and the second Mrs Day appeared in view, looking fixedly at the
table as she advanced towards it, with apparent obliviousness
of the presence of any other human being than herself. In short,
if the table had been the personage, and the persons the table,
her glance would have been the most natural imaginable.

She showed herself to possess an ordinary woman's face,
iron-grey hair, hardly any hips, and a great deal of cleanliness
in a broad white apron-string as it appeared upon the waist of
her dark stuff dress.

'People will run away with a story now, I suppose,' she began
saying, 'that Jane Day's tablecloths are as poor and ragged as
any union[49] beggar's!'

Dick now perceived that the tablecloth was a little the worse
for wear, and reflecting for a moment concluded that 'people'
in step-mother language probably meant himself. On lifting his
eyes he found that Mrs Day had vanished again upstairs, and
presently returned with an armful of new damask-linen tablecloths folded square and hard as boards by long compression.

These she flounced down into a chair; then took one, shook it out from its folds, and spread it on the table by instalments, transferring the plates and dishes one by one from the old to the new cloth.

'And I suppose they'll say, too, that she ha'n't a decent knife and fork in her house!'

'I shouldn't say any such ill-natured thing, I am sure –' began Dick. But Mrs Day had vanished into the next room. Fancy appeared distressed.

'Very strange woman, isn't she?' said Geoffrey, quietly going on with his dinner. 'But 'tis too late to attempt curing. My heart! 'tis so growed into her that 'twould kill her to take it out. Ay, she's very queer: you'd be amazed to see what valuable goods we've got stowed away upstairs.'

Back again came Mrs Day with a box of bright steel horn-handled knives, silver-plated forks, carver, and all complete. These were wiped of the preservative oil which coated them, and then a knife and fork were laid down to each individual with a bang, the carving knife and fork thrust into the meat dish, and the old ones they had hitherto used tossed away.

Geoffrey placidly cut a slice with the new knife and fork, and asked Dick if he wanted any more.

The table had been spread for the mixed midday meal of dinner and tea which was common among frugal countryfolk. 'The parishioners about here,' continued Mrs Day, not looking at any living being, but snatching up the brown delf tea-things, 'are the laziest, gossipest, poachest, jailest set of any ever I came among. And they'll talk about my teapot and tea-things next, I suppose!' She vanished with the teapot, cups, and saucers, and reappeared with a tea-service in white china, and a packet wrapped in brown paper. This was removed, together with folds of tissue-paper underneath; and a brilliant silver teapot appeared.

'I'll help to put the things right,' said Fancy soothingly, and rising from her seat. 'I ought to have laid out better things, I suppose. But' (here she enlarged her looks so as to include Dick) 'I have been away from home a good deal, and I make shocking blunders in my housekeeping.' Smiles and suavity were then dispensed all around by this bright little bird.

After a little more preparation and modification Mrs Day took her seat at the head of the table, and during the latter or tea division of the meal presided with much composure. It may cause some surprise to learn that, now her vagary was over, she showed herself to be an excellent person with much common sense, and even a religious seriousness of tone on matters pertaining to her afflictions.

* VII *

Dick makes himself Useful

THE effect of Geoffrey's incidental allusions to Mr Shiner was to restrain a considerable flow of spontaneous chat that would otherwise have burst from young Dewy along the drive homeward. And a certain remark he had hazarded to her, in rather too blunt and eager a manner, kept the young lady herself even more silent than Dick. On both sides there was an unwillingness to talk on any but the most trivial subjects, and their sentences rarely took a larger form than could be expressed in two or three words.

Owing to Fancy being later in the day than she had promised the charwoman had given up expecting her; whereupon Dick could do no less than stay and see her comfortably tided over the disagreeable time of entering and establishing herself in an empty house after an absence of a week. The additional furniture and utensils that had been brought (a canary and cage among the rest) were taken out of the vehicle, and the horse was unharnessed and put in the plot opposite, where there was some tender grass. Dick lighted the fire already laid; and activity began to loosen their tongues a little.

'There!' said Fancy, 'we forgot to bring the fire-irons!'

She had originally found in her sitting-room, to bear out the expression 'nearly furnished' which the school-manager had used in his letter to her, a table, three chairs, a fender, and a piece of carpet. This 'nearly' had been supplemented hitherto by a kind friend, who had lent her fire-irons and crockery until she should fetch some from home.

Dick attended to the young lady's fire, using his whip-handle for a poker till it was spoilt, and then flourishing a hurdle stick for the remainder of the time.

'The kettle boils; now you shall have a cup of tea,' said Fancy, diving into the hamper she had brought.

'Thank you,' said Dick, whose drive had made him ready for some, especially in her company.

'Well, here's only one cup-and-saucer, as I breathe! Whatever could mother be thinking about? Do you mind making shift, Mr Dewy?'

'Not at all, Miss Day,' said that civil person.

'— And only having a cup by itself? or a saucer by itself?'

'Don't mind in the least.'

'Which do you mean by that?'

'I mean the cup if you like the saucer.'

'And the saucer if I like the cup?'

'Exactly, Miss Day.'

'Thank you, Mr Dewy, for I like the cup decidedly. Stop a minute; there are no spoons now!' She dived into the hamper again, and at the end of two or three minutes looked up and said, 'I suppose you don't mind if I can't find a spoon?'

'Not at all,' said the agreeable Richard.

'The fact is the spoons have slipped down somewhere; right under the other things. O yes, here's one, and only one. You would rather have one than not I suppose, Mr Dewy?'

'Rather not. I never did care much about spoons.'

'Then I'll have it. I do care about them. You must stir up your tea with a knife. Would you mind lifting the kettle off, that it may not boil dry?'

Dick leapt to the fireplace, and earnestly removed the kettle.

'There! you did it so wildly that you have made your hand black. We always use kettle-holders; didn't you learn housewifery as far as that, Mr Dewy? Well, never mind the soot on your hand. Come here. I am going to rinse mine, too.'

They went to a basin she had placed in the back room. 'This is the only basin I have,' she said. 'Turn up your sleeves, and by that time my hands will be washed, and you can come.'

Her hands were in the water now. 'O, how vexing!' she exclaimed. 'There's not a drop of water left for you unless you draw it, and the well is I don't know how many furlongs deep; all that was in the pitcher I used for the kettle and this basin. Do you mind dipping the tips of your fingers in the same?'

'Not at all. And to save time I won't wait till you have done, if you have no objection?'

Thereupon he plunged in his hands, and they paddled together. It being the first time in his life that he had touched female fingers under water, Dick duly registered the sensation as rather a nice one.

'Really, I hardly know which are my own hands and which are yours, they have got so mixed up together,' she said, withdrawing her own very suddenly.

'It doesn't matter at all,' said Dick, 'at least as far as I am concerned.'

'There! no towel! Whoever thinks of a towel till the hands are wet?'

'Nobody.'

' "Nobody." How very dull it is when people are so friendly! Come here, Mr Dewy. Now do you think you could lift the lid of that box with your elbow, and then, with something or other, take out a towel you will find under the clean clothes? Be *sure* don't touch any of them with your wet hands, for the things at the top are all Starched and Ironed.'

Dick managed by the aid of a knife and fork to extract a towel from under a muslin dress without wetting the latter; and for a moment he ventured to assume a tone of criticism.

'I fear for that dress,' he said, as they wiped their hands together.

'What?' said Miss Day, looking into the box at the dress alluded to. 'O, I know what you mean – that the vicar will never let me wear muslin?'

'Yes.'

'Well, I know it is condemned by all orders in the church as flaunting, and unfit for common wear for girls who've their living to get; but we'll see.'

'In the interest of the church I hope you don't speak seriously.'

'Yes, I do; but we'll see.' There was a comely determination on her lip, very pleasant to a beholder who was neither bishop, priest, nor deacon. 'I think I can manage any vicar's views about me if he's under forty.'

Dick rather wished she had never thought of managing vicars.

'I certainly shall be glad to get some of your delicious tea,' he said in rather a free way, yet modestly, as became one in a position between that of visitor and inmate, and looking wistfully at his lonely saucer.

'So shall I. Now is there anything else we want, Mr Dewy?'

'I really think there's nothing else, Miss Day.'

She prepared to sit down, looking musingly out of the window at Smart's enjoyment of the rich grass. 'Nobody seems to care about me,' she murmured, with large lost eyes fixed upon the sky beyond Smart.

'Perhaps Mr Shiner does,' said Dick, in the tone of a slightly injured man.

'Yes, I forgot – he does, I know.' Dick precipitately regretted that he had suggested Shiner since it had produced such a miserable result as this.

'I'll warrant you'll care for somebody very much indeed another day, won't you, Mr Dewy?' she continued, looking very feelingly into the mathematical centre of his eyes.

'Ah, I'll warrant I shall,' said Dick, feelingly too, and looking back into her dark pupils, whereupon they were turned aside.

'I meant,' she went on, preventing him from speaking just as he was going to narrate a forcible story about his feelings; 'I meant that nobody comes to see if I have returned – not even the vicar.'

'If you want to see him, I'll call at the vicarage directly we have had some tea.'

'No, no! Don't let him come down here, whatever you do, whilst I am in such a state of disarrangement. Parsons look so miserable and awkward when one's house is in a muddle; walking about and making impossible suggestions in quaint academic phrases till your flesh creeps and you wish them dead. Do you take sugar?'

Mr Maybold was at this instant seen coming up the path.

'There! That's he coming! How I wish you were not here! — that is, how awkward — dear, dear!' she exclaimed, with a quick ascent of blood to her face, and irritated with Dick rather than the vicar, as it seemed.

'Pray don't be alarmed on my account, Miss Day — good-afternoon!' said Dick in a huff, putting on his hat and leaving the room hastily by the back-door.

The horse was caught and put in, and on mounting the shafts to start he saw through the window the vicar, standing upon some books piled in a chair, and driving a nail into the wall; Fancy, with a demure glance, holding the canary-cage up to him as if she had never in her life thought of anything but vicars and canaries.

* VIII *

Dick meets his Father

FOR several minutes Dick drove along homeward, with the inner eye of reflection so anxiously set on his passages at arms with Fancy that the road and scenery were as a thin mist over the real pictures of his mind. Was she a coquette? The balance between the evidence that she did love him and that she did not was so nicely struck that his opinion had no stability. She had let him put his hand upon hers; she had allowed her gaze to drop plumb into the depths of his – his into hers – three or four times; her manner had been very free with regard to the basin and towel; she had appeared vexed at the mention of Shiner. On the other hand, she had driven him about the house like a quiet dog or cat, said Shiner cared for her, and seemed anxious that Mr Maybold should do the same.

Thinking thus as he neared the handpost at Mellstock Cross, sitting on the front board of the spring cart – his legs on the outside, and his whole frame jigging up and down like a candle-flame to the time of Smart's trotting – who should he see coming down the hill but his father in the light wagon, quivering up and down on a smaller scale of shakes, those merely caused by the stones in the road. They were soon crossing each other's front.

'Weh-hey!' said the tranter to Smiler.

'Weh-hey!' said Dick to Smart, in an echo of the same voice.

'Th'st hauled her back, I suppose?' Reuben inquired peaceably.

'Yes,' said Dick, with such a clinching period at the end that it seemed he was never going to add another word. Smiler, thinking this the close of the conversation, prepared to move on.

'Weh-hey!' said the tranter. 'I tell thee what it is, Dick. That there maid is taking up thy thoughts more than's good for thee, my sonny. Thou'rt never happy now unless th'rt making thyself miserable about her in one way or another.'

'I don't know about that, father,' said Dick rather stupidly.

'But I do – Wey, Smiler! – 'Od rot the women, 'tis nothing else wi' 'em nowadays but getting young men and leading 'em astray.'

'Pooh, father! you just repeat what all the common world says; that's all you do.'

'The world's a very sensible feller on things in jineral, Dick; very sensible indeed.'

Dick looked into the distance at a vast expanse of mortgaged estate. 'I wish I was as rich as a squire when he's as poor as a crow,' he murmured; 'I'd soon ask Fancy something.'

'I wish so too, wi' all my heart, sonny; that I do. Well, mind what beest about, that's all.'

Smart moved on a step or two. 'Supposing now, father, – We-hey, Smart! – I did think a little about her, and I had a chance, which I ha'n't; don't you think she's a very good sort of – of – one?'

'Ay, good; she's good enough. When you've made up your mind to marry, take the first respectable body that comes to hand – she's as good as any other; they be all alike in the groundwork; 'tis only in the flourishes there's a difference. She's good enough; but I can't see what the nation a young feller like you – wi' a comfortable house and home, and father and mother to take care o' thee, and who sent 'ee to a school so good that 'twas hardly fair to the other children – should want to go hollering after a young woman for, when she's quietly making a husband in her pocket, and not troubled by chick nor chiel, to make a poverty-stric' wife and family of her, and neither hat, cap, wig, nor waistcoat to set 'em up with: be drowned if I can see it, and that's the long and short o't, my sonny!'

Dick looked at Smart's ears, then up the hill; but no reason was suggested by any object that met his gaze.

'For about the same reason that you did, father, I suppose.'

'Dang it, my sonny, thou'st got me there!' And the tranter

gave vent to a grim admiration, with the mien of a man who was too magnanimous not to appreciate artistically a slight rap on the knuckles, even if they were his own.

'Whether or no,' said Dick, 'I asked her a thing going along the road.'

'Come to that, is it? Turk! won't thy mother be in a taking! Well, she's ready, I don't doubt?'

'I didn't ask her anything about having me; and if you'll let me speak, I'll tell 'ee what I want to know. I just said, Did she care about me?'

'Piph-ph-ph!'

'And then she said nothing for a quarter of a mile, and then she said she didn't know. Now, what I want to know is, what was the meaning of that speech?' The latter words were spoken resolutely, as if he didn't care for the ridicule of all the fathers in creation.

'The meaning of that speech is,' the tranter replied deliberately, 'that the meaning is meant to be rather hid at present. Well, Dick, as an honest father to thee, I don't pretend to deny what you d'know well enough; that is, that her father being rather better in the pocket than we, I should welcome her ready enough if it must be somebody.'

'But what d'ye think she really did mean?' said the unsatisfied Dick.

'I'm afeard I am not o' much account in guessing, especially as I was not there when she said it, and seeing that your mother was the only 'ooman I ever cam' into such close quarters as that with.'

'And what did mother say to you when you asked her?' said Dick musingly.

'I don't see that that will help 'ee.'

'The principle is the same.'

'Well — ay: what did she say? Let's see. I was oiling my working-day boots without taking 'em off, and wi' my head hanging down, when she just brushed on by the garden hatch like a flittering leaf. "Ann," I said says I, and then, – but, Dick, I'm afeard 'twill be no help to thee; for we were such a rum couple, your mother and I, leastways one half was, that is myself – and your mother's charms was more in the manner than the material.'

'Never mind! "Ann," said you.'

' "Ann," said I, as I was saying . . . "Ann," I said to her when I was oiling my working-day boots wi' my head hanging down, "Woot hae me?" . . . What came next I can't quite call up at this distance o' time. Perhaps your mother would know, – she's got a better memory for her little triumphs than I. However, the long and the short o' the story is that we were married somehow, as I found afterwards. 'Twas on White Tuesday, – Mellstock Club walked the same day,[50] every man two and two, and a fine day 'twas, – hot as fire; how the sun did strike down upon my back going to church! I well can mind what a bath o' sweating I was in, body and soul! But Fance will ha' thee, Dick – she won't walk with another chap – no such good luck.'

'I don't know about that,' said Dick, whipping at Smart's flank in a fanciful way which, as Smart knew, meant nothing in connection with going on. 'There's Pa'son Maybold, too – that's all against me.'

'What about he? She's never been stuffing into thy innocent heart that he's in love with her? Lord, the vanity o' maidens!'

'No, no. But he called, and she looked at him in such a way, and at me in such a way – quite different the ways were, – and as I was coming off there was he hanging up her birdcage.'

'Well, why shouldn't the man hang up her birdcage? Turk seize it all, what's that got to do wi' it? Dick, that thou beest a white-lyvered chap I don't say, but if thou beestn't as mad as a cappel-faced bull[51] let me smile no more.'

'O, ay.'

'And what's think now, Dick?'

'I don't know.'

'Here's another pretty kettle o' fish for thee. Who d'ye think's the bitter weed in our being turned out? Did our party tell 'ee?'

'No. Why, Pa'son Maybold, I suppose.'

'Shiner, – because he's in love with thy young woman, and

d'want to see her young figure sitting up at that queer instrument, and her young fingers rum-strumming upon the keys.'

A sharp ado of sweet and bitter was going on in Dick during this communication from his father. 'Shiner's a fool! – no, that's not it; I don't believe any such thing, father. Why, Shiner would never take a bold step like that unless she'd been a little made up to, and had taken it kindly. Pooh!'

'Who's to say she didn't?'

'I do.'

'The more fool you.'

'Why, father of me?'

'Has she ever done more to thee?'

'No.'

'Then she has done as much to he –rot 'em! Now, Dick, this is how a maid is. She'll swear she's dying for thee; and she is dying for thee, and she will die for thee; but she'll fling a look over t'other shoulder at another young feller, though never leaving off dying for thee just the same.'

'She's not dying for me, and so she didn't fling a look at him.'

'But she may be dying for him, for she looked at thee.'

'I don't know what to make of it at all,' said Dick gloomily.

'All I can make of it is,' the tranter said, raising his whip, arranging his different joints and muscles, and motioning to the horse to move on, 'that if you can't read a maid's mind by her motions, nature d'seem to say thou'st ought to be a bachelor. Clk, clk! Smiler!' And the tranter moved on.

Dick held Smart's rein firmly, and the whole concern of horse, cart, and man remained rooted in the lane. How long this condition would have lasted is unknown, had not Dick's thoughts, after adding up numerous items of misery, gradually wandered round to the fact that as something must be done it could not be done by staying there all night.

Reaching home he went up to his bedroom, shut the door as if he were going to be seen no more in this life, and taking a sheet of paper and uncorking the ink-bottle he began a letter. The dignity of the writer's mind was so powerfully apparent in every line of this effusion that it obscured the logical sequence of facts and intentions to an appreciable degree; and it was not at all clear to a reader whether he there and then left off loving Miss Fancy Day; whether he had never loved her seriously and never meant to; whether he had been dying up to the present moment and now intended to get well again; or whether he had hitherto been in good health and intended to die for her forthwith.

He put this letter in an envelope, sealed it up, directed it in a stern handwriting of straight dashes – easy flourishes being rigorously excluded. He walked with it in his pocket down the lane in strides not an inch less than three feet long. Reaching her gate he put on a resolute expression – then put it off again, turned back homeward, tore up his letter, and sat down.

That letter was altogether in a wrong tone – that he must own. A heartless man-of-the-world tone was what the juncture required. That he rather wanted her, and rather did not want her – the latter for choice; but that as a member of society he didn't mind making a query in jaunty terms, which could only be answered in the same way: did she mean anything by her bearing towards him, or did she not?

This letter was considered so satisfactory in every way that, being put into the hands of a little boy and the order given that he was to run with it to the school, he was told in addition not to look behind him if Dick called after him to bring it back, but to run along with it just the same. Having taken this precaution against vacillation Dick watched his messenger down the road, and turned into the house whistling an air in such ghastly jerks and starts that whistling seemed to be the act the very furthest removed from that which was instinctive in such a youth.

The letter was left as ordered: the next morning came and passed – and no answer. The next. The next. Friday night came. Dick resolved that if no answer or sign were given by her the next day, on Sunday he would meet her face to face, and have it all out by word of mouth.

'Dick,' said his father, coming in from the garden at that moment – in each hand a hive of bees tied in a cloth to prevent their egress – 'I think you'd better take these two swarms of bees to Mrs Maybold's tomorrow, instead o' me, and I'll go wi' Smiler and the wagon.'

It was a relief; for Mrs Maybold, the vicar's mother, who had just taken into her head a fancy for keeping bees (pleasantly disguised under the pretence of its being an economical wish to produce her own honey), lived near the watering-place of Budmouth Regis, ten miles off, and the business of transporting the hives thither would occupy the whole day, and to some extent annihilate the vacant time between this evening and the coming Sunday. The best spring-cart was washed throughout, the axles oiled, and the bees placed therein for the journey.

PART THE THIRD

SUMMER

* I *

Driving out of Budmouth

An easy bend of neck and graceful set of head; full and wavy bundles of dark-brown hair; light fall of little feet; pretty devices on the skirt of the dress; clear deep eyes; in short, a bunch of sweets: it was Fancy! Dick's heart went round to her with a rush.

The scene was the corner of Mary Street in Budmouth-Regis,[52] near the King's statue, at which point the white angle of the last house in the row cut perpendicularly an embayed and nearly motionless expanse of salt water projected from the outer ocean – today lit in bright tones of green and opal. Dick and Smart had just emerged from the street, and there on the right, against the brilliant sheet of liquid colour, stood Fancy Day; and she turned and recognized him.

Dick suspended his thoughts of the letter and wonder at how she came there by driving close to the chains of the Esplanade – incontinently displacing two chairmen, who had just come to life for the summer in new clean shirts and revivified clothes, and being almost displaced in turn by a rigid boy rattling along with a baker's cart and looking neither to the right nor the left. He asked if she were going to Mellstock that night.

'Yes, I'm waiting for the carrier,' she replied, seeming, too, to suspend thoughts of the letter.

'Now I can drive you home nicely, and you save half an hour. Will ye come with me?'

As Fancy's power to will anything seemed to have departed in some mysterious manner at that moment, Dick settled the matter by getting out and assisting her into the vehicle without another word.

The temporary flush upon her cheek changed to a lesser hue which was permanent, and at length their eyes met; there was present between them a certain feeling of embarrassment, which arises at such moments when all the instinctive acts dictated by the position have been performed. Dick, being engaged with the reins, thought less of this awkwardness than did Fancy, who had nothing to do but to feel his presence, and to be more and more conscious of the fact that by accepting a seat beside him in this way she succumbed to the tone of his note. Smart jogged along, and Dick jogged, and the helpless Fancy necessarily jogged too; and she felt that she was in a measure captured and made a prisoner.

'I am so much obliged to you for your company, Miss Day,' he observed, as they drove past the two semicircular bays of the Old Royal Hotel, where His Majesty King George the Third had many a time attended the balls of the burgesses.

To Miss Day, crediting him with the same consciousness of mastery – a consciousness of which he was perfectly innocent – this remark sounded like a magnanimous intention to soothe her, the captive.

'I didn't come for the pleasure of obliging you with my company,' she said.

The answer had an unexpected manner of incivility in it that must have been rather surprising to young Dewy. At the same time it may be observed that when a young woman returns a rude answer to a young man's civil remark her heart is in a state which argues rather hopefully for his case than otherwise.

There was silence between them till they had left the sea-front and passed about twenty of the trees that ornamented the road leading up out of the town towards Casterbridge and Mellstock.

'Though I didn't come for that purpose either, I would have done it,' said Dick at the twenty-first tree.

'Now, Mr Dewy, no flirtation, because it's wrong, and I don't wish it.'

Dick seated himself afresh just as he had been sitting before, arranged his looks very emphatically, and cleared his throat.

'Really, anybody would think you had met me on business and were just going to commence,' said the lady intractably.

'Yes, they would.'

'Why, you never have, to be sure!'

This was a shaky beginning. He chopped round and said cheerily, as a man who had resolved never to spoil his jollity by loving one of womankind —

'Well, how are you getting on Miss Day at the present time? Gaily, I don't doubt for a moment.'

'I am not gay, Dick; you know that.'

'Gaily doesn't mean decked in gay dresses.'

'I didn't suppose gaily was gaily dressed. Mighty me, what a scholar you've grown!'

'Lots of things have happened to you this spring, I see.'

'What have you seen?'

'O, nothing; I've heard, I mean!'

'What have you heard?'

'The name of a pretty man with brass studs, and a copper ring, and a tin watch-chain, a little mixed up with your own. That's all.'

'That's a very unkind picture of Mr Shiner, for that's who you mean! The studs are gold as you know, and its a real silver chain; the ring I can't conscientiously defend, and he only wore it once.'

'He might have worn it a hundred times without showing it half so much.'

'Well, he's nothing to me,' she serenely observed.

'Not any more than I am?'

'Now, Mr Dewy,' said Fancy severely, 'certainly he isn't any more to me than you are!'

'Not so much?'

She looked aside to consider the precise compass of that question. 'That I can't exactly answer,' she replied with soft archness.

As they were going rather slowly another spring-cart, containing a farmer, farmer's wife, and farmer's man, jogged past them; and the farmer's wife and farmer's man eyed the couple very curiously. The farmer never looked up from the horse's tail.

'Why can't you exactly answer?' said Dick, quickening Smart a little, and jogging on just behind the farmer and farmer's wife and man.

As no answer came, and as their eyes had nothing else to do, they both contemplated the picture presented in front, and noticed how the farmer's wife sat flattened between the two men, who bulged over each end of the seat to give her room till they almost sat upon their respective wheels; and they looked too at the farmer's wife's silk mantle inflating itself between her shoulders like a balloon and sinking flat again at each jog of the horse. The farmer's wife, feeling their eyes sticking into her back, looked over her shoulder. Dick dropped ten yards further behind.

'Fancy, why can't you answer?' he repeated.

'Because how much you are to me depends upon how much I am to you,' said she in low tones.

'Everything,' said Dick, putting his hand towards hers and casting emphatic eyes upon the upper curve of her cheek.

'Now, Richard Dewy, no touching me! I didn't say in what way your thinking of me affected the question – perhaps inversely, don't you see? No touching, sir! Look; goodness me, don't, Dick!'

The cause of her sudden start was the unpleasant appearance over Dick's right shoulder of an empty timber-wagon and four journeymen-carpenters reclining in lazy postures inside it, their eyes directed upwards at various oblique angles into the surrounding world, the chief object of their existence being apparently to criticize to the very backbone and marrow every animate object that came within the compass of their vision. This difficulty of Dick's was overcome by trotting on till the wagon and carpenters were beginning to look rather misty by reason of a film of dust that accompanied their wagon-wheels and rose around their heads like a fog.

'Say you love me, Fancy.'

'No, Dick, certainly not; 'tisn't time to do that yet.'

'Why, Fancy?'

' "Miss Day" is better at present – don't mind my saying so; and I ought not to have called you Dick.'

'Nonsense! when you know that I would do anything on earth for your love. Why, you make any one think that loving is a thing that can be done and undone, and put on and put off at a mere whim.'

'No, no, I don't,' she said gently; 'but there are things which tell me I ought not to give way to much thinking about you, even if –'

'But you want to, don't you? Yes, say you do; it is best to be truthful. Whatever they may say about a woman's right to conceal where her love lies, and pretend it doesn't exist, and things like that, it is not best; I do know it, Fancy. And an honest woman in that, as well as in all her daily concerns, shines most brightly, and is thought most of in the long-run.'

'Well then, perhaps, Dick, I do love you a little,' she whispered tenderly; 'but I wish you wouldn't say any more now.'

'I won't say any more now, then, if you don't like it, dear. But you do love me a little, don't you?'

'Now you ought not to want me to keep saying things twice; I can't say any more now, and you must content with what you have.'

'I may at any rate call you Fancy? There's no harm in that.'

'Yes, you may.'

'And you'll not call me Mr Dewy any more?'

'Very well.'

* II *

Further along the Road

DICK'S spirits having risen in the course of these admissions of his sweetheart he now touched Smart with the whip; and on Smart's neck, not far behind his ears. Smart, who had been lost in thought for some time, never dreaming that Dick could reach so far with a whip which, on this particular journey, had never been extended further than his flank, tossed his head and scampered along with exceeding briskness, which was very pleasant to the young couple behind him till, turning a bend in the road, they came instantly upon the farmer, farmer's man, and farmer's wife with the flapping mantle, all jogging on just the same as ever.

'Bother those people! Here we are upon them again.'

'Well, of course. They have as much right to the road as we.'

'Yes, but it is provoking to be overlooked so. I like a road all to myself. Look what a lumbering affair theirs is!' The wheels of the farmer's cart just at that moment jogged into a depression running across the road, giving the cart a twist, whereupon all three nodded to the left, and on coming out of it all three nodded to the right, and went on jerking their backs in and out as usual. 'We'll pass them when the road gets wider.'

When an opportunity seemed to offer itself for carrying this intention into effect they heard light flying wheels behind, and on their quartering there whizzed along past them a brand-new gig, so brightly polished that the spokes of the wheels sent forth a continual quivering light at one point in their circle, and all the panels glared like mirrors in Dick and Fancy's eyes. The driver, and owner as it appeared, was really a handsome man; his companion was Shiner. Both turned round as they passed Dick and Fancy and stared with bold admiration in her face till they were obliged to attend to the operation of passing the farmer. Dick glanced for an instant at Fancy while she was undergoing their scrutiny; then returned to his driving with rather a sad countenance.

'Why are you so silent?' she said after a while, with real concern.

'Nothing.'

'Yes, it is, Dick. I couldn't help those people passing.'

'I know that.'

'You look offended with me. What have I done?'

'I can't tell without offending you.'

'Better out.'

'Well,' said Dick, who seemed longing to tell even at the risk of offending her, 'I was thinking how different you in love are from me in love. Whilst those men were staring you dismissed me from your thoughts altogether and –'

'You can't offend me further now; tell all!'

'And showed upon your face a pleased sense of being attractive to 'em.'

'Don't be silly, Dick! You know very well I didn't.'

Dick shook his head sceptically and smiled.

'Dick, I always believe flattery *if possible* – and it was possible then. Now there's an open confession of weakness. But I showed no consciousness of it.'

Dick, perceiving by her look that she would adhere to her statement, charitably forbore saying anything that could make her prevaricate. The sight of Shiner, too, had recalled another branch of the subject to his mind; that which had been his greatest trouble till her company and words had obscured its probability.

'By the way, Fancy, do you know why our quire is to be dismissed?'

'No: except that it is Mr Maybold's wish for me to play the organ.'

'Do you know how it came to be his wish?'

'That I don't.'

'Mr Shiner, being churchwarden, has persuaded the vicar; who, however, was willing enough before. Shiner, I know, is crazy to see you playing every Sunday; I suppose he'll turn over your music, for the organ will be close to his pew. But – I know you have never encouraged him?'

'Never once!' said Fancy emphatically, and with eyes full of earnest truth. 'I don't like him indeed, and I never heard of his doing this before! I have always felt that I should like to play in a church, but I never wished to turn you and your choir out; and I never even said that I could play till I was asked. You don't think for a moment that I did, surely, do you?'

'I know you didn't, dear.'

'Or that I care the least morsel of a bit for him?'

'I know you don't.'

The distance between Budmouth and Mellstock was ten or eleven miles, and there being a good inn, 'The Ship', four miles out of Budmouth, with a mast and cross-trees in front, Dick's custom in driving thither was to divide his journey into three stages by resting at this inn going and coming, and not troubling the Budmouth stables at all, whenever his visit to the town was a mere call and deposit, as today.

Fancy was ushered into a little tea-room and Dick went to the stables to see to the feeding of Smart. In face of the significant twitches of feature that were visible in the ostler and labouring men idling around, Dick endeavoured to look unconscious of the fact that there was any sentiment between him and Fancy beyond a tranter's desire to carry a passenger home. He presently entered the inn and opened the door of Fancy's room.

'Dick, do you know, it has struck me that it is rather awkward my being here alone with you like this. I don't think you had better come in with me.'

'That's rather unpleasant, dear.'

'Yes, it is, and I wanted you to have some tea as well as myself too, because you must be tired.'

'Well, let me have some with you, then. I was denied once before, if you recollect, Fancy.'

'Yes, yes, never mind! And it seems unfriendly of me now, but I don't know what to do.'

'It shall be as you say, then.' Dick began to retreat with a dissatisfied wrinkling of face, and a farewell glance at the cosy tea-tray.

'But you don't see how it is, Dick, when you speak like that,' she said with more earnestness than she had ever shown before. 'You do know that even if I care very much for you I must remember that I have a difficult position to maintain. The vicar would not like me, as his schoolmistress, to indulge in a *tête-à-tête* anywhere with anybody.'

'But I am not *any* body!' exclaimed Dick.

'No, no, I mean with a young man;' and she added softly, 'unless I were really engaged to be married to him.'

'Is that all? Then, dearest, dearest, why we'll be engaged at once, to be sure we will, and down I sit! There it is, as easy as a glove!'

'Ah! but suppose I won't! And, goodness me, what have I done!' she faltered, getting very red. 'Positively, it seems as if I meant you to say that!'

'Let's do it! I mean get engaged,' said Dick. 'Now, Fancy, will you be my wife?'

'Do you know, Dick, it was rather unkind of you to say what you did coming along the road,' she remarked as if she had not heard the latter part of his speech; though an acute observer might have noticed about her breast as the word 'wife' fell from Dick's lips a soft silent escape of breaths, with very short rests between each.

'What did I say?'

'About my trying to look attractive to those men in the gig.'

'You couldn't help looking so, whether you tried or no. And, Fancy, you do care for me?'

'Yes.'

'Very much?'

'Yes.'

'And you'll be my own wife?'

Her heart quickened, adding to and withdrawing from her cheek varying tones of red to match each varying thought. Dick looked expectantly at the ripe tint of her delicate mouth, waiting for what was coming forth.

'Yes – if father will let me.'

Dick drew himself close to her, compressing his lips and pouting them out as if he were about to whistle the softest melody known.

'O no!' said Fancy solemnly.

The modest Dick drew back a little.

'Dick, Dick, kiss me and let me go instantly! – here's somebody coming!' she whisperingly exclaimed.

Half an hour afterwards Dick emerged from the inn, and if Fancy's lips had been real cherries probably Dick's would have appeared deeply stained. The landlord was standing in the yard.

'Heu-heu! hay-hay, Master Dewy? Ho-ho!' he laughed, letting the laugh slip out gently and by degrees that it might make little noise in its exit, and smiting Dick under the fifth rib at the same time. 'This will never do, upon my life, Master Dewy! calling for tay for a feymel passenger, and then going in and sitting down and having some too, and biding such a fine long time!'

'But surely you know?' said Dick, with great apparent surprise. 'Yes, yes! Ha-ha!' smiting the landlord under the ribs in return.

'Why, what? Yes, yes; ha-ha!'

'You know, of course!'

'Yes, of course! But – that is – I don't.'

'Why about – between that young lady and me?' nodding to the window of the room that Fancy occupied.

'No; not I!' said the innkeeper, bringing his eyes into circles.

'And you don't!'

'Not a word, I'll take my oath!'

'But you laughed when I laughed.'

'Ay, that was me sympathy; so did you when I laughed!'

'Really, you don't know? Goodness – not knowing that!'

'I'll take my oath I don't!'

'O yes,' said Dick, with frigid rhetoric of pitying astonishment, 'we're engaged to be married, you see, and I naturally look after her.'

'Of course, of course! I didn't know that, and I hope ye'll excuse any little freedom of mine, Mr Dewy. But it is a very odd thing; I was talking to your father very intimate about family matters only last Friday in the world, and who should come in but Keeper Day, and we all then fell a-talking o' family matters; but neither one o' them said a mortal word about it; knowen me too so many years, and I at your father's own wedding. 'Tisn't what I should have expected from an old neighbour!'

'Well, to say the truth, we hadn't told father of the engagement at that time; in fact, 'twasn't settled.'

'Ah! the business was done Sunday. Yes, yes, Sunday's the courting day. Heu-heu!'

'No, 'twasn't done Sunday in particular.'

'After school-hours this week? Well, a very good time, a very proper good time.'

'O no, 'twasn't done then.'

'Coming along the road today then, I suppose?'

'Not at all; I wouldn't think of getting engaged in a dog-cart.'

'Dammy — might as well have said at once the *when* be blowed! Anyhow, 'tis a fine day, and I hope next time you'll come as one.'

Fancy was duly brought out and assisted into the vehicle, and the newly affianced youth and maiden passed up the steep hill to the Ridgeway, and vanished in the direction of Mellstock.

* III *

A Confession

It was a morning of the latter summer-time; a morning of lingering dews, when the grass is never dry in the shade. Fuchsias and dahlias were laden till eleven o'clock with small drops and dashes of water, changing the colour of their sparkle at every movement of the air; and elsewhere hanging on twigs like small silver fruit. The threads of garden-spiders appeared thick and polished. In the dry and sunny places dozens of long-legged crane-flies whizzed off the grass at every step the passer took.

Fancy Day and her friend Susan Dewy the tranter's daughter were in such a spot as this, pulling down a bough laden with early apples. Three months had elapsed since Dick and Fancy had journeyed together from Budmouth, and the course of their love had run on vigorously during the whole time. There had been just enough difficulty attending its development, and just enough finesse required in keeping it private, to lend the passion an ever-increasing freshness on Fancy's part, whilst, whether from these accessories or not, Dick's heart had been at all times as fond as could be desired. But there was a cloud on Fancy's horizon now.

'She is so well off – better than any of us,' Susan Dewy was saying. 'Her father farms five hundred acres, and she might marry a doctor or curate or anything of that kind if she contrived a little.'

'I don't think Dick ought to have gone to that gipsy-party at all when he knew I couldn't go,' replied Fancy uneasily.

'He didn't know that you would not be there till it was too late to refuse the invitation,' said Susan.

'And what was she like? Tell me.'

'Well, she was rather pretty, I must own.'

'Tell straight on about her, can't you! Come, do, Susan. How many times did you say he danced with her?'

'Once.'

'Twice, I think you said?'

'Indeed I'm sure I didn't.'

'Well, and he wanted to again, I expect.'

'No; I don't think he did. She wanted to dance with him again bad enough, I know. Everybody does with Dick, because he's so handsome and such a clever courter.'

'O, I wish! – How did you say she wore her hair?'

'In long curls, – and her hair is light, and it curls without being put in paper: that's how it is she's so attractive.'

'She's trying to get him away! yes, yes, she is! And through keeping this miserable school I mustn't wear my hair in curls! But I will; I don't care if I leave the school and go home, I will wear my curls! Look, Susan, do! is her hair as soft and long as this?' Fancy pulled from its coil under her hat a twine of her own hair and stretched it down her shoulder to show its length, looking at Susan to catch her opinion from her eyes.

'It is about the same length as that, I think,' said Miss Dewy.

Fancy paused hopelessly. 'I wish mine was lighter, like hers!' she continued mournfully. 'But hers isn't so soft, is it? Tell me, now.'

'I don't know.'

Fancy abstractedly extended her vision to survey a yellow butterfly and a red-and-black butterfly that were flitting along in company, and then became aware that Dick was advancing up the garden.

'Susan, here's Dick coming; I suppose that's because we've been talking about him.'

'Well, then, I shall go indoors now – you won't want me;' and Susan turned practically and walked off.

Enter the single-minded Dick, whose only fault at the gipsy-ing, or picnic, had been that of loving Fancy too exclusively and depriving himself of the innocent pleasure the gathering might have afforded him, by sighing regretfully at her absence, – who had danced with the rival in sheer despair of ever being able to get through that stale, flat, and unprofitable afternoon in any other way; but this she would not believe.

Fancy had settled her plan of emotion. To reproach Dick? O no, no. 'I am in great trouble,' said she, taking what was intended to be a hopelessly melancholy survey of a few small apples lying under the tree; yet a critical ear might have noticed in her voice a tentative tone as to the effect of the words upon Dick when she uttered them.

'What are you in trouble about? Tell me of it,' said Dick earnestly. 'Darling, I will share it with 'ee and help 'ee.'

'No, no: you can't! Nobody can!'

'Why not? You don't deserve it, whatever it is. Tell me, dear.'

'O, it isn't what you think! It is dreadful: my own sin!'

'Sin, Fancy! as if you could sin! I know it can't be.'

' 'Tis, 'tis!' said the young lady, in a pretty little frenzy of sorrow. 'I have done wrong, and I don't like to tell it! Nobody will forgive me, nobody! and you above all will not!... I have allowed myself to – to – fl –'

'What, – not flirt!' he said, controlling his emotion as it were by a sudden pressure inward from his surface. 'And you said only the day before yesterday that you hadn't flirted in your life!'

'Yes, I did; and that was a wicked story! I have let another love me, and –'

'Good G –! Well, I'll forgive you, – yes, if you couldn't help it, – yes, I will!' said the now dismal Dick. 'Did you encourage him?'

'O, – I don't know, – yes – no. O, I think so!'

'What was it?'

A pause.

'Tell me!'

'Mr Shiner.'

After a silence that was only disturbed by the fall of an apple, a long-checked sigh from Dick, and a sob from Fancy, he said with real austerity –

'Tell it all; – every word!'

'He looked at me, and I looked at him, and he said, "Will you let me show you how to catch bullfinches down here by the stream?" And I – wanted to know very much – I did so long to have a bullfinch! I couldn't help that! – and I said, "Yes!" and then he said, "Come here." And I went with him down to the lovely river, and then he said to me, "Look and see how I do it, and then you'll know: I put this birdlime round this twig, and then I go here," he said, "and hide away under a bush; and presently clever Mister Bird comes and perches upon the twig, and flaps his wings, and you've got him before you can say Jack" – something; O, O, O, I forget what!'

'Jack Sprat,' mournfully suggested Dick through the cloud of his misery.

'No, not Jack Sprat,' she sobbed.

'Then 'twas Jack Robinson!' he said with the emphasis of a man who had resolved to discover every iota of the truth or die.

'Yes, that was it! And then I put my hand upon the rail of the bridge to get across, and – That's all.'

'Well, that isn't much, either,' said Dick critically and more cheerfully. 'Not that I see what business Shiner has to take upon himself to teach you anything. But it seems – it do seem there must have been more than that to set you up in such a dreadful taking?'

He looked into Fancy's eyes. Misery of miseries! – guilt was written there still.

'Now, Fancy, you've not told me all!' said Dick, rather sternly for a quiet young man.

'O, don't speak so cruelly! I am afraid to tell now! If you hadn't been harsh I was going on to tell all; now I can't!'

'Come, dear Fancy, tell: come. I'll forgive; I must. – by heaven and earth, I must, whether I will or no; I love you so!'

'Well, when I put my hand on the bridge, he touched it –'

'A scamp!' said Dick, grinding an imaginary human frame to powder.

'And then he looked at me, and at last he said, "Are you in love with Dick Dewy?" And I said, "Perhaps I am!" and then he said, "I wish you weren't then, for I want to marry you, with all my soul." '

'There's a villain now! Want to marry you!' And Dick quivered with the bitterness of satirical laughter. Then suddenly remembering that he might be reckoning without his host: 'Unless, to be sure, you are willing to have him, – perhaps you are,' he said, with the wretched indifference of a castaway.

'No, indeed I am not!' she said, her sobs just beginning to take a favourable turn towards cure.

'Well, then,' said Dick, coming a little to his senses, 'you've been stretching it very much in giving such a dreadful beginning to such a mere nothing. And I know what you've done it for, – just because of that gipsy-party!' He turned away from her and took five paces decisively, as if he were tired of an ungrateful country, including herself. 'You did it to make me jealous, and I won't stand it!' He flung the words to her over his shoulder and then stalked on, apparently very anxious to walk to the remotest of the Colonies that very minute.

'O, O, O, Dick – Dick!' she cried, trotting after him like a pet lamb and really seriously alarmed at last, 'you'll kill me! My impulses are bad – miserably wicked, – and I can't help it; forgive me, Dick! And I love you always; and those times when you look silly and don't seem quite good enough for me, – just the same, I do, Dick! And there is something more serious, though not concerning that walk with him.'

'Well, what is it?' said Dick, altering his mind about walking to the Colonies; in fact, passing to the other extreme, and standing so rooted to the road that he was apparently not even going home.

'Why this,' she said, drying the beginning of a new flood of tears she had been going to shed, 'this is the serious part. Father has told Mr Shiner that he would like him for a son-in-law if he could get me; – that he has his right hearty consent to come courting me!'

IV

An Arrangement

'THAT *is* serious,' said Dick, more intellectually than he had spoken for a long time.

The truth was that Geoffrey knew nothing about his daughter's continued walks and meetings with Dick. When a hint that there were symptoms of an attachment between them had first reached Geoffrey's ears he stated so emphatically that he must think the matter over before any such thing could be allowed that, rather unwisely on Dick's part, whatever it might have been on the lady's, the lovers were careful to be seen together no more in public; and Geoffrey, forgetting the report, did not think over the matter at all. So Mr Shiner resumed his old position in Geoffrey's brain by mere flux of time. Even Shiner began to believe that Dick existed for Fancy no more, — though that remarkably easy-going man had taken no active steps on his own account as yet.

'And father has not only told Mr Shiner that,' continued Fancy, 'but he has written me a letter to say he should wish me to encourage Mr Shiner if 'twas convenient!'

'I must start off and see your father at once!' said Dick, taking two or three vehement steps to the south, recollecting that Mr Day lived to the north, and coming back again.

'I think we had better see him together. Not tell him what you come for, or anything of the kind, until he likes you, and so win his brain through his heart, which is always the way to manage people. I mean in this way: I am going home on Saturday week to help them in the honey-taking. You might come there to me, have something to eat and drink, and let him guess what your coming signifies, without saying it in so many words.'

'We'll do it, dearest. But I shall ask him for you, flat and plain; not wait for his guessing.' And the lover then stepped close to her, and attempted to give her one little kiss on the cheek, his lips alighting, however, on an outlying tract of her back hair by reason of an impulse that had caused her to turn her head with a jerk. 'Yes, and I'll put on my second-best suit and a clean shirt and collar, and black my boots as if 'twas a Sunday. 'Twill have a good appearance, you see, and that's a great deal to start with.'

'You won't wear that old waistcoat, will you, Dick?'

'Bless you, no! Why I —'

'I didn't mean to be personal, dear Dick,' she said, fearing she had hurt his feelings. ' 'Tis a very nice waistcoat, but what I meant was, that though it is an excellent waistcoat for a settled-down man, it is not quite one for' (she waited, and a blush expanded over her face, and then she went on again) — 'for going courting in.'

'No, I'll wear my best winter one, with the leather lining, that mother made. It is a beautiful, handsome waistcoat inside, yes, as ever anybody saw. In fact, only the other day, I unbuttoned it to show a chap that very lining, and he said it was the strongest handsomest lining you could wish to see on the king's waistcoat himself.'

'*I* don't quite know what to wear,' she said, as if her habitual indifference alone to dress had kept back so important a subject till now.

'Why, that blue frock you wore last week.'

'Doesn't set well round the neck. I couldn't wear that.'

'But I shan't care.'

'No, you won't mind.'

'Well, then it's all right. Because you only care how you look to me, do you, dear? I only dress for you, that's certain.'

'Yes, but you see I couldn't appear in it again very well.'

'Any strange gentleman you mid meet in your journey might notice the set of it, I suppose. Fancy, men in love don't think so much about how they look to other women.' It is difficult to say whether a tone of playful banter or of gentle reproach prevailed in the speech.

'Well then, Dick,' she said, with good-humoured frankness,

'I'll own it. I shouldn't like a stranger to see me dressed badly even though I am in love. 'Tis our nature, I suppose.'

'You perfect woman!'

'Yes; if you lay the stress on "woman",' she murmured, looking at a group of hollyhocks in flower, round which a crowd of butterflies had gathered like female idlers round a bonnet-shop.

'But about the dress. Why not wear the one you wore at our party?'

'That sets well, but a girl of the name of Bet Tallor, who lives near our house, has had one made almost like it (only in pattern, though of miserably cheap stuff), and I couldn't wear it on that account. Dear me, I am afraid I can't go now.'

'O yes, you must; I know you will!' said Dick, with dismay. 'Why not wear what you've got on?'

'What! this old one! After all, I think that by wearing my grey one Saturday, I can make the blue one do for Sunday. Yes, I will. A hat or a bonnet, which shall it be? Which do I look best in?'

'Well, I think the bonnet is nicest, more quiet and matronly.'

'What's the objection to the hat? Does it make me look old?'

'O no; the hat is well enough; but it makes you look rather too – you won't mind me saying it, dear?'

'Not at all, for I shall wear the bonnet.'

'– Rather too coquettish and flirty for an engaged young woman.'

She reflected a minute. 'Yes; yes. Still, after all, the hat would do best; hats *are* best, you see. Yes, I must wear the hat, dear Dicky, because I ought to wear a hat, you know.'

PART THE FOURTH

AUTUMN

I

Going Nutting

DICK, dressed in his second-best suit, burst into Fancy's sitting-room with a glow of pleasure on his face.

It was two o'clock on Friday, the day before her contemplated visit to her father, and for some reason connected with cleaning the school the children had been given this Friday afternoon for pastime, in addition to the usual Saturday.

'Fancy! it happens just right that it is a leisure half day with you. Smart is lame in his near-foot-afore, and so, as I can't do anything, I've made a holiday afternoon of it, and am come for you to go nutting with me!'

She was sitting by the parlour window with a blue frock lying across her lap and scissors in her hand.

'Go nutting! Yes. But I'm afraid I can't go for an hour or so.'

'Why not? 'Tis the only spare afternoon we may both have together for weeks.'

'This dress of mine, that I am going to wear on Sunday at Yalbury; – I find it fits so badly that I must alter it a little, after all. I told the dressmaker to make it by a pattern I gave her at the time; instead of that, she did it her own way, and made me look a perfect fright.'

'How long will you be?' he inquired, looking rather disappointed.

'Not long. Do wait and talk to me; come, do, dear.'

Dick sat down. The talking progressed very favourably amid the snipping and sewing till about half-past two, at which time his conversation began to be varied by a slight tapping upon his toe with a walking-stick he had cut from the hedge as he came along. Fancy talked and answered him, but sometimes the answers were so negligently given that it was evident her thoughts lay for the greater part in her lap with the blue dress.

The clock struck three. Dick arose from his seat, walked

round the room with his hands behind him, examined all the furniture, then sounded a few notes on the harmonium, then looked inside all the books he could find, then smoothed Fancy's head with his hand. Still the snipping and sewing went on.

The clock struck four. Dick fidgeted about, yawned privately; counted the knots in the table, yawned publicly; counted the flies on the ceiling, yawned horribly; went into the kitchen and scullery and so thoroughly studied the principle upon which the pump was constructed that he could have delivered a lecture on the subject. Stepping back to Fancy, and finding still that she had not done, he went into her garden and looked at her cabbages and potatoes, and reminded himself that they seemed to him to wear a decidedly feminine aspect; then pulled up several weeds and came in again. The clock struck five, and still the snipping and sewing went on.

Dick attempted to kill a fly, peeled all the rind off his walking-stick, then threw the stick into the scullery because it was spoilt, produced hideous discords from the harmonium, and accidentally overturned a vase of flowers, the water from which ran in a rill across the table and dribbled to the floor, where it formed a lake, the shape of which, after the lapse of a few minutes, he began to modify considerably with his foot till it was like a map of England and Wales.

'Well, Dick, you needn't have made quite such a mess.'

'Well, I needn't, I suppose.' He walked up to the blue dress, and looked at it with a rigid gaze. Then an idea seemed to cross his brain.

'Fancy.'

'Yes.'

'I thought you said you were going to wear your grey gown all day tomorrow on your trip to Yalbury, and in the evening too, when I shall be with you, and ask your father for you?'

'So I am.'

'And the blue one only on Sunday?'

'And the blue one Sunday.'

'Well, dear, I shan't be at Yalbury Sunday to see it.'

'No, but I shall walk to Longpuddle church in the afternoon

with father, and such lots of people will be looking at me there, you know; and it did set so badly round the neck.'

'I never noticed it, and 'tis like nobody else would.'

'They might.'

'Then why not wear the grey one on Sunday as well? 'Tis as pretty as the blue one.'

'I might make the grey one do, certainly. But it isn't so good; it didn't cost half so much as this one, and besides, it would be the same I wore Saturday.'

'Then wear the striped one, dear.'

'I might.'

'Or the dark one.'

'Yes, I might; but I want to wear a fresh one they haven't seen.'

'I see, I see,' said Dick, in a voice in which the tones of love were decidedly inconvenienced by a considerable emphasis, his thoughts meanwhile running as follows: 'I, the man she loves best in the world, as she says, am to understand that my poor half-holiday is to be lost, because she wants to wear on Sunday a gown there is not the slightest necessity for wearing, simply, in fact, to appear more striking than usual in the eyes of the Longpuddle young men; and I not there, either.'

'Then there are three dresses good enough for my eyes, but neither is good enough for the youths of Longpuddle,' he said.

'No, not that exactly, Dick. Still, you see, I do want – to look pretty to them – there, that's honest! But I shan't be much longer.'

'How much?'

'A quarter of an hour.'

'Very well; I'll come in in a quarter of an hour.'

'Why go away?'

'I mid as well.'

He went out, walked down the road, and sat upon a gate. Here he meditated and meditated, and the more he meditated the more decidedly did he begin to fume, and the more positive was he that his time had been scandalously trifled with by Miss Fancy Day – that, so far from being the simple girl who had never had a sweetheart before, as she had solemnly assured him time after time, she was, if not a flirt, a woman who had had no end of admirers; a girl most certainly too anxious about her frocks; a girl, whose feelings, though warm, were not deep; a girl who cared a great deal too much how she appeared in the eyes of other men. 'What she loves best in the world,' he thought, with an incipient spice of his father's grimness, 'is her hair and complexion. What she loves next best, her gowns and hats; what she loves next best, myself, perhaps!'

Suffering great anguish at this disloyalty in himself and harshness to his darling, yet disposed to persevere in it, a horribly cruel thought crossed his mind. He would not call for her, as he had promised, at the end of a quarter of an hour! Yes, it would be a punishment she well deserved. Although the best part of the afternoon had been wasted he would go nutting as he had intended, and go by himself.

He leaped over the gate, and pushed up the lane for nearly two miles, till a winding path called Snail-Creep sloped up a hill and entered a hazel copse by a hole like a rabbit's burrow.[53] In he plunged, vanished among the bushes, and in a short time there was no sign of his existence upon earth save an occasional rustling of boughs and snapping of twigs in divers points of Grey's Wood.

Never man nutted as Dick nutted that afternoon. He worked like a galley slave. Half-hour after half-hour passed away, and still he gathered without ceasing. At last, when the sun had set, and bunches of nuts could not be distinguished from the leaves which nourished them, he shouldered his bag, containing quite two pecks of the finest produce of the wood, about as much use to him as two pecks of stones from the road, strolled down the woodland track, crossed the highway and entered the homeward lane, whistling as he went.

Probably, Miss Fancy Day never before or after stood so low in Mr Dewy's opinion as on that afternoon. In fact, it is just possible that a few more blue dresses on the Longpuddle young men's account would have clarified Dick's brain entirely, and made him once more a free man.

But Venus had planned other developments, at any rate for the present. Cuckoo-Lane, the way he pursued, passed over a

ridge which rose keenly against the sky about fifty yards in his
van. Here, upon the bright after-glow about the horizon, was
now visible an irregular shape, which at first he conceived to be
a bough standing a little beyond the line of its neighbours.
Then it seemed to move, and, as he advanced still further, there
was no doubt that it was a living being sitting in the bank, head
bowed on hand. The grassy margin entirely prevented his footsteps from being heard, and it was not till he was close that the
figure recognized him. Up it sprang, and he was face to face
with Fancy.

'Dick, Dick! O, is it you, Dick!'

'Yes, Fancy,' said Dick, in a rather repentant tone, and
lowering his nuts.

She ran up to him, flung her parasol on the grass, put her
little head against his breast, and then there began a narrative
disjointed by such a hysterical weeping as was never surpassed
for intensity in the whole history of love.

'O Dick,' she sobbed out, 'where have you been away from
me? O, I have suffered agony, and thought you would never
come any more! 'Tis cruel, Dick; no 'tisn't, it is justice! I've
been walking miles and miles up and down Grey's Wood, trying
to find you, till I was wearied and worn out, and I could walk
no further, and had come back this far! O Dick, directly you
were gone I thought I had offended you and I put down the
dress; 'tisn't finished now, and I never will finish it, and I'll
wear an old one Sunday! Yes, Dick, I will, because I don't care
what I wear when you are not by my side – ha, you think I do,
but I don't! – and I ran after you, and I saw you go up Snail-
Creep and not look back once, and then you plunged in, and I
after you; but I was too far behind. O, I did wish the horrid
bushes had been cut down so that I could see your dear shape
again! And then I called out to you and nobody answered, and
I was afraid to call very loud lest anybody else should hear me.
Then I kept wandering and wandering about, and it was dreadful misery, Dick. And then I shut my eyes and fell to picturing
you looking at some other woman, very pretty and nice, but
with no affection or truth in her at all, and then imagined you
saying to yourself, "Ah, she's as good as Fancy, for Fancy told

me a story, and was a flirt, and cared for herself more than me, so now I'll have this one for my sweetheart." O, you won't, will you, Dick, for I do love you so!'

It is scarcely necessary to add that Dick renounced his freedom there and then, and kissed her ten times over, and promised that no pretty woman of the kind alluded to should ever engross his thoughts; in short, that though he had been vexed with her all such vexation was past, and that henceforth and for ever it was simply Fancy or death for him. And then they set about proceeding homewards, very slowly on account of Fancy's weariness, she leaning upon his shoulder and in addition receiving support from his arm round her waist; though she had sufficiently recovered from her desperate condition to sing to him, 'Why are you wandering here, I pray?' during the latter part of their walk. Nor is it necessary to describe in detail how the bag of nuts was quite forgotten until three days later, when it was found among the brambles and restored empty to Mrs Dewy, her initials being marked thereon in red cotton; and how she puzzled herself till her head ached upon the question of how on earth her meal-bag could have got into Cuckoo-Lane.

II

Honey-taking, and Afterwards

SATURDAY evening saw Dick Dewy journeying on foot to Yalbury Wood, according to the arrangement with Fancy.

The landscape being concave, at the going down of the sun
everything suddenly assumed a uniform robe of shade. The
evening advanced from sunset to dusk long before Dick's arrival, and his progress during the latter portion of his walk
through the trees was indicated by the flutter of terrified birds
that had been roosting over the path. And in crossing the
glades, masses of hot dry air that had been formed on the hills
during the day greeted his cheeks alternately with clouds of
damp night air from the valleys. He reached the keeper-
steward's house, where the grass-plot and the garden in front
appeared light and pale against the unbroken darkness of the
grove from which he had emerged, and paused at the garden
gate.

He had scarcely been there a minute when he beheld a sort
of procession advancing from the door in his front. It consisted
first of Enoch the trapper, carrying a spade on his shoulder and
a lantern dangling in his hand; then came Mrs Day, the light of
the lantern revealing that she bore in her arms curious objects
about a foot long in the form of Latin crosses (made of lath and
brown paper dipped in brimstone – called matches by bee-
masters); next came Miss Day with a shawl thrown over her
head; and behind all, in the gloom, Mr Frederic Shiner.

Dick in his consternation at finding Shiner present was at a
loss how to proceed, and retired under a tree to collect his
thoughts.

'Here I be, Enoch,' said a voice; and the procession advancing
further, the lantern's rays illuminated the figure of Geoffrey
awaiting their arrival beside a row of bee-hives in front of the
path. Taking the spade from Enoch he proceeded to dig two

holes in the earth beside the hives, the others standing round in a circle except Mrs Day, who deposited her matches in the fork of an apple-tree and returned to the house. The party remaining were now lit up in front by the lantern in their midst, their shadows radiating each way upon the garden-plot like the spokes of a wheel. An apparent embarrassment of Fancy at the presence of Shiner caused a silence in the assembly, during which the preliminaries of execution were arranged, the matches fixed, the stake kindled, the two hives placed over the two holes, and the earth stopped round the edges. Geoffrey then stood erect, and rather more, to straighten his backbone after the digging.

'They were a peculiar family,' said Mr Shiner, regarding the hives reflectively.

Geoffrey nodded.

'Those holes will be the grave of thousands!' said Fancy. 'I think 'tis rather a cruel thing to do.'

Her father shook his head. 'No,' he said, tapping the hives to shake the dead bees from their cells, 'if you suffocate 'em this way, they only die once: if you fumigate 'em in the new way, they come to life again, and die o' starvation; so the pangs o' death be twice upon 'em.'

'I incline to Fancy's notion,' said Mr Shiner, laughing lightly.

'The proper way to take honey, so that the bees be neither starved nor murdered, is a puzzling matter,' said the keeper steadily.

'I should like never to take it from them,' said Fancy.

'But 'tis the money,' said Enoch musingly. 'For without money man is a shadder!'

The lantern-light had disturbed many bees that had escaped from hives destroyed some days earlier, and, demoralized by affliction, were now getting a living as marauders about the doors of other hives. Several flew round the head and neck of Geoffrey; then darted upon him with an irritated bizz.

Enoch threw down the lantern and ran off and pushed his head into a currant bush; Fancy scudded up the path; and Mr Shiner floundered away helter-skelter among the cabbages. Geoffrey stood his ground, unmoved and firm as a rock. Fancy was the first to return, followed by Enoch picking up the lantern. Mr Shiner still remained invisible.

'Have the craters stung ye?' said Enoch to Geoffrey.

'No, not much – on'y a little here and there,' he said with leisurely solemnity, shaking one bee out of his shirt sleeve, pulling another from among his hair, and two or three more from his neck. The rest looked on during this proceeding with a complacent sense of being out of it, – much as a European nation in a state of internal commotion is watched by its neighbours.

'Are those all of them, father?' said Fancy, when Geoffrey had pulled away five.

'Almost all, – though I feel one or two more sticking into my shoulder and side. Ah! there's another just begun again upon my backbone. You lively young mortals, how did you get inside there? However, they can't sting me many times more, poor things, for they must be getting weak. They mid as well stay in me till bedtime now, I suppose.'

As he himself was the only person affected by this arrangement it seemed satisfactory enough; and after a noise of feet kicking against cabbages in a blundering progress among them the voice of Mr Shiner was heard from the darkness in that direction.

'Is all quite safe again?'

No answer being returned to this query he apparently assumed that he might venture forth, and gradually drew near the lantern again. The hives were now removed from their position over the holes, one being handed to Enoch to carry indoors, and one being taken by Geoffrey himself.

'Bring hither the lantern, Fancy: the spade can bide.'

Geoffrey and Enoch then went towards the house, leaving Shiner and Fancy standing side by side on the garden-plot.

'Allow me,' said Shiner, stooping for the lantern and seizing it at the same time with Fancy.

'I can carry it,' said Fancy, religiously repressing all inclination to trifle. She had thoroughly considered that subject after the tearful explanation of the bird-catching adventure to Dick, and had decided that it would be dishonest in her as an engaged young woman to trifle with men's eyes and hands any more. Finding that Shiner still retained his hold of the lantern she relinquished it, and he, having found her retaining it, also let go. The lantern fell and was extinguished. Fancy moved on.

'Where is the path?' said Mr Shiner.

'Here,' said Fancy. 'Your eyes will get used to the dark in a minute or two.'

'Till that time will ye lend me your hand?'

Fancy gave him the extreme tips of her fingers and they stepped from the plot into the path.

'You don't accept attentions very freely.'

'It depends upon who offers them.'

'A fellow like me, for instance.'

A dead silence.

'Well, what do you say, Missie?'

'It then depends upon how they are offered.'

'Not wildly, and yet not careless-like; not purposely, and yet not by chance; not too quick nor yet too slow.'

'How then?' said Fancy.

'Coolly and practically,' he said. 'How would that kind of love be taken?'

'Not anxiously, and yet not indifferently; neither blushing nor pale; nor religiously not yet quite wickedly.'

'Well, how?'

'Not at all.'[54]

Geoffrey Day's storehouse at the back of his dwelling was hung with bunches of dried horehound, mint, and sage; brown-paper bags of thyme and lavender; and long ropes of clean onions. On shelves were spread large red and yellow apples, and choice selections of early potatoes for seed next year; – vulgar crowds of commoner kind lying beneath in heaps. A few empty beehives were clustered around a nail in one corner, under which stood two or three barrels of new cider of the first crop, each bubbling and squirting forth from the yet open bunghole.

Fancy was now kneeling beside the two inverted hives, one of which rested against her lap for convenience in operating upon the contents. She thrust her sleeves above her elbows, and inserted her small pink hand edgewise between each white lobe of honeycomb, performing the act so adroitly and gently as not to unseal a single cell. Then cracking the piece off at the crown of the hive by a slight backward and forward movement she lifted each portion as it was loosened into a large blue platter placed on a bench at her side.

'Bother these little mortals!' said Geoffrey, who was holding the light to her and giving his back an uneasy twist. 'I really think I may as well go indoors and take 'em out, poor things! for they won't let me alone. There's two a stinging wi' all their might now. I'm sure I wonder their strength can last so long.'

'All right, friend; I'll hold the candle whilst you are gone,' said Mr Shiner, leisurely taking the light and allowing Geoffrey to depart, which he did with his usual long paces.

He could hardly have gone round to the housedoor when other footsteps were heard approaching the outbuilding; the tip of a finger appeared in the hole through which the wood latch was lifted, and Dick Dewy came in, having been all this time walking up and down the wood vainly waiting for Shiner's departure.

Fancy looked up and welcomed him rather confusedly. Shiner grasped the candlestick more firmly, and, lest doing this in silence should not imply to Dick with sufficient force that he was quite at home and cool, he sang invincibly –

'King Arthur he had three sons.' [55]

'Father here?' said Dick.

'Indoors, I think,' said Fancy, looking pleasantly at him.

Dick surveyed the scene and did not seem inclined to hurry off just at that moment. Shiner went on singing –

'The miller was drown'd in his pond,
    The weaver was hung in his yarn,
And the d— ran away with the little tail-or,
    With the broadcloth under his arm.'

'That's a terrible crippled rhyme, if that's your rhyme!' said Dick, with a grain of superciliousness in his tone.

177

'It's no use your complaining to me about the rhyme!' said Mr Shiner. 'You must go to the man that made it.'

Fancy by this time had acquired confidence.

'Taste a bit, Mr Dewy,' she said, holding up to him a small circular piece of honeycomb that had been the last in the row of layers, remaining still on her knees and flinging back her head to look in his face; 'and then I'll taste a bit too.'

'And I, if you please,' said Mr Shiner. Nevertheless the farmer looked superior, as if he could even now hardly join the trifling from very importance of station; and after receiving the honeycomb from Fancy he turned it over in his hand till the cells began to be crushed, and the liquid honey ran down from his fingers in a thin string.

Suddenly a faint cry from Fancy caused them to gaze at her.

'What's the matter, dear?' said Dick.

'It is nothing, but – O-o! – a bee has stung the inside of my lip! He was in one of the cells I was eating!'

'We must keep down the swelling or it may be serious!' said Shiner, stepping up and kneeling beside her. 'Let me see it.'

'No, no!'

'Just let *me* see it,' said Dick kneeling on the other side; and after some hesitation she pressed down her lip with one finger to show the place. 'O, I hope 'twill soon be better! I don't mind a sting in ordinary places, but it is so bad upon your lip,' she added with tears in her eyes, and writhing a little from the pain.

Shiner held the light above his head and pushed his face close to Fancy's, as if the lip had been shown exclusively to himself, upon which Dick pushed closer, as if Shiner were not there at all.

'It is swelling,' said Dick to her right aspect.

'It isn't swelling,' said Shiner to her left aspect.

'Is it dangerous on the lip?' cried Fancy. 'I know it is dangerous on the tongue.'

'O no, not dangerous,' answered Dick.

'Rather dangerous,' had answered Shiner simultaneously.

'I must try to bear it!' said Fancy, turning again to the hives.

'Hartshorn-and-oil is a good thing to put to it, Miss Day,' said Shiner with great concern.

'Sweet-oil-and-hartshorn I've found to be a good thing to cure stings, Miss Day,' said Dick with greater concern.

'We have some mixed indoors; would you kindly run and get it for me?' she said.

Now whether by inadvertence or whether by mischievous intention, the individuality of the *you* was so carelessly denoted that both Dick and Shiner sprang to their feet like twin acrobats, and marched abreast to the door; both seized the latch and lifted it, and continued marching on shoulder to shoulder in the same manner to the dwelling-house. Not only so but, entering the room, they marched as before straight up to Mrs Day's chair, letting the door in the oak partition slam so forcibly that the rows of pewter on the dresser rang like a bell.

'Mrs Day, Fancy has stung her lip and wants you to give me the hartshorn, please,' said Mr Shiner, very close to Mrs Day's face.

'O, Mrs Day, Fancy has asked me to bring out the hartshorn, please, because she has stung her lip!' said Dick, a little closer to Mrs Day's face.

'Well, men alive! that's no reason why you should eat me, I suppose!' said Mrs Day, drawing back.

She searched in the corner-cupboard, produced the bottle, and began to dust the cork, the rim, and every other part very carefully, Dick's hand and Shiner's hand waiting side by side.

'Which is head man?' said Mrs Day. 'Now, don't come mum-budgeting[56] so close again. Which is head man?'

Neither spoke; and the bottle was inclined towards Shiner. Shiner, as a high-class man, would not look in the least triumphant, and turned to go off with it as Geoffrey came downstairs after the search in his linen for concealed bees.

'O – that you, Master Dewy?'

Dick assured the keeper that it was; and the young man then determined upon a bold stroke for the attainment of his end, forgetting that the worst of bold strokes is the disastrous consequences they involve if they fail.

'I've come on purpose to speak to you very particular, Mr Day,' he said, with a crushing emphasis intended for the ears of

Mr Shiner, who was vanishing round the door-post at that moment.

'Well, I've been forced to go upstairs and unrind myself, and shake some bees out o' me,' said Geoffrey, walking slowly towards the open door and standing on the threshold. 'The young rascals got into my shirt and wouldn't be quiet nohow.'

Dick followed him to the door.

'I've come to speak a word to you,' he repeated, looking out at the pale mist creeping up from the gloom of the valley. 'You may perhaps guess what it is about.'

The keeper lowered his hands into the depths of his pockets, twirled his eyes, balanced himself on his toes, looked as perpendicularly downward as if his glance were a plumb-line, then horizontally, collecting together the cracks that lay about his face till they were all in the neighbourhood of his eyes.

'Maybe I don't know,' he replied.

Dick said nothing; and the stillness was disturbed only by some small bird that was being killed by an owl in the adjoining wood, whose cry passed into the silence without mingling with it.

'I've left my hat up in chammer,'[57] said Geoffrey; 'wait while I step up and get en.'

'I'll be in the garden,' said Dick.

He went round by a side wicket into the garden, and Geoffrey went upstairs. It was the custom in Mellstock and its vicinity to discuss matters of pleasure and ordinary business inside the house, and to reserve the garden for very important affairs, a custom which, as is supposed, originated in the desirability of getting away at such times from the other members of the family when there was only one room for living in, though it was now quite as frequently practised by those who suffered from no such limitation to the size of their domiciles.

The head-keeper's form appeared in the dusky garden, and Dick walked towards him. The elder paused and leant over the rail of a piggery that stood on the left of the path, upon which Dick did the same; and they both contemplated a whitish shadowy shape that was moving about and grunting among the straw of the interior.

'I've come to ask for Fancy,' said Dick.

'I'd as lief you hadn't.'

'Why should that be, Mr Day?'

'Because it makes me say that you've come to ask what ye be'n't likely to have. Have ye come for anything else?'

'Nothing.'

'Then I'll just tell 'ee you've come on a very foolish errand. D'ye know what her mother was?'

'No.'

'A teacher in a landed family's nursery, who was foolish enough to marry the keeper of the same establishment; for I was only a keeper then, though now I've a dozen other irons in the fire as steward here for my lord, what with the timber sales and the yearly fellings, and the gravel and sand sales, and one thing and t'other. However, d'ye think Fancy picked up her good manners, the smooth turn of her tongue, her musical notes, and her knowledge of books, in a homely hole like this?'

'No.'

'D'ye know where?'

'No.'

'Well, when I went a-wandering after her mother's death she lived with her aunt, who kept a boarding-school, till her aunt married Lawyer Green – a man as sharp as a needle – and the school was broke up. Did ye know that then she went to the training-school, and that her name stood first among the Queen's scholars of her year?'[58]

'I've heard so.'

'And that when she sat for her certificate as Government teacher, she had the highest of the first class?'

'Yes.'

'Well, and do ye know what I live in such a miserly way for when I've got enough to do without it, and why I make her work as a schoolmistress instead of living here?'

'No.'

'That if any gentleman, who sees her to be his equal in polish, should want to marry her, and she want to marry him, he shan't be superior to her in pocket. Now do ye think after this that you be good enough for her?'

'No.'

'Then good-night t'ee, Master Dewy.'

'Good-night, Mr Day.'

Modest Dick's reply had faltered upon his tongue, and he turned away wondering at his presumption in asking for a woman whom he had seen from the beginning to be so superior to him.

* III *

Fancy in the Rain

THE next scene is a tempestuous afternoon in the following month, and Fancy Day is discovered walking from her father's home towards Mellstock.

A single vast grey cloud covered the country, from which the small rain and mist had just begun to blow down in wavy sheets, alternately thick and thin. The trees of the fields and plantations writhed like miserable men as the air wound its way swiftly among them: the lowest portions of their trunks, that had hardly ever been known to move, were visibly rocked by the fiercer gusts, distressing the mind by its painful un-wontedness, as when a strong man is seen to shed tears. Low-hanging boughs went up and down; high and erect boughs went to and fro; the blasts being so irregular, and divided into so many cross-currents, that neighbouring branches of the same tree swept the skies in independent motions, crossed each other, or became entangled. Across the open spaces flew flocks of green and yellowish leaves which, after travelling a long distance from their parent trees, reached the ground and lay there with their under-sides upward.

As the rain and wind increased, and Fancy's bonnet-ribbons leapt more and more snappishly against her chin, she paused on entering Mellstock Lane to consider her latitude, and the dist-ance to a place of shelter. The nearest house was Elizabeth Endorfield's in Higher Mellstock, whose cottage and garden stood not far from the junction of that hamlet with the road she followed. Fancy hastened onward, and in five minutes entered a gate which shed upon her toes a flood of water-drops as she opened it.

'Come in, chiel!' a voice exclaimed before Fancy had knocked: a promptness that would have surprised her had she not known that Mrs Endorfield was an exceedingly and exceptionally sharp woman in the use of her eyes and ears.

Fancy went in and sat down. Elizabeth was paring potatoes for her husband's supper.

Scrape, scrape, scrape; then a toss, and splash went a potato into a bucket of water.

Now as Fancy listlessly noted these proceedings of the dame she began to reconsider an old subject that lay uppermost in her heart. Since the interview between her father and Dick the days had been melancholy days for her. Geoffrey's firm opposition to the notion of Dick as a son-in-law was more than she had expected. She had frequently seen her lover since that time, it is true, and had loved him more for the opposition than she would have otherwise dreamt of doing – which was a happiness of a certain kind. Yet, though love is thus an end in itself it must be believed to be the means to another end if it is to assume the rosy hues of an unalloyed pleasure. And such a belief Fancy and Dick were emphatically denied just now.

Elizabeth Endorfield had a repute among women which was in its nature something between distinction and notoriety. It was founded on the following items of character. She was shrewd and penetrating; her house stood in a lonely place; she never went to church; she wore a red cloak; she always retained her bonnet indoors; and she had a pointed chin. Thus far her attributes were distinctly Satanic; and those who looked no further called her, in plain terms, a witch. But she was not gaunt, nor ugly in the upper part of her face, nor particularly strange in manner; so that, when her more intimate acquaintances spoke of her the term was softened, and she became simply a Deep Body, who was as long-headed as she was high. It may be stated that Elizabeth belonged to a class of suspects who were gradually losing their mysterious characteristics under the administration of the young vicar; though during the long reign of Mr Grinham the parish of Mellstock had proved extremely favourable to the growth of witches.

While Fancy was revolving all this in her mind, and putting it to herself whether it was worth while to tell her troubles to

Elizabeth, and ask her advice in getting out of them, the witch spoke.

'You be down – proper down,' she said suddenly, dropping another potato into the bucket.

Fancy took no notice.

'About your young man.'

Fancy reddened. Elizabeth seemed to be watching her thoughts. Really one would almost think she must have the powers people ascribed to her.

'Father not in the humour for't hey?' Another potato was finished and flung in. 'Ah, I know about it. Little birds tell me things that people don't dream of my knowing.'

Fancy was desperate about Dick, and here was a chance – O, such a wicked chance! – of getting help; and what was goodness beside love!

'I wish you'd tell me how to put him in the humour for it?' she said.

'That I could soon do,' said the witch quietly.

'Really? O, do; anyhow – I don't care – so that it is done! How could I do it, Mrs Endorfield?'

'Nothing so mighty wonderful in it.'

'Well, but how?'

'By witchery, of course!' said Elizabeth.

'No!' said Fancy.

' 'Tis, I assure ye. Didn't you ever hear I was a witch?'

'Well,' hesitated Fancy, 'I have heard you called so.'

'And you believed it?'

'I can't say that I did exactly believe it, for 'tis very horrible and wicked; but, O, how I do wish it was possible for you to be one!'

'So I am. And I'll tell you how to bewitch your father to let you marry Dick Dewy.'

'Will it hurt him, poor thing?'

'Hurt who?'

'Father.'

'No; the charm is worked by common sense, and the spell can only be broke by your acting stupidly.'

Fancy looked rather perplexed, and Elizabeth went on:

185

'This fear of Lizz – whatever 'tis –
  By great and small,
She makes pretence to common sense,
  And that's all.

You must do it like this.' The witch laid down her knife and potato, and then poured into Fancy's ear a long and detailed list of directions, glancing up from the corner of her eye into Fancy's face with an expression of sinister humour. Fancy's face brightened, clouded, rose and sank, as the narrative proceeded. 'There,' said Elizabeth at length, stooping for the knife and another potato, 'do that, and you'll have him by-long and by-late, my dear.'

'And do it I will!' said Fancy.

She then turned her attention to the external world once more. The rain continued as usual, but the wind had abated considerably during the discourse. Judging that it was now possible to keep an umbrella erect she pulled her hood again over her bonnet, bade the witch good-bye, and went her way.

* IV *

The Spell

MRS ENDORFIELD'S advice was duly followed.

'I be proper sorry that your daughter isn't so well as she might be,' said a Mellstock man to Geoffrey one morning.

'But is there anything in it?' said Geoffrey uneasily, as he shifted his hat to the right. 'I can't understand the report. She didn't complain to me a bit when I saw her.'

'No appetite at all, they say.'

Geoffrey crossed to Mellstock and called at the school that afternoon. Fancy welcomed him as usual, and asked him to stay and take tea with her.

'I be'n't much for tea this time o' day,' he said, but stayed.

During the meal he watched her narrowly. And to his great consternation discovered the following unprecedented change in the healthy girl – that she cut herself only a diaphanous slice of bread-and-butter, and, laying it on her plate, passed the meal-time in breaking it into pieces, but eating no more than about one-tenth of the slice. Geoffrey hoped she would say something about Dick and finish up by weeping, as she had done after the decision against him a few days subsequent to the interview in the garden. But nothing was said, and in due time Geoffrey departed again for Yalbury Wood.

' 'Tis to be hoped poor Miss Fancy will be able to keep on her school,' said Geoffrey's man Enoch to Geoffrey the following week, as they were shovelling up ant-hills in the wood.

Geoffrey stuck in the shovel, swept seven or eight ants from his sleeve, and killed another that was prowling round his ear, then looked perpendicularly into the earth, as usual, waiting for Enoch to say more. 'Well, why shouldn't she?' said the keeper at last.

'The baker told me yesterday,' continued Enoch, shaking out

another emmet[59] that had run merrily up his thigh, 'that the bread he've left at that there school-house this last month would starve any mouse in the three creations; that 'twould so! And afterwards I had a pint o' small down at Morris's, and there I heard more.'

'What might that ha' been?'

'That she used to have a pound o' the best rolled butter a week, regular as clockwork, from Dairyman Viney's for herself, as well as just so much salted for the helping girl, and the 'ooman she calls in; but now the same quantity d'last her three weeks, and then 'tis thoughted she throws it away sour.'

'Finish doing the emmets, and carry the bag home-along.' The keeper resumed his gun, tucked it under his arm, and went on without whistling to the dogs, who however followed with a bearing meant to imply that they did not expect any such attentions when their master was reflecting.

On Saturday morning a note came from Fancy. He was not to trouble about sending her the couple of rabbits as was intended, because she feared she should not want them. Later in the day Geoffrey went to Casterbridge and called upon the butcher who served Fancy with fresh meat, which was put down to her father's account.

'I've called to pay up our little bill, Neighbour Haylock, and you can gie me the chiel's account at the same time.'

Mr Haylock turned round three-quarters of a circle in the midst of a heap of joints, altered the expression of his face from meat to money, went into a little office consisting only of a door and a window, looked very vigorously into a book which possessed length but no breadth; and then, seizing a piece of paper and scribbling thereupon, handed the bill.

Probably it was the first time in the history of commercial transactions that the quality of shortness in a butcher's bill was a cause of tribulation to the debtor. 'Why, this isn't all she've had in a whole month!' said Geoffrey.

'Every mossel,' said the butcher – '(now, Dan, take that leg and shoulder to Mrs White's, and this eleven pound here to Mr Martin's) – you've been treating her to smaller joints lately, to my thinking, Mr Day?'

'Only two or three little scram rabbits this last week, as I am alive – I wish I had!'

'Well, my wife said to me – (Dan! not too much, not too much on that tray at a time; better go twice) – my wife said to me as she posted up the books: "Haylock," she says, "Miss Day must have been affronted this summer during that hot muggy weather that spoilt so much for us; for depend upon't," she says, "she've been trying John Grimmett unknown to us: see her account else." 'Tis little, of course, at the best of times, being only for one, but now 'tis next kin to nothing.'

'I'll inquire,' said Geoffrey despondingly.

He returned by way of Mellstock, and called upon Fancy in fulfilment of a promise. It being Saturday the children were enjoying a holiday, and on entering the residence Fancy was nowhere to be seen. Nan the charwoman was sweeping the kitchen.

'Where's my da'ter?' said the keeper.

'Well, you see she was tired with the week's teaching, and this morning she said, "Nan, I shan't get up till the evening." You see, Mr Day, if people don't eat they can't work; and as she've gie'd up eating she must gie up working.'

'Have ye carried up any dinner to her?'

'No; she don't want any. There, we all know that such things don't come without good reason – not that I wish to say anything about a broken heart, or anything of the kind.'

Geoffrey's own heart felt inconveniently large just then. He went to the staircase and ascended to his daughter's door.

'Fancy!'

'Come in, father.'

To see a person in bed from any cause whatever on a fine afternoon is depressing enough; and here was his only child Fancy not only in bed, but looking very pale. Geoffrey was visibly disturbed.

'Fancy, I didn't expect to see thee here, chiel,' he said. 'What's the matter?'

'I'm not well, father.'

'How's that?'

'Because I think of things.'

'What things can you have to think o' so mortal much?'

'You know, father.'

'You think I've been cruel to thee in saying that that penniless Dick o' thine shan't marry thee, I suppose?'

No answer.

'Well, you know, Fancy, I do it for the best, and he isn't good enough for thee. You know that well enough.' Here he again looked at her as she lay. 'Well, Fancy, I can't let my only chiel die; and if you can't live without en, you must ha' en, I suppose.'

'O, I don't want him like that; all against your will, and everything so disobedient!' sighed the invalid.

'No, no, 'tisn't against my will. My wish is, now I d'see how 'tis hurten thee to live without en, that he shall marry thee as soon as we've considered a little. That's my wish flat and plain, Fancy. There, never cry, my little maid! You ought to have cried afore; no need o' crying now 'tis all over. Well, howsoever, try to step over and see me and mother-law tomorrow, and ha' a bit of dinner wi' us.'

'And – Dick too?'

'Ay, Dick too, 'far's I know.'

'And *when* do you think you'll have considered, father, and he may marry me?' she coaxed.

'Well, there, say next Midsummer; that's not a day too long to wait.'

On leaving the school Geoffrey went to the tranter's. Old William opened the door.

'Is your grandson Dick in 'ithin, William?'

'No, not just now, Mr Day. Though he've been at home a good deal lately.'

'O, how's that?'

'What wi' one thing, and what wi' t'other, he's all in a mope, as might be said. Don't seem the feller he used to. Ay, 'a will sit studding and thinking as if 'a were going to turn chapel-member, and then do nothing but traypse and wamble[60] about. Used to be such a chatty boy, too, Dick did; and now 'a don't speak at all. But won't ye step inside? Reuben will be home soon, 'a b'lieve.'

'No, thank you, I can't stay now. Will ye just ask Dick if he'll do me the kindness to step over to Yalbury tomorrow with my da'ter Fancy, if she's well enough? I don't like her to come by herself, now she's not so terrible topping in health.'

'So I've heard. Ay, sure, I'll tell him without fail.'

V

After gaining her Point

THE visit to Geoffrey passed off as delightfully as a visit might
have been expected to pass off when it was the first day of
smooth experience in a hitherto obstructed love-course. And
then came a series of several happy days of the same undis-
turbed serenity. Dick could court her when he chose; stay away
when he chose, – which was never; walk with her by winding
streams and waterfalls and autumn scenery till dews and twilight sent them home. And thus they drew near the day of the
Harvest Thanksgiving, which was also the time chosen for
opening the organ in Mellstock Church.

It chanced that Dick on that very day was called away from
Mellstock. A young acquaintance had died of consumption at
Charmley, a neighbouring village, on the previous Monday,
and Dick in fulfilment of a long-standing promise was to assist
in carrying him to the grave. When on Tuesday Dick went towards the school to acquaint Fancy with the fact it is difficult
to say whether his own disappointment at being denied the
sight of her triumphant *début* as organist, was greater than his
vexation that his pet should on this great occasion be deprived
of the pleasure of his presence. However, the intelligence was
communicated. She bore it as she best could, not without many
expressions of regret and convictions that her performance
would be nothing to her now.

Just before eleven o'clock on Sunday he set out upon his sad
errand. The funeral was to be immediately after the morning
service, and as there were four good miles to walk, driving
being inconvenient, it became necessary to start comparatively
early. Half an hour later would certainly have answered his purpose quite as well, yet at the last moment nothing would content his ardent mind but that he must go a mile out of his way

in the direction of the school, in the hope of getting a glimpse of his Love as she started for church.

Striking therefore into the lane towards the school, instead of across the ewelease direct to Charmley, he arrived opposite her door as his goddess emerged.

If ever a woman looked a divinity Fancy Day appeared one that morning as she floated down those school steps, in the form of a nebulous collection of colours inclining to blue. With an audacity unparalleled in the whole history of village-schoolmistresses at this date – partly owing, no doubt, to papa's respectable accumulation of cash, which rendered her profession not altogether one of necessity – she had actually donned a hat and feather and lowered her hitherto plainly looped-up hair, which now fell about her shoulders in a profusion of curls. Poor Dick was astonished: he had never seen her look so distractingly beautiful before save on Christmas-eve, when her hair was in the same luxuriant condition of freedom. But his first burst of delighted surprise was followed by less comfortable feelings as soon as his brain recovered its power to think.

Fancy had blushed; – was it with confusion? She had also involuntarily pressed back her curls. She had not expected him.

'Fancy, you didn't know me for a moment in my funeral clothes, did you?'

'Good-morning, Dick – no, really, I didn't know you for an instant in such a sad suit.'

He looked again at the gay tresses and hat. 'You've never dressed so charming before, dearest.'

'I like to hear you praise me in that way, Dick,' she said, smiling archly. 'It is meat and drink to a woman. Do I look nice really?'

'Fie! you know it. Did you remember, – I mean didn't you remember about my going away today?'

'Well, yes, I did, Dick; but, you know, I wanted to look well; – forgive me.'

'Yes, darling; yes, of course, – there's nothing to forgive. No, I was only thinking that when we talked on Tuesday and Wednesday and Thursday and Friday about my absence today, and

I was so sorry for it, you said, Fancy, so were you sorry, and almost cried, and said it would be no pleasure to you to be the attraction of the church today since I could not be there.'

'My dear one, neither will it be so much pleasure to me... But I do take a little delight in my life, I suppose,' she pouted.

'Apart from mine?'

She looked at him with perplexed eyes. 'I know you are vexed with me, Dick, and it is because the first Sunday I have curls and a hat and feather since I have been here happens to be the very day you are away and won't be with me. Yes, say it is, for that is it! And you think that all this week I ought to have remembered you wouldn't be here today, and not have cared to be better dressed than usual. Yes, you do, Dick, and it is rather unkind!'

'No, no,' said Dick earnestly and simply, 'I didn't think so badly of you as that. I only thought that — if *you* had been going away, I shouldn't have tried new attractions for the eyes of other people. But then of course you and I are different, naturally.'

'Well, perhaps we are.'

'Whatever will the vicar say, Fancy?'

'I don't fear what he says in the least!' she answered proudly. 'But he won't say anything of the sort you think. No, no.'

'He can hardly have conscience to, indeed.'

'Now come, you say, Dick, that you quite forgive me, for I must go,' she said with sudden gaiety, and skipped backwards into the porch. 'Come here, sir; — say you forgive me, and then you shall kiss me; — you never have yet when I have worn curls, you know. Yes, just where you want to so much, — yes, you may!'

Dick followed her into the inner corner, where he was probably not slow in availing himself of the privilege offered.

'Now that's a treat for you, isn't it?' she continued. 'Goodbye, or I shall be late. Come and see me tomorrow: you'll be tired tonight.'

Thus they parted, and Fancy proceeded to the church. The organ stood on one side of the chancel, close to and under the immediate eye of the vicar when he was in the pulpit and also in full view of the congregation. Here she sat down, for the first time in such a conspicuous position, her seat having previously been in a remote spot in the aisle.

'Good heavens – disgraceful! Curls and a hat and feather!' said the daughters of the small gentry, who had either only curly hair without a hat and feather, or a hat and feather without curly hair. 'A bonnet for church always!' said sober matrons.

That Mr Maybold was conscious of her presence close beside him during his sermon; that he was not at all angry at her development of costume; that he admired her, she perceived. But she did not see that he loved her during that sermon-time as he had never loved a woman before; that her proximity was a strange delight to him; and that he gloried in her musical success that morning in a spirit quite beyond a mere cleric's glory at the inauguration of a new order of things.

The old choir, with humbled hearts, no longer took their seats in the gallery as heretofore (which was now given up to the school-children who were not singers, and a pupil-teacher), but were scattered about with their wives in different parts of the church. Having nothing to do with conducting the service for almost the first time in their lives they all felt awkward, out of place, abashed, and inconvenienced by their hands. The tranter had proposed that they should stay away today and go nutting, but grandfather William would not hear of such a thing for a moment. 'No,' he replied reproachfully, and quoted a verse: ' "Though this has come upon us let not our hearts be turned back, or our steps go out of the way." '[61]

So they stood and watched the curls of hair trailing down the back of the successful rival, and the waving of her feather as she swayed her head. After a few timid notes and uncertain touches her playing became markedly correct, and towards the end full and free. But, whether from prejudice or unbiased judgement, the venerable body of musicians could not help thinking that the simpler notes they had been wont to bring forth were more in keeping with the simplicity of their old church than the crowded chords and interludes it was her pleasure to produce.

* VI *

Into Temptation

THE day was done, and Fancy was again in the school-house. About five o'clock it began to rain, and in rather a dull frame of mind she wandered into the schoolroom for want of something better to do. She was thinking – of her lover Dick Dewy? Not precisely. Of how weary she was of living alone; how unbearable it would be to return to Yalbury under the rule of her strange-tempered step-mother; that it was far better to be married to anybody than do that; that eight or nine long months had yet to be lived through ere the wedding could take place.

At the side of the room were high windows of Ham-hill stone, upon either sill of which she could sit by first mounting a desk and using it as a footstool. As the evening advanced here she perched herself, as was her custom on such wet and gloomy occasions, put on a light shawl and bonnet, opened the window, and looked out at the rain.

The window overlooked a field called the Grove, and it was the position from which she used to survey the crown of Dick's passing hat in the early days of their acquaintance and meetings. Not a living soul was now visible anywhere; the rain kept all people indoors who were not forced abroad by necessity, and necessity was less importunate on Sundays than during the week.

Sitting here and thinking again – of her lover, or of the sensation she had created at church that day? – well, it is unknown – thinking and thinking she saw a dark masculine figure arising into distinctness at the further end of the Grove – a man without an umbrella. Nearer and nearer he came, and she perceived that he was in deep mourning, and then that it was Dick. Yes, in the fondness and foolishness of his young heart, after walking four miles in a drizzling rain without overcoat or umbrella and in face of a remark from his love that he was not to come because he would be tired, he had made it his business to wander this mile out of his way again from sheer wish of spending ten minutes in her presence.

'O Dick, how wet you are!' she said, as he drew up under the window. 'Why, your coat shines as if it had been varnished, and your hat – my goodness, there's a streaming hat!'

'O, I don't mind, darling!' said Dick cheerfully. 'Wet never hurts me, though I am rather sorry for my best clothes. However, it couldn't be helped; we lent all the umbrellas to the women. I don't know when I shall get mine back.'

'And look, there's a nasty patch of something just on your shoulder.'

'Ah, that's japanning; it rubbed off the clamps of poor Jack's coffin when we lowered him from our shoulders upon the bier! I don't care about that, for 'twas the last deed I could do for him; and 'tis hard if you can't afford a coat for an old friend.'

Fancy put her hand to her mouth for half a minute. Underneath the palm of that little hand there existed for that half-minute a little yawn.

'Dick, I don't like you to stand there in the wet. And you mustn't sit down. Go home and change your things. Don't stay another minute.'

'One kiss after coming so far,' he pleaded.

'If I can reach, then.'

He looked rather disappointed at not being invited round to the door. She twisted from her seated position and bent herself downwards, but not even by standing on the plinth was it possible for Dick to get his lips into contact with hers as she held them. By great exertion she might have reached a little lower; but then she would have exposed her head to the rain.

'Never mind, Dick; kiss my hand,' she said, flinging it down to him. 'Now, good-bye.'

'Good-bye.'

He walked slowly away, turning and turning again to look at her till he was out of sight. During the retreat she said to herself, almost involuntarily, and still conscious of that morning's triumph –

'I like Dick, and I love him; but how plain and sorry a man looks in the rain, with no umbrella, and wet through!'

As he vanished she made as if to descend from her seat; but glancing in the other direction she saw another form coming along the same track. It was also that of a man. He, too, was in black from top to toe; but he carried an umbrella.

He drew nearer, and the direction of the rain caused him so to slant his umbrella that from her height above the ground his head was invisible, as she was also to him. He passed in due time directly beneath her, and in looking down upon the exterior of his umbrella her feminine eyes perceived it to be of superior silk – less common at that date than since – and of elegant make. He reached the entrance to the building, and Fancy suddenly lost sight of him. Instead of pursuing the roadway as Dick had done he had turned sharply round into her own porch.

She jumped to the floor, hastily flung off her shawl and bonnet, smoothed and patted her hair till the curls hung in passable condition, and listened. No knock. Nearly a minute passed, and still there was no knock. Then there arose a soft series of raps no louder than the tapping of a distant woodpecker, and barely distinct enough to reach her ears. She composed herself and flung open the door.

In the porch stood Mr Maybold.

There was a warm flush upon his face and a bright flash in his eyes which made him look handsomer than she had ever seen him before.

'Good-evening, Miss Day.'

'Good-evening, Mr Maybold,' she said, in a strange state of mind. She had noticed, beyond the ardent hue of his face, that his voice had a singular tremor in it, and that his hand shook like an aspen leaf when he laid his umbrella in the corner of the porch. Without another word being spoken by either he came into the schoolroom, shut the door, and moved close to her. Once inside the expression of his face was no more discernible by reason of the increasing dusk of evening.

'I want to speak to you,' he then said; 'seriously – on a perhaps unexpected subject, but one which is all the world to me — I don't know what it may be to you, Miss Day.'

No reply.

'Fancy, I have come to ask you if you will be my wife?'

As a person who has been idly amusing himself with rolling a snowball might start at finding he had set in motion an avalanche, so did Fancy start at these words from the young vicar. And in the dead silence which followed them the breathings of the man and of the woman could be distinctly and separately heard; and there was this difference between them — his respirations gradually grew quieter and less rapid after the enunciation; hers, from having been low and regular, increased in quickness and force till she almost panted.

'I cannot, I cannot, Mr Maybold — I cannot! Don't ask me!' she said.

'Don't answer in a hurry!' he entreated. 'And do listen to me. This is no sudden feeling on my part. I have loved you for more than six months! Perhaps my late interest in teaching the children here has not been so single-minded as it seemed. You will understand my motive — like me better, perhaps, for honestly telling you that I have struggled against my emotion continually, because I have thought that it was not well for me to love you! But I resolved to struggle no longer; I have examined the feeling; and the love I bear you is as genuine as that I could bear any woman! I see your great charm; I respect your natural talents, and the refinement they have brought into your nature — they are quite enough, and more than enough for me! They are equal to anything ever required of the mistress of a quiet parsonage-house — the place in which I shall pass my days, wherever it may be situated. O Fancy, I have watched you, criticized you even severely, brought my feelings to the light of judgement, and still have found them rational, and such as any man might have expected to be inspired with by a woman like you! So there is nothing hurried, secret, or untoward in my desire to do this. Fancy, will you marry me?'

No answer was returned.

'Don't refuse; don't,' he implored. 'It would be foolish of you

— I mean cruel! Of course we would not live here, Fancy. I have had for a long time the offer of an exchange of livings with a friend in Yorkshire, but I have hitherto refused on account of my mother. There we would go. Your musical powers shall be still further developed; you shall have whatever pianoforte you like; you shall have anything, Fancy, anything to make you happy — pony-carriage, flowers, birds, pleasant society; yes, you have enough in you for any society, after a few months of travel with me! Will you, Fancy, marry me?'

Another pause ensued, varied only by the surging of the rain against the window-panes, and then Fancy spoke, in a faint and broken voice.

'Yes, I will,' she said.

'God bless you, my own!' He advanced quickly, and put his arm out to embrace her. She drew back hastily. 'No no, not now!' she said in an agitated whisper. 'There are things; — but the temptation is, O, too strong, and I can't resist it; I can't tell you now, but I must tell you! Don't, please, don't come near me now! I want to think. I can scarcely get myself used to the idea of what I have promised yet.' The next minute she turned to a desk, buried her face in her hands, and burst into a hysterical fit of weeping. 'O, leave me to myself!' she sobbed; 'leave me! O, leave me!'

'Don't be distressed; don't, dearest!' It was with visible diffi-culty that he restrained himself from approaching her. 'You shall tell me at your leisure what it is that grieves you so; I am happy — beyond all measure happy! — at having your simple promise.'

'And do go and leave me now!'

'But I must not, in justice to you, leave for a minute, until you are yourself again.'

'There then,' she said, controlling her emotion, and standing up; 'I am not disturbed now.'

He reluctantly moved towards the door. 'Good-bye!' he mur-mured tenderly. 'I'll come tomorrow about this time.'

VII

Second Thoughts

THE next morning the vicar rose early. The first thing he did
was to write a long and careful letter to his friend in Yorkshire.
Then, eating a little breakfast, he crossed the meadows in the
direction of Casterbridge, bearing his letter in his pocket, that
he might post it at the town office, and obviate the loss of one
day in its transmission that would have resulted had he left
it for the foot-post through the village.

It was a foggy morning, and the trees shed in noisy water-
drops the moisture they had collected from the thick air, an
acorn occasionally falling from its cup to the ground in company with the drippings. In the meads sheets of spiders'-web,
almost opaque with wet, hung in folds over the fences, and
the falling leaves appeared in every variety of brown, green, and
yellow hue.

A low and merry whistling was heard on the highway he was
approaching, then the light footsteps of a man going in the
same direction as himself. On reaching the junction of his path
with the road the vicar beheld Dick Dewy's open and cheerful
face. Dick lifted his hat, and the vicar came out into the highway that Dick was pursuing.

'Good-morning, Dewy. How well you are looking!' said Mr
Maybold.

'Yes, sir, I am well — quite well! I am going to Casterbridge
now, to get Smart's collar; we left it there Saturday to be
repaired.'

'I am going to Casterbridge, so we'll walk together,' the vicar
said. Dick gave a hop with one foot to put himself in step with
Mr Maybold, who proceeded: 'I fancy I didn't see you at church
yesterday, Dewy. Or were you behind the pier?'

'No; I went to Charmley. Poor John Dunford chose me to be
one of his bearers a long time before he died, and yesterday was

the funeral. Of course I couldn't refuse, though I should have liked particularly to have been at home as 'twas the day of the new music.'

'Yes, you should have been. The musical portion of the service was successful – very successful indeed; and what is more to the purpose no ill-feeling whatever was evinced by any of the members of the old choir. They joined in the singing with the greatest good-will.'

' 'Twas natural enough that I should want to be there, I suppose,' said Dick, smiling a private smile; 'considering who the organ-player was.'

At this the vicar reddened a little, and said, 'Yes, yes,' though not at all comprehending Dick's true meaning, who, as he received no further reply, continued hesitatingly, and with another smile denoting his pride as a lover –

'I suppose you know what I mean, sir? You've heard about me and – Miss Day?'

The red in Maybold's countenance went away: he turned and looked Dick in the face.

'No,' he said constrainedly, 'I've heard nothing whatever about you and Miss Day.'

'Why, she's my sweetheart, and we are going to be married next Midsummer. We are keeping it rather close just at present, because 'tis a good many months to wait; but it is her father's wish that we don't marry before, and of course we must submit. But the time 'ill soon slip along.'

'Yes, the time will soon slip along – Time glides away every day – yes.'

Maybold said these words, but he had no idea of what they were. He was conscious of a cold and sickly thrill throughout him; and all he reasoned was this that the young creature whose graces had intoxicated him into making the most imprudent resolution of his life was less an angel than a woman.

'You see, sir,' continued the ingenuous Dick, ' 'twill be better in one sense. I shall by that time be the regular manager of a branch o' father's business which we think of starting elsewhere. It has very much increased lately, and we expect next year to keep a' extra couple of horses. We've already our eye on one – brown as a berry, neck like a rainbow, fifteen hands, and not a grey hair in her – offered us at twenty-five want a crown. And to kip pace with the times I have had some cards prented, and I beg leave to hand you one, sir.'

'Certainly,' said the vicar, mechanically taking the card that Dick offered him.

'I turn in here by Grey's Bridge,'[62] said Dick. 'I suppose you go straight on and up town?'

'Yes.'

'Good-morning, sir.'

'Good-morning, Dewy.'

Maybold stood still upon the bridge, holding the card as it had been put into his hand, and Dick's footsteps died away towards Durnover Mill. The vicar's first voluntary action was to read the card: –

DEWY AND SON,

TRANTERS AND HAULIERS,

MELLSTOCK.

N.B. – *Furniture, Coals, Potatoes, Live and Dead Stock,*
removed to any distance on the shortest notice.

Mr Maybold leant over the parapet of the bridge and looked into the river. He saw – without heeding – how the water came rapidly from beneath the arches, glided down a little steep, then spread itself over a pool in which dace, trout, and minnows sported at ease among the long green locks of weed that lay heaving and sinking with their roots towards the current. At the end of ten minutes spent leaning thus he drew from his pocket the letter to his friend, tore it deliberately into such minute fragments that scarcely two syllables remained in juxtaposition, and sent the whole handful of shreds fluttering into the water. Here he watched them eddy, dart, and turn, as they were carried downwards towards the ocean and gradually disappeared from his view. Finally he moved off, and pursued his way at a rapid pace back again to Mellstock Vicarage.

Nerving himself by a long and intense effort he sat down in his study and wrote as follows:

DEAR MISS DAY, – The meaning of your words, 'the temptation is too strong,' of your sadness and your tears, has been brought home to me by an accident. I know today what I did not know yesterday – that you are not a free woman.

Why did you not tell me – why didn't you? Did you suppose I knew? No. Had I known, my conduct in coming to you as I did would have been reprehensible.

But I don't chide you! Perhaps no blame attaches to you – I can't tell. Fancy, though my opinion of you is assailed and disturbed in a way which cannot be expressed, I love you still, and my word to you holds good yet. But will you, in justice to an honest man who relies upon your word to him, consider whether, under the circumstances, you can honourably forsake him? – yours ever sincerely.

ARTHUR MAYBOLD.

He rang the bell. 'Tell Charles to take these copybooks and this note to the school at once.'

The maid took the parcel and the letter, and in a few minutes a boy was seen to leave the vicarage gate with the one under his arm and the other in his hand. The vicar sat with his hand to his brow, watching the lad as he descended Church Lane and entered the waterside path which intervened between that spot and the school.

Here he was met by another boy, and after a free salutation and pugilistic frisk had passed between the two the second boy came on his way to the vicarage, and the other vanished out of sight.

The boy came to the door, and a note for Mr Maybold was brought in.

He knew the writing. Opening the envelope with an unsteady hand he read the subjoined words:

DEAR MR MAYBOLD, – I have been thinking seriously and sadly through the whole of the night of the question you put to me last evening; and of my answer. That answer, as an honest woman, I had no right to give.

It is my nature – perhaps all women's – to love refinement of mind and manners; but even more than this, to be ever fascinated with the idea of surroundings more elegant and pleasing than those which have been customary. And you praised me, and praise is life to me. It was alone my sensations at these things which prompted my reply. Ambition and vanity they would be called; perhaps they are so.

After this explanation I hope you will generously allow me to withdraw the answer I too hastily gave.

And one more request. To keep the meeting of last night, and all that passed between us there, for ever a secret. Were it to become known it would utterly blight the happiness of a trusting and generous man, whom I love still, and shall love always. – yours sincerely,

FANCY DAY

The last written communication that ever passed from the vicar to Fancy was a note containing these words only:

Tell him everything; it is best. He will forgive you.

PART THE FIFTH

CONCLUSION

I

'The Knot there's no Untying'[63]

THE last day of the story is dated just subsequent to that point in the development of the seasons when country people go to bed among nearly naked trees, are lulled to sleep by a fall of rain, and awake next morning among green ones; when the landscape appears embarrassed with the sudden weight and brilliancy of its leaves; when the night-jar comes and strikes up for the summer his tune of one note; when the apple-trees have bloomed, and the roads and orchard-grass become spotted with fallen petals; when the faces of the delicate flowers are darkened and their heads weighed down by the throng of honey-bees, which increase their humming till humming is too mild a term for the all-pervading sound; and when cuckoos, blackbirds, and sparrows, that have hitherto been merry and respectful neighbours, become noisy and persistent intimates.

The exterior of Geoffrey Day's house in Yalbury Wood appeared exactly as was usual at that season, but a frantic barking of the dogs at the back told of unwonted movements somewhere within. Inside the door the eyes beheld a gathering which was a rarity indeed for the dwelling of the solitary wood-steward and keeper.

About the room were sitting and standing, in various gnarled attitudes, our old acquaintance grandfathers James and William, the tranter, Mr Penny, two or three children, including Jimmy and Charley, besides three or four country ladies and gentlemen from a greater distance who do not require any distinction by name. Geoffrey was seen and heard stamping about the outhouse and among the bushes of the garden, attending to details of daily routine before the proper time arrived for their performance, in order that they might be off his hands for the day. He appeared with his shirt-sleeves rolled up; his best new nether garments, in which he had arrayed himself that morning, being temporarily disguised under a week-day apron whilst these proceedings were in operation. He occasionally glanced at the hives in passing to see if his wife's bees were swarming, ultimately rolling down his shirt-sleeves and going indoors, talking to tranter Dewy whilst buttoning the wristbands, to save time; next going upstairs for his best waistcoat, and coming down again to make another remark whilst buttoning that, during the time looking fixedly in the tranter's face as if he were a looking-glass.

The furniture had undergone attenuation to an alarming extent, every duplicate piece having been removed, including the clock by Thomas Wood; Ezekiel Saunders being at last left sole referee in matters of time.

Fancy was stationary upstairs, receiving her layers of clothes and adornments and answering by short fragments of laughter which had more fidgetiness than mirth in them, remarks that were made from time to time by Mrs Dewy and Mrs Penny, who were assisting her at the toilet, Mrs Day having pleaded a queerness in her head as a reason for shutting herself up in an inner bedroom for the whole morning. Mrs Penny appeared with nine corkscrew curls on each side of her temples, and a back comb stuck upon her crown like a castle on a steep.

The conversation just now going on was concerning the banns, the last publication of which had been on the Sunday previous.

'And how did they sound?' Fancy subtly inquired.

'Very beautiful indeed,' said Mrs Penny. 'I never heard any sound better.'

'But *how*?'

'O, *so* natural and elegant, didn't they, Reuben!' she cried through the chinks of the unceiled floor to the tranter downstairs.

'What's that?' said the tranter, looking up inquiringly at the floor above him for an answer.

'Didn't Dick and Fancy sound well when they were called home in church last Sunday?' came downwards again in Mrs Penny's voice.

'Ay, that they did, my sonnies! – especially the first time.

There was a terrible whispering piece of work in the congregation, wasn't there, neighbour Penny?' said the tranter, taking up the thread of conversation on his own account and, in order to be heard in the room above, speaking very loud to Mr Penny, who sat at the distance of three feet from him, or rather less.

'I never can mind seeing such a whispering as there was,' said Mr Penny, also loudly, to the room above. 'And such sorrowful envy on the maidens' faces; really, I never did see such envy as there was!'

Fancy's lineaments varied in innumerable little flushes and her heart palpitated innumerable little tremors of pleasure. 'But perhaps,' she said, with assumed indifference, 'it was only because no religion was going on just then?'

'O, no; nothing to do with that. 'Twas because of your high standing in the parish. It was just as if they had one and all caught Dick kissing and coling[64] ye to death, wasn't it, Mrs Dewy?'

'Ay; that 'twas.'

'How people will talk about one's doings!' Fancy exclaimed.

'Well, if you make songs about yourself, my dear, you can't blame other people for singing 'em.'

'Mercy me! how shall I go through it?' said the young lady again, but merely to those in the bedroom, with a breathing of a kind between a sigh and a pant, round shining eyes, and warm face.

'O, you'll get through it well enough, child,' said Mrs Dewy placidly. 'The edge of the performance is took off at the calling home; and when once you get up to the chancel end o' the church you feel as saucy as you please. I'm sure I felt as brave as a sodger all through the deed – though of course I dropped my face and looked modest, as was becoming to a maid. Mind you do that, Fancy.'

'And I walked into the church as quiet as a lamb, I'm sure,' subjoined Mrs Penny. 'There, you see Penny is such a little small man. But certainly I was flurried in the inside o' me. Well, thinks I, 'tis to be, and here goes! And do you do the same: say, " 'Tis to be, and here goes!" '

'Is there such wonderful virtue in " 'Tis to be, and here goes!"' inquired Fancy.

'Wonderful! 'Twill carry a body through it all from wedding to churching, if you only let it out with spirit enough.'

'Very well, then,' said Fancy, blushing. ' 'Tis to be, and here goes!'

'That's a girl for a husband!' said Mrs Dewy.

'I do hope he'll come in time!' continued the bride-elect, inventing a new cause of affright now that the other was demolished.

' 'Twould be a thousand pities if he didn't come, now you be so brave,' said Mrs Penny.

Grandfather James, having overheard some of these remarks, said downstairs with mischievous loudness –

'I've known some would-be weddings when the men didn't come.'

'They've happened not to come, before now, certainly,' said Mr Penny, cleaning one of the glasses of his spectacles.

'O, do hear what they are saying downstairs,' whispered Fancy. 'Hush, hush!'

She listened.

'They have, haven't they, Geoffrey?' continued grim grandfather James, as Geoffrey entered.

'Have what?' said Geoffrey.

'The men have been known not to come.'

'That they have,' said the keeper.

'Ay; I've knowed times when the wedding had to be put off through his not appearing, being tired of the woman. And another case I knowed was when the man was catched in a man-trap crossing Oaker's Wood, and the three months had run out before he got well, and the banns had to be published over again.'

'How horrible!' said Fancy.

'They only say it on purpose to tease 'ee, my dear,' said Mrs Dewy.

' 'Tis quite sad to think what wretched shifts poor maids have been put to,' came again from downstairs. 'Ye should hear Clerk Wilkins, my brother-law, tell his experiences in marrying couples these last thirty year: sometimes one thing, sometimes another – 'tis quite heart-rending – enough to make your hair stand on end.'

'Those things don't happen very often, I know,' said Fancy with smouldering uneasiness.

'Well, really 'tis time Dick was here,' said the tranter.

'Don't keep on at me so, grandfather James and Mr Dewy, and all you down there!' Fancy broke out, unable to endure any longer. 'I am sure I shall die, or do something, if you do!'

'Never you hearken to these old chaps, Miss Day!' cried Nat Callcome the best man, who had just entered, and threw his voice upward through the chinks of the floor as the others had done. ' 'Tis all right; Dick's coming on like a wild feller; he'll be here in a minute. The hive o' bees his mother gie'd en for his new garden swarmed jist as he was starting, and he said, "I can't afford to lose a stock o' bees; no, that I can't, though I fain would; and Fancy wouldn't wish it on any account." So he jist stopped to ting[65] to 'em and shake 'em.'

'A genuine wise man,' said Geoffrey.

'To be sure what a day's work we had yesterday!' Mr Callcome continued, lowering his voice as if it were not necessary any longer to include those in the room above among his audience, and selecting a remote corner of his best clean handkerchief for wiping his face. 'To be sure!'

'Things so heavy, I suppose,' said Geoffrey, as if reading through the chimney-window from the far end of the vista.

'Ay,' said Nat, looking round the room at points from which furniture had been removed. 'And so awkward to carry, too. 'Twas ath'art and across Dick's garden; in and out Dick's door; up and down Dick's stairs; round and round Dick's chammers[66] till legs were worn to stumps: and Dick is so particular, too. And the stores of victuals and drink that lad has laid in: why, 'tis enough for Noah's ark! I'm sure I never wish to see a choicer half-dozen of hams than he's got there in his chimley; and the cider I tasted was a very pretty drop, indeed; – none could desire a prettier cider.'

'They be for the love and the stalled ox both. Ah, the greedy martels!' said grandfather James.

'Well, may-be they be. "Surely," says I, "that couple between 'em have heaped up so much furniture and victuals that
anybody would think they were going to take hold the big end
of married life first, and begin wi' a grown-up family." Ah, what
a bath of heat we two chaps were in, to be sure, a-getting that
furniture in order!'

'I do so wish the room below was ceiled,' said Fancy as the
dressing went on; 'we can hear all they say and do down there.'

'Hark! Who's that?' exclaimed a small pupil-teacher, who
also assisted this morning to her great delight. She ran half-way
down the stairs and peeped round the banister. 'O, you should,
you should, you should!' she exclaimed, scrambling up to the
room again.

'What?' said Fancy.

'See the bridesmaids! They've just a-come! 'Tis wonderful,
really! 'tis wonderful how muslin can be brought to it. There,
they don't look a bit like themselves, but like some very rich
sisters o' theirs that nobody knew they had!'

'Make them come up to me, make them come up!' cried
Fancy ecstatically; and the four damsels appointed, namely,
Miss Susan Dewy, Miss Bessie Dewy, Miss Vashti Sniff, and
Miss Mercy Onmey surged upstairs and floated along the
passage.

'I wish Dick would come!' was again the burden of Fancy.

The same instant a small twig and flower from the creeper
outside the door flew in at the open window, and a masculine
voice said, 'Ready, Fancy dearest?'

'There he is, he is!' cried Fancy, tittering spasmodically and
breathing as it were for the first time that morning.

The bridesmaids crowded to the window and turned their
heads in the direction pointed out, at which motion eight ear-
rings all swung as one: – not looking at Dick because they
particularly wanted to see him, but with an important sense of
their duty as obedient minister of the will of that apotheosised
being – the Bride.

'He looks very taking!' said Miss Vashti Sniff, a young lady
who blushed cream-colour and wore yellow bonnet-ribbons.

Dick was advancing to the door in a painfully new coat of

shining cloth, primrose-coloured waistcoat, hat of the same painful style of newness, and with an extra quantity of whiskers shaved off his face and hair cut to an unwonted shortness in honour of the occasion.

'Now I'll run down,' said Fancy, looking at herself over her shoulder in the glass, and flitting off.

'O Dick!' she exclaimed, 'I am so glad you are come! I knew you would, of course, but I thought, O, if you shouldn't!'

'Not come, Fancy! Het or wet, blow or snow, here come I today! Why, what's possessing your little soul? You never used to mind such things a bit.'

'Ah, Mr Dick, I hadn't hoisted my colours and committed myself then!' said Fancy.

' 'Tis a pity I can't marry the whole five of ye!' said Dick, surveying them all round.

'Heh-heh-heh!' laughed the four bridesmaids, and Fancy privately touched Dick and smoothed him down behind his shoulder as if to assure herself that he was there in flesh and blood as her own property.

'Well, whoever would have thought such a thing?' said Dick, taking off his hat, sinking into a chair, and turning to the elder members of the company.

The latter arranged their eyes and lips to signify that in their opinion nobody could have thought such a thing, whatever it was.

'That my bees should ha' swarmed just then, of all times and seasons!' continued Dick, throwing a comprehensive glance like a net over the whole auditory. 'And 'tis a fine swarm, too: I haven't seen such a fine swarm for these ten years.'

'A' excellent sign,' said Mrs Penny, from the depths of experience. 'A' excellent sign.'

'I am glad everything seems so right,' said Fancy with a breath of relief.

'And so am I,' said the four bridesmaids with much sympathy.

'Well, bees can't be put off,' observed the inharmonious grandfather James. 'Marrying a woman is a thing you can do at any moment; but a swarm o' bees won't come for the asking.'

Dick fanned himself with his hat. 'I can't think,' he said thoughtfully, 'whatever 'twas I did to offend Mr Maybold, – a man I like so much, too. He rather took to me when he came first, and used to say he should like to see me married, and that he'd marry me, whether the young woman I chose lived in his parish or no. I just hinted to him of it when I put in the banns, but he didn't seem to take kindly to the notion now, and so I said no more. I wonder how it was.'

'I wonder!' said Fancy, looking into vacancy with those beautiful eyes of hers – too refined and beautiful for a tranter's wife; but, perhaps, not too good.

'Altered his mind, as folks will, I suppose,' said the tranter. 'Well, my sonnies, there'll be a good strong party looking at us today as we go along.'

'And the body of the church,' said Geoffrey, 'will be lined with females, and a row of young fellers' heads, as far down as the eyes, will be noticed just above the sills of the chancel-winders.'

'Ay, you've been through it twice,' said Reuben, 'and well mid know.'

'I can put up with it for once,' said Dick, 'or twice either, or a dozen times.'

'O Dick!' said Fancy reproachfully.

'Why, dear, that's nothing, – only just a bit of a flourish. You be as nervous as a cat today.'

'And then, of course, when 'tis all over,' continued the tranter, 'we shall march two and two round the parish.'

'Yes, sure,' said Mr Penny: 'two and two: every man hitched up to his woman, 'a b'lieve.'

'I never can make a show of myself in that way!' said Fancy, looking at Dick to ascertain if he could.

'I'm agreed to anything you and the company like, my dear!' said Mr Richard Dewy heartily.

'Why, we did when we were married, didn't we, Ann?' said the tranter; 'and so do everybody, my sonnies.'

'And so did we,' said Fancy's father.

'And so did Penny and I,' said Mrs Penny: 'I wore my best

Bath clogs, I remember, and Penny was cross because it made me look so tall.'

'And so did father and mother,' said Miss Mercy Onmey.

'And I mean to, come next Christmas!' said Nat the grooms-man vigorously, and looking towards the person of Miss Vashti Sniff.

'Respectable people don't nowadays,' said Fancy. 'Still, since poor mother did, I will.'

'Ay,' resumed the tranter, ' 'twas on a White Tuesday when I committed it. Mellstock Club walked the same day, and we new-married folk went a-gaying round the parish behind 'em. Everybody used to wear something white at Whitsuntide in them days. My sonnies, I've got the very white trousers that I wore, at home in box now. Ha'n't I, Ann?'

'You had till I cut 'em up for Jimmy,' said Mrs Dewy.

'And we ought, by rights, after doing this parish, to go round Higher and Lower Mellstock, and call at Viney's, and so work our way hither again across He'th,' said Mr Penny, recovering scent of the matter in hand. 'Dairyman Viney is a very respect-able man, and so is Farmer Kex, and we ought to show our-selves to them.'

'True,' said the tranter, 'we ought to go round Mellstock to do the thing well. We shall form a very striking object walking along in rotation, good-now, neighbours?'

'That we shall: a proper pretty sight for the nation,' said Mrs Penny.

'Hullo!' said the tranter, suddenly catching sight of a singu-lar human figure standing in the doorway, and wearing a long smock-frock of pillow-case cut and of snowy whiteness. 'Why, Leaf! whatever dost thou do here?'

'I've come to know if so be I can come to the wedding – hee-hee!' said Leaf in a voice of timidity.

'Now, Leaf,' said the tranter reproachfully, 'you know we don't want 'ee here today: we've got no room for 'ee, Leaf.'

'Thomas Leaf, Thomas Leaf, fie upon 'ee for prying!' said old William.

'I know I've got no head, but I thought, if I washed and put on a clane shirt and smock-frock, I might just call,' said Leaf, turning away disappointed and trembling.

'Poor feller!' said the tranter, turning to Geoffrey. 'Suppose we must let en come? His looks are rather against en, and he is terrible silly; but 'a have never been in jail, and 'a won't do no harm.'

Leaf looked with gratitude at the tranter for these praises, and then anxiously at Geoffrey, to see what effect they would have in helping his cause.

'Ay, let en come,' said Geoffrey decisively. 'Leaf, th'rt welcome, 'st know'; and Leaf accordingly remained.

They were now all ready for leaving the house, and began to form a procession in the following order: Fancy and her father, Dick and Susan Dewy, Nat Callcome and Vashti Sniff, Ted Waywood and Mercy Onmey, and Jimmy and Bessie Dewy. These formed the executive, and all appeared in strict wedding attire. Then came the tranter and Mrs Dewy, and last of all Mr and Mrs Penny; – the tranter conspicuous by his enormous gloves, size eleven and threequarter, which appeared at a distance like boxing gloves bleached and sat rather awkwardly upon his brown hands; this hall-mark of respectability having been set upon himself today (by Fancy's special request) for the first time in his life.

'The proper way is for the bridesmaids to walk together,' suggested Fancy.

'What? 'Twas always young man and young woman, arm in crook, in my time!' said Geoffrey, astounded.

'And in mine!' said the tranter.

'And in ours!' said Mr and Mrs Penny.

'Never heard o' such a thing as woman and woman!' said old William; who, with grandfather James and Mrs Day, was to stay at home.

'Whichever way you and the company like, my dear!' said Dick, who, being on the point of securing his right to Fancy, seemed willing to renounce all other rights in the world with the greatest pleasure. The decision was left to Fancy.

'Well, I think I'd rather have it the way mother had it,' she said, and the couples moved along under the trees, every man to his maid.

'Ah!' said grandfather James to grandfather William as they retired, 'I wonder which she thinks most about, Dick or her wedding raiment!'

'Well, 'tis their nature,' said grandfather William. 'Remember the words of the prophet Jeremiah: "Can a maid forget her ornaments, or a bride her attire?"'

Now among dark perpendicular firs, like the shafted columns of a cathedral; now through a hazel copse, matted with primroses and wild hyacinths; now under broad beeches in bright young leaves they threaded their way into the high road over Yalbury Hill, which dipped at that point directly into the village of Geoffrey Day's parish; and in the space of a quarter of an hour Fancy found herself to be Mrs Richard Dewy, though, much to her surprise, feeling no other than Fancy Day still.

On the circuitous return walk through the lanes and fields, amid much chattering and laughter, especially when they came to stiles, Dick discerned a brown spot far up a turnip field.

'Why, tis' Enoch!' he said to Fancy. 'I thought I missed him at the house this morning. How is it he's left you?'

'He drank too much cider, and it got into his head, and they put him in Weatherbury[67] stocks for it. Father was obliged to get somebody else for a day or two, and Enoch hasn't had anything to do with the woods since.'

'We might ask him to call down tonight. Stocks are nothing for once, considering 'tis our wedding day.' The bridal party was ordered to halt.

'Eno-o-o-och!' cried Dick at the top of his voice.

'Y-a-a-a-a-a-as!' said Enoch from the distance.

'D'ye know who I be-e-e-e-e?'

'No-o-o-o-o-o-o!'

'Dick Dew-w-w-w-wy!'

'O-h-h-h-h-h!'

'Just a-ma-a-a-a-a-arried!'

'O-h-h-h-h-h!'

'This is my wife, Fa-a-a-a-a-ancy!' (holding her up to Enoch's view as if she had been a nosegay).

'O-h-h-h-h-h!'

'Will ye come across to the party to-ni-i-i-i-i-ight!'

'Ca-a-a-a-a-an't!'

'Why n-o-o-o-o-ot?'

'Don't work for the family no-o-o-o-ow!'

'Not nice of Master Enoch,' said Dick as they resumed their walk.

'You mustn't blame en,' said Geoffrey; 'the man's not hisself now; he's in his morning frame of mind. When he's had a gallon o' cider or ale, or a pint or two of mead, the man's well enough, and his manners be as good as anybody's in the kingdom.'

II

Under the Greenwood Tree

THE point in Yalbury Wood which abutted on the end of Geoffrey Day's premises was closed with an ancient tree, horizontally of enormous extent, though having no great pretensions
to height. Many hundreds of birds had been born amidst the
boughs of this single tree; tribes of rabbits and hares had
nibbled at its bark from year to year; quaint tufts of fungi had
sprung from the cavities of its forks; and countless families of
moles and earthworms had crept about its roots. Beneath and
beyond its shade spread a carefully-tended grass-plot, its purpose being to supply a healthy exercise-ground for young
chickens and pheasants: the hens, their mothers, being en-
closed in coops placed upon the same green flooring.

All these encumbrances were now removed, and as the afternoon advanced the guests gathered on the spot, where music,
dancing, and the singing of songs went forward with great
spirit throughout the evening. The propriety of every one was
intense, by reason of the influence of Fancy, who, as an additional precaution in this direction had strictly charged her
father and the tranter to carefully avoid saying 'thee' and 'thou'
in their conversation, on the plea that those ancient words
sounded so very humiliating to persons of newer taste; also
that they were never to be seen drawing the back of the hand
across the mouth after drinking — a local English custom of
extraordinary antiquity, but stated by Fancy to be decidedly
dying out among the better classes of society.

In addition to the local musicians present a man who had a
thorough knowledge of the tambourine was invited from the
village of Tantrum Clangley, — a place long celebrated for the
skill of its inhabitants as performers on instruments of per-
cussion. These important members of the assembly were relegated to a height of two or three feet from the ground, upon a

temporary erection of planks supported by barrels. Whilst the dancing progressed the older persons sat in a group under the trunk of the tree, – the space being allotted to them somewhat grudgingly by the young ones, who were greedy of pirouetting room, – and fortified by a table against the heels of the dancers. Here the gaffers and gammers whose dancing days were over told stories of great impressiveness, and at intervals surveyed the advancing and retiring couples from the same retreat, as people on shore might be supposed to survey a naval engagement in the bay beyond; returning again to their tales when the pause was over. Those of the whirling throng who, during the rests between each figure, turned their eyes in the direction of these seated ones, were only to discover, on account of the music and bustle, that a very striking circumstance was in course of narration – denoted by an emphatic sweep of the hand, snapping of the fingers, close of the lips, and fixed look into the centre of the listener's eye for the space of a quarter of a minute, which raised in that listener such a reciprocating working of face as to sometimes make the distant dancers half wish to know what such an interesting tale could refer to.

Fancy caused her looks to wear as much matronly expression as was obtainable out of six hours' experience as a wife, in order that the contrast between her own state of life and that of the unmarried young women present might be duly impressed upon the company: occasionally stealing glances of admiration at her left hand, but this quite privately; for her ostensible bearing concerning the matter was intended to show that, though she undoubtedly occupied the most wondrous position in the eyes of the world that had ever been attained, she was almost unconscious of the circumstances, and that the somewhat prominent position in which that wonderfully-emblazoned left hand was continually found to be placed when handing cups and saucers, knives, forks, and glasses, was quite the result of accident. As to wishing to excite envy in the bosoms of her maiden companions by the exhibition of the shining ring, every one was to know it was quite foreign to the dignity of such an experienced married woman. Dick's imagination in the meantime was far less capable of drawing so much

wontedness from his new condition. He had been for two or
three hours trying to feel himself merely a newly-married man,
but had been able to get no further in the attempt than to
realize that he was Dick Dewy, the tranter's son, at a party
given by Lord Wessex's head man-in-charge, on the outlying
Yalbury estate, dancing and chatting with Fancy Day.

Five country dances, including 'Haste to the Wedding', two
reels, and three fragments of hornpipes, brought them to the
time for supper which, on account of the dampness of the grass
from the immaturity of the summer season, was spread indoors.
At the conclusion of the meal Dick went out to put the horse
in; and Fancy, with the elder half of the four bridesmaids,
retired upstairs to dress for the journey to Dick's new cottage
near Mellstock.

'How long will you be putting on your bonnet, Fancy?' Dick
inquired at the foot of the staircase. Being now a man of business and married he was strong on the importance of time, and
doubled the emphasis of his words in conversing, and added
vigour to his nods.

'Only a minute.'

'How long is that?'

'Well, dear, five.'

'Ah, sonnies!' said the tranter, as Dick retired, ' 'tis a talent
of the female race that low numbers should stand for high,
more especially in matters of waiting, matters of age, and
matters of money.'

'True, true, upon my body,' said Geoffrey.

'Ye spak with feeling, Geoffrey, seemingly.'

'Anybody that d'know my experience might guess that.'

'What's she doing now, Geoffrey?'

'Claning out all the upstairs drawers and cupboards, and
dusting the second-best chainey – a thing that's only done once
a year. "If there's work to be done I must do it," says she,
"wedding or no." '

' 'Tis my belief she's a very good woman at bottom.'

'She's terrible deep, then.'

Mrs Penny turned round. 'Well, 'tis humps and hollers with
the best of us; but still and for all that, Dick and Fancy stand

as fair a chance of having a bit of sunsheen as any married pair in the land.'

'Ay, there's no gainsaying it.'

Mrs Dewy came up, talking to one person and looking at another. 'Happy, yes,' she said. ' 'Tis always so when a couple is so exactly in tune with one another as Dick and she.'

'When they be'n't too poor to have time to sing,' said grandfather James.

'I tell ye, neighbours, when the pinch comes,' said the tranter: 'when the oldest daughter's boots be only a size less than her mother's, and the rest o' the flock close behind her. A sharp time for a man that, my sonnies; a very sharp time! Chanticleer's comb is a-cut then, 'a believe.'

'That's about the form o't,' said Mr Penny. 'That'll put the stuns upon[68] a man, when you must measure mother and daughters' lasts to tell 'em apart.'

'You've no cause to complain, Reuben, of such a close-coming flock,' said Mrs Dewy; 'for ours was a straggling lot enough, God knows!'

'I d'know it, I d'know it,' said the tranter. 'You be a well-enough woman, Ann.'

Mrs Dewy put her mouth in the form of a smile and put it back again without smiling.

'And if they come together, they go together,' said Mrs Penny, whose family had been the reverse of the tranter's; 'and a little money will make either fate tolerable. And money can be made by our young couple, I know.'

'Yes, that it can!' said the impulsive voice of Leaf, who had hitherto humbly admired the proceedings from a corner. 'It can be done – all that's wanted is a few pounds to begin with. That's all! I know a story about it!'

'Let's hear thy story, Leaf,' said the tranter. 'I never knew you were clever enough to tell a story. Silence, all of ye! Mr Leaf will tell a story.'

'Tell your story, Thomas Leaf,' said grandfather William in the tone of a schoolmaster.

'Once,' said the delighted Leaf, in an uncertain voice, 'there was a man who lived in a house! Well, this man went thinking and thinking night and day. At last, he said to himself, as I might, "If I had only ten pound, I'd make a fortune." At last by hook or by crook, behold he got the ten pounds!'

'Only think of that!' said Nat Callcome satirically.

'Silence!' said the tranter.

'Well, now comes the interesting part of the story! In a little time he made that ten pounds twenty. Then a little time after that he doubled it, and made it forty. Well, he went on, and a good while after that he made it eighty, and on to a hundred. Well, by-and-by he made it two hundred! Well, you'd never believe it, but – he went on and made it four hundred! He went on, and what did he do? Why, he made it eight hundred! Yes, he did,' continued Leaf in the highest pitch of excitement, bringing down his fist upon his knee with such force that he quivered with the pain; 'yes, and he went on and made it A THOUSAND!'

'Hear, hear!' said the tranter. 'Better than the history of England, my sonnies!'

'Thank you for your story, Thomas Leaf,' said grandfather William; and then Leaf gradually sank into nothingness again.

Amid a medley of laughter, old shoes, and elderwine, Dick and his bride took their departure side by side in the excellent new spring-cart which the young tranter now possessed. The moon was just over the full, rendering any light from lamps or their own beauties quite unnecessary to the pair. They drove slowly along Yalbury Bottom, where the road passed between two copses. Dick was talking to his companion.

'Fancy,' he said, 'why we are so happy is because there is such full confidence between us. Ever since that time you confessed to that little flirtation with Shiner by the river (which was really no flirtation at all), I have thought how artless and good you must be to tell me o' such a trifling thing, and to be so frightened about it as you were. It has won me to tell you my every deed and word since then. We'll have no secrets from each other, darling, will we ever? – no secret at all.'

'None from today,' said Fancy. 'Hark! what's that?'

From a neighbouring thicket was suddenly heard to issue in a loud, musical, and liquid voice –

'Tippiwit! swe-e-et! ki-ki-ki! Come hither, come hither, come hither!'

'O, 'tis the nightingale,' murmured she, and thought of a secret she would never tell.

GENERAL PREFACE TO THE
WESSEX EDITION OF 1912

In accepting a proposal for a definite edition of these productions in prose and verse I have found an opportunity of classifying the novels under heads that show approximately the author's aim, if not his achievement, in each book of the series at the date of its composition. Sometimes the aim was lower than at other times; sometimes, where the intention was primarily high, force of circumstances (among which the chief were the necessities of magazine publication) compelled a modification, great or slight, of the original plan. Of a few, however, of the longer novels, and of many of the shorter tales, it may be assumed that they stand today much as they would have stood if no accidents had obstructed the channel between the writer and the public. That many of them, if any, stand as they would stand if written *now* is not to be supposed.

In the classification of these fictitious chronicles – for which the name of 'The Wessex Novels' was adopted, and is still retained – the first group is called 'Novels of Character and Environment', and contains those which approach most nearly to uninfluenced works; also one or two which, whatever their quality in some few of their episodes, may claim a verisimilitude in general treatment and detail.

The second group is distinguished as 'Romances and Fantasies,' a sufficiently descriptive definition. The third class – 'Novels of Ingenuity' – show a not infrequent disregard of the probable in the chain of events, and depend for their interest mainly on the incidents themselves. They might also be characterized as 'Experiments', and were written for the nonce simply; though despite the artificiality of their fable some of their scenes are not without fidelity to life.

It will not be supposed that these differences are distinctly perceptible in every page of every volume. It was inevitable that blendings and alternations should occur in all. Moreover, as it was not thought desirable in every instance to change the arrangement of the shorter stories to which readers have grown accustomed, certain of these may be found under headings to which an acute judgement might deny appropriateness.

It has sometimes been conceived of novels that evolve their action on a circumscribed scene – as do many (though not all) of these – that they cannot be so inclusive in their exhibition of human nature as novels wherein the scenes cover large extents of country, in which events figure amid towns and cities, even wander over the four quarters of the globe. I am not concerned to argue this point further than to suggest that the conception is an untrue one in respect of the elementary passions. But I would state that the geographical limits of the stage here trodden were not absolutely forced upon the writer by circumstances; he forced them upon himself from judgement. I considered that our magnificent heritage from the Greeks in dramatic literature found sufficient room for a large proportion of its action in an extent of their country not much larger than the half-dozen counties here reunited under the old name of Wessex, that the domestic emotions have throbbed in Wessex nooks with as much intensity as in the palaces of Europe, and that, anyhow, there was quite enough human nature in Wessex for one man's literary purpose. So far was I possessed by this idea that I kept within the frontiers when it would have been easier to overlap them and give more cosmopolitan features to the narrative.

Thus, though the people in most of the novels (and in much of the shorter verse) are dwellers in a province bounded on the north by the Thames, on the south by the English Channel, on the east by a line running from Hayling Island to Windsor Forest, and on the west by the Cornish coast, they were meant to be typically and essentially those of any and every place where

> Thought's the slave of life, and life time's fool

– beings in whose hearts and minds that which is apparently local should be really universal.

But whatever the success of this intention, and the value of these novels as delineations of humanity, they have at least a humble supplementary quality of which I may be justified in reminding the reader, though it is one that was quite unintentional and unforeseen. At the dates represented in the various narrations things were like that in Wessex: the inhabitants lived in certain ways, engaged in certain occupations, kept alive certain customs, just as they are shown doing in these pages. And in particularizing such I have often been reminded of Boswell's remarks on the trouble to which he was put and the pilgrimages he was obliged to make to authenticate some detail, though the labour was one which would bring him no praise. Unlike his achievement, however, on which an error would as he says have brought discredit, if these country customs and vocations, obsolete and obsolescent, had been detailed wrongly, nobody would have discovered such errors to the end of Time. Yet I have instituted inquiries to correct tricks of memory, and striven against temptations to exaggerate, in order to preserve for my own satisfaction a fairly true record of a vanishing life.

It is advisable also to state here, in response to inquiries from readers interested in landscape, prehistoric antiquities, and especially old English architecture, that the description of these backgrounds has been done from the real – that is to say, has something real for its basis, however illusively treated. Many features of the first two kinds have been given under their existing names; for instance, the Vale of Blackmoor or Blakemore, Hambledon Hill, Bulbarrow, Nettlecombe Tout, Dogbury Hill, High-Stoy, Bubb-Down Hill, The Devil's Kitchen, Cross-in-Hand, Long-Ash Lane, Benvill Lane, Giant's Hill, Crimmercrock Lane, and Stonehenge. The rivers Froom, or Frome, and Stour, are, of course, well known as such. And the further idea was that large towns and points tending to mark the outline of Wessex – such as Bath, Plymouth, The Start, Portland Bill, Southampton, etc. – should be named clearly. The scheme was not greatly elaborated, but, whatever its value, the names remain still.

In respect of places described under fictitious or ancient names in the novels – for reasons that seemed good at the time of writing them – and kept up in the poems – discerning people have affirmed in print that they clearly recognize the originals: such as Shaftesbury in 'Shaston', Sturminster Newton in 'Stourcastle', Dorchester in 'Casterbridge', Salisbury Plain in 'The Great Plain', Cranborne Chase in 'The Chase', Beaminster in 'Emminster', Bere Regis in 'Kingsbere', Woodbury Hill in 'Greenhill', Wool Bridge in 'Wellbridge', Harfoot or Harput Lane in 'Stagfoot Lane', Hazlebury in 'Nuttlebury', Bridport in 'Port Bredy', Maiden Newton in 'Chalk Newton', a farm near Nettlecombe Tout in 'Flintcomb Ash', Sherborne in 'Sherton Abbas', Milton Abbey in 'Middleton Abbey', Cerne Abbas in 'Abbot's Cernel', Evershot in 'Evershed', Taunton in 'Toneborough', Bournemouth in 'Sandbourne', Winchester in 'Wintoncester', Oxford in 'Christminster', Reading in 'Aldbrickham', Newbury in 'Kennetbridge', Wantage in 'Alfredston', Basingstoke in 'Stoke Barehills', and so on. Subject to the qualifications above given, that no detail is guaranteed – that the portraiture of fictitiously named towns and villages was only suggested by certain real places, and wantonly wanders from inventorial descriptions of them – I do not contradict these keen hunters for the real; I am satisfied with their statements as at least an indication of their interest in the scenes.

Thus much for the novels. Turning now to the verse – to myself the more individual part of my literary fruitage – I would say that, unlike some of the fiction, nothing interfered with the writer's freedom in respect of its form or content. Several of the poems – indeed many – were produced before novel-writing had been thought of as a pursuit; but few saw the light till all the novels had been published. The limited stage to which the majority of the latter confine their exhibitions has not been adhered to here in the same proportion, the dramatic part especially having a very broad theatre of action. It may thus relieve the circumscribed areas treated in the prose, if such relief be needed. To be sure, one might argue that by surveying Europe from a celestial point of vision – as in *The Dynasts* – that continent becomes virtually a province – a

Wessex, an Attica, even a mere garden – and hence is made to conform to the principle of the novels, however far it out-measures their region. But that may be as it will.

The few volumes filled by the verse cover a producing period of some eighteen years first and last, while the seventeen or more volumes of novels represent correspondingly about four-and-twenty years. One is reminded by this disproportion in time and result how much more concise and quintessential expression becomes when given in rhythmic form than when shaped in the language of prose.

One word on what has been called the present writer's philosophy of life, as exhibited more particularly in this metrical section of his compositions. Positive views on the Whence and the Wherefore of things have never been advanced by this pen as a consistent philosophy. Nor is it likely, indeed, that imaginative writings extended over more than forty years would exhibit a coherent scientific theory of the universe even if it had been attempted – of that universe concerning which Spencer owns to the 'paralysing thought' that possibly there exists no comprehension of it anywhere. But such objectless consistency never has been attempted, and the sentiments in the following pages have been stated truly to be mere impressions of the moment, and not convictions or arguments.

That these impressions have been condemned as 'pessimistic' – as if that were a very wicked adjective – shows a curious muddle-mindedness. It must be obvious that there is a higher characteristic of philosophy than pessimism, or than meliorism, or even than the optimism of these critics – which is truth. Existence is either ordered in a certain way, or it is not so ordered, and conjectures which harmonize best with experience are removed above all comparison with other conjectures which do not so harmonize. So that to say one view is worse than other views without proving it erroneous implies the possibility of a false view being better or more expedient than a true view; and no pragmatic proppings can make that *idolum specus* stand on its feet, for it postulates a prescience denied to humanity.

And there is another consideration. Differing natures find their tongue in the presence of differing spectacles. Some natures become vocal at tragedy, some are made vocal by comedy, and it seems to me that to whichever of these aspects of life a writer's instinct for expression the more readily responds, to that he should allow it to respond. That before a contrasting side of things he remains undemonstrative need not be assumed to mean that he remains unperceiving.

It was my hope to add to these volumes of verse as many more as would make a fairly comprehensive cycle of the whole. I had wished that those in dramatic, ballad, and narrative form should include most of the cardinal situations which occur in social and public life, and those in lyric form a round of emotional experiences of some completeness. But

> The petty done, the undone vast!

The more written the more seems to remain to be written; and the night cometh. I realize that these hopes and plans, except possibly to the extent of a volume or two, must remain unfulfilled.

October 1911   T.H.

NOTE ON THE TEXT

THE text followed is that of the Macmillan Wessex Edition of 1912, the last to be revised by Hardy. It differs in minor details from that of the first edition published by Tinsley Brothers in 1872. When the American firm of Osgood, McIlvaine & Co. proposed a uniform edition of all Hardy's novels in 1895, Hardy revised *Under the Greenwood Tree*, bringing its 'Wessex' place-names into line with those of the later Wessex novels, and adding quite a lot of small topographical detail. The game-keeper Geoffrey Day was given increased status (see note 47) and Dick Dewy's speech further rusticated, probably to widen the social gap between Dick and Fancy Day. Some of the words spoken by members of the Mellstock Quire were changed in favour of dialect expressions, apparently to meet the criticisms of Hardy's friend Horace Moule in the *Saturday Review*. Hardy also added a slightly ungenteel anecdote that might have been thought coarse when the book was first published (see note 36).

ACKNOWLEDGEMENTS

THE present edition, and the introduction to it, is indebted to the information and suggestions contained in F. B. Pinion's invaluable *A Hardy Companion* (Macmillan, 1968), W. R. Rutland's *Thomas Hardy* (Blackwell, 1938), Carl J. Weber's *Hardy of Wessex* (1940), Merryn Williams's *Thomas Hardy and Rural England* (Macmillan, 1972), Douglas Brown's *Thomas Hardy* (Longman, 1954), and Robert Gittings's *The Young Thomas Hardy* (Macmillan, 1975).

NOTES

1 (p. 32). *It was customary to inscribe a few jigs, reels, hornpipes, and ballads in the same book ...*: Three MS. music-books belonging to Thomas Hardy's grandfather and father have been preserved. They are described in W. R. Rutland's *Thomas Hardy* (Oxford, 1938). See Notes 11 and 22.

2 (p. 33). *Mellstock Quire*: The 'Mellstock Quire' or members of it find mention in many of Hardy's poems, in particular *Friends Beyond, The Rash Pride, The Dead Quire, Church Romance, Winter Night in the Woodlands, The Country Wedding, The Paphian Ball*. Other references are to be found in the short stories – *The Fiddler of the Reels, The Grave by the Handpost*, and *The Waiting Supper*. Old William Dewy appears as a character in an anecdote in chapter XVII of *Tess of the D'Urbervilles*, and in *Absentmindedness in a Parish Choir*, one of the tales in *A Few Crusted Characters*. Out of the characters who make up 'The Mellstock Quire' Hardy took elements from which he constructed the Wessex rustics who appear in his later novels. Traces of the 'Mellstock Quire' can also be found in *Two on a Tower*, and *The Mayor of Casterbridge*.

3 (p. 39). *With the rose and the lily etc.*: These lines are from 'The Sheep-Shearing Song', a version of which can be found in *The Folk-Song Journal*, vol. I, pp. 262–3.

4 (p. 39). *Mellstock parish*: 'Mellstock Parish' in Hardy's fictional 'Wessex' stands for the real village of Stinsford and the hamlets of Higher and Lower Bockhampton two miles east of Dorchester ('Casterbridge'). Hardy was born in his grandfather's cottage at Higher Bockhampton ('Upper Mellstock') and his heart is buried in his first wife's grave beside his parents at Stinsford. 'Mellstock Cross' (Bockhampton Cross) is not mentioned in the first edition (1872) of *Under the Greenwood Tree*. Hardy revised the texts of all his novels for the uniform edition of 1895, and took the opportunity of regularizing all their 'Wessex' place-names. In the case of *Under the Greenwood Tree* he intensified its geographical particularity by expanding most references to places, in the course of which he inserted a great many new 'Wessex' place-names in the text.

5 (p. 41). *Mr Robert Penny*: According to Hardy's disguised autobiography (F. E. Hardy: *The Early Life of Thomas Hardy*), his actual name was Robert Reason. He is buried in Stinsford churchyard near the tombs of the Hardys, along with other members of the 'Mellstock Quire' – the three Dewys, Michael Mail, and Joseph Bowman. See Hardy's famous poem *Friends Beyond*, and *The Dead Quire*:

> There Dewy lay by the gaunt yew tree,
> There Reuben and Michael, a pace behind,
> And Bowman with his family
> By the wall that the ivies bind.

The members of the Stinsford choir were Thomas Hardy's grandfather, his sons Thomas and James, and one James Dart. According to the *Life*, William Dewy, Reuben Dewy, Dick Dewy and Michael Mail occupied the same seats and played the same instruments. But although the Hardy family home at Higher Bockhampton serves as a model for the Dewys' house in 'Upper Mellstock' the characters of the Dewys are not based on the Hardys.

6 (p. 43). *It was a long low cottage with a hipped roof of thatch . . .*: The Dewy cottage is based on Hardy's birthplace, described in *The Early Life of Thomas Hardy* as

> the seven-room rambling house that stands easternmost of the few scattered dwellings called Higher Bockhampton, in the parish of Stinsford. The domiciles were quaint, brass-knockered, and green-shuttered then... The Hardy homestead, too, is weather-worn and reduced, having comprised, in addition to the house, two gardens (one of them part orchard) a horse-paddock, and sand-and-gravel pits, afterwards exhausted and overgrown, also stabling and like buildings since removed... The wide, brilliantly white chimney-corner, in his childhood such a feature of the sitting-room, is also gone.

It was in this cottage that Hardy wrote *Under the Greenwood Tree*.

7 (p. 45). '*. . . The water-cider from 'em is as good as most people's best cider is*': Some of the characteristics of Reuben Dewy, the Tranter, are based on those of James Dart, one of the members of the original Stinsford choir. In *The Early Life of Thomas Hardy* appears this extract from Hardy's notebooks: 'Met J.D. (James Dart), one of the old Mellstock fiddlers – who kept me talking interminably: a man who speaks neither truth nor lies, but a sort of Not Proven compound which is very relishable.' Hardy often helped his father at cider-making – 'a proceeding he had always enjoyed from childhood – the apples being from huge old trees that have now perished'. It was the cider-making scene in Hardy's first novel, *Desperate Remedies*, which was otherwise poorly received, that the *Athenaeum* and *Spectator* reviews united in praising.

8 (p. 45). *Fourteens*: candles sold at fourteen to the lb.

9 (p. 46). *husbird*: rascal.

10 (p. 47). *martel*: individual, person.

11 (p. 51). *Christmas-carol books*: W. R. Rutland's *Thomas Hardy* (Oxford, 1938) describes three MS. music-books belonging to Hardy's father and grandfather, used at Puddletown and later at Stinsford ('Mellstock') according to inscriptions in Thomas Hardy's own hand. The third of these, autographed by Hardy's father 'Thomas Hardy. Bock-

hampton' bears a note by the novelist: 'The Carol Book of T.H. II (used on the rounds on Xmas Eve in "Mellstock Quire" down to about 1842).' Rutland remarks: 'This volume contains only Christmas Carols and Hymns. The great interest of this volume is that it is clearly similar to the ones which are several times mentioned in *Under the Greenwood Tree*.' See further, note 22.

12 (p. 51). *linnit*: lint.

13 (p. 52). *thirtingill as a chiel*: obstinate as a child.

14 (p. 52). *bradded*: nailed.

15 (p. 52). *pomace*: pulped apples.

16 (p. 54). *teaving*: toiling, struggling.

17 (p. 57). *metheglin*: a kind of mead.

According to Hardy, Voss was the only real person in his novels introduced under his own name (though Robert Gittings, in *The Young Thomas Hardy*, points out that he forgot 'poor deaf Grammer Cates' in *A Pair of Blue Eyes*). It is impossible to resist quoting the sketch of Voss in the autobiographical *Early Life of Thomas Hardy*:

> T. Voss used to take casts of heads of executed convicts. He took those of Preedy and Stone. Dan Pouncy held the heads while it was being done. Voss oiled the faces, and took them in halves, afterwards making casts from the masks. There was a groove where the rope went, and Voss saw a little blood in the case of Stone, where the skin had been broken – not in Preedy's.

18 (p. 58). '... *Barrel-organs, and the things next door to 'em that you blow with your foot* ...': Michael Mail is referring to the harmonium, or American organ, invented 1840.

19 (p. 58). *serpent*: a bass wind-instrument 8 ft long, a tube twisted into three U-shaped turns, made of thin wood covered with leather and with four keys (though some had as many as fourteen). It was in vogue during the eighteenth century, when George III introduced it into the British Army. Now obsolete, though still to be found in France (where it was invented at Auxerre in the sixteenth century).

20 (p. 59). *rafting*: rousing.

21 (p. 59). *dumbledores*: bumblebees. The first edition reads, 'Miserable machines!' one of the phrases that Horace Moule picked out as incongruous in the mouth of a rustic in his *Saturday Review* notice of the book. Hardy changed it in his 1895 revision.

22 (p. 61). '*Four breaths, and then, "O, what unbounded goodness!", number fifty-nine,' said William*: In the Hardy Carol Book mentioned by Rutland (see note 11) No. 59 is 'O what unbounded goodness, Lord'. No. 78 is a blank page, but according to Hardy's sister Katharine he got the words of 'Remember Adam's Fall' from their mother. An early version of this carol appears in *Melismata: Musicall Phansies fitting the Court Citie & Countrie Humours*, ed. T. Ravenscroft, printed in London, 1611. It is also found in *Cantus: Songs and Fancies*, compiled by John Forbes, 1682,

23 (p. 65). *scram*: puny, contemptible.

24 (p. 66). *snap*: snack.

25 (p. 69). *ewe-lease*: sheep-pasture.

26 (p. 70). The service *'which chronologically follows'* the marriage service: i.e. 'The Thanksgiving of Women after Childbirth'.

27 (p. 76). *'... I'd "How'st do" him indeed!...'*: Throughout his novels Hardy underlines the mild snobbism among the peasantry that was beginning to erode dialect and local usages. Cf. *The Mayor of Casterbridge*, chapter XX, where Henchard flies into a rage because his daughter uses a dialect phrase. See also pp. 87–8 and 221 of *Under the Greenwood Tree*.

28 (p. 78). *the 'Triumph, or Follow my Lover'*: this was a six-handed reel usually danced longways by six couples, with the women on one side and the men on the other at the beginning of the formation. This, like the other country dance named in *Under the Greenwood Tree* (see the last chapter of the book), is included in the Hardy music notebooks (cf. Elna Sherman, 'Thomas Hardy: Lyricist, Symphonist', *Music and Letters*, xxi, April 1940). Hardy also mentions it in his poems 'The Dance at the Phoenix', 'One we knew'.

29 (p. 82). *six-hands-round*: According to Hardy, this dance must have been 'The College Hornpipe'.

30 (p. 87). *the Dree Mariners at Casterbridge*: the 'Dree Mariners' was Hardy's name for 'The King of Prussia' public-house which stood in the High Street, Dorchester, near the 'King's Arms'. It plays a significant role in *The Mayor of Casterbridge*. In the original 1872 edition of *Under the Greenwood Tree* it is called 'The Three Choughs'. Hardy made a drawing of it, reproduced in F. B. Pinion's *A Hardy Companion*.

31 (p. 89). *a Nasmyth hammer*: the steam-hammer invented by James Nasmyth (1808–90).

32 (p. 91). *'cross-dadder'*: a children's game, presumably one like 'prisoner's base' (*sic* in the original 1872 edition of *Under the Greenwood Tree*).

33 (p. 98). *Moroni*: Giambattista Moroni, c. 1525–78, Italian portrait-painter of the Brescian school. His portrait of a tailor is in the National Gallery.

34 (p. 99). *gawk-hammer*: gaping idiot.

35 (p. 100). *mumbudgeting*: taking by surprise, without notice.

36 (p. 102). *'Yes; he was a right sensible pa'son ... Which was no compliment to us, come to that.'*: this anecdote does not appear in the original 1872 edition of *Under the Greenwood Tree*. Hardy added it when he revised the novel in 1895. It might have seemed to him a little too strong for the sensibilities of the audience he was writing for in the 1870s.

37 (p. 102). *borus-snorus*: outspoken.

38 (p. 102). *drong*: walled alley, or hedged lane.

39 (p. 102). *full-buff*: face to face.

NOTES

40 (p. 102). *strent*: rent or slit.

41 (p. 106). *het*: gulp.

42 (p. 110). *good-now*: sure enough. Among Hardy's papers at Max Gate was found his answer to a query respecting the origin of this phrase:

> The expression 'good now' is still much in use in the interior of this country, though it is dying away hereabout. Its tone is one of conjectural assurance, its precise meaning being 'You may be sure' and such phrases as 'I'll warrant', 'methinks', 'sure enough' would be used as alternatives. The Americanism 'I guess' is near it.
>
> Though I should know exactly how and when to say it, I have never thought about its root meaning. As the people who use it are those who pronounce enough in the old way 'enow', it is possible that 'good now' is 'true enow', sure enough.
>
> The commentators are quite in error in taking 'good' to be vocative meaning 'goodman', 'my good fellow', as is proved by the frequency of such a sentence as this: 'You won't do it my lad, good now,' which would otherwise be redundant.

43 (p. 113). '... *A Laodicean lukewarmness* ...': cf. Revelations, iii 14–16:

> And unto the angel of the church of the Laodiceans write; These things saith the Amen, the faithful and true Witness, the beginning of the creation of God.
>
> I know thy works that thou art neither cold nor hot: I would thou wert cold or hot.
>
> So because thou art lukewarm, and neither cold nor hot, I will spue thee out of my mouth.

44 (p. 117). *mischty*: mischief.

45 (p. 118). *stud*: quandary.

46 (p. 119). '... *up-country London ink-bottle chaps* ...': see the quotations from Hardy's essay *The Dorsetshire Labourer* in the Introduction, pp. 14–15.

47 (p. 120). *Yalbury Wood*: Yalbury Wood is Hardy's 'Wessex' name for Yellowham Wood, between Dorchester and Puddletown. The road up Yellowham Hill intersects the wood, and on the north side stands Geoffrey Day's cottage, though the 'greenwood tree' that once stood near it was felled in 1934. Yalbury Wood is also mentioned in *Far from the Madding Crowd* and *The Mayor of Casterbridge*. The opening sentence of this paragraph was rewritten by Hardy in 1895, apparently to increase Day's status (in the original version he is merely a gamekeeper).

48 (p. 124). '... *He is as true as the town time* ...': the 1872 edition reads, 'He was as true as the Squire's time.' An interesting emendation.

49 (p. 127). *union*: i.e. workhouse.

50 (p. 138). '... *'Twas on White Tuesday, – Mellstock Club walked the same day* ...': according to William Barnes (as quoted by J. S. Udal in

Dorsetshire Folklore) 'Whitsuntide is now a time commonly chosen for
the yearly meeting of the Friendly Societies – Club-Walken as it is
mostly called in Dorset.' They were mostly burial or sickness clubs, and
some existed as late as 1939. See Chapter II of *Tess of the D'Urbervilles*,
and Barnes's fine poem, *Whitsuntide an' Club Walken*, reprinted in *The
Penguin Book of Everyday Verse*.

51 (p. 138). *cappel-faced*: white, dappled with red.

52 (p. 145). *Budmouth-Regis*: 'Budmouth-Regis' is Weymouth, where
Hardy worked as an architect from 1869 to 1870.

53 (p. 170). *Snail-Creep*: the real name (derived from a country dance)
of the path that climbs from near the Hardy cottage at Higher Bockhampton to the main road to London.

54 (p. 176). *'Allow me'* ... *'Not at all.'*: this dialogue between Fancy
Day and Shiner is somewhat artificial and incongruous. The *Athenaeum*
reviewer remarked that 'it would have drawn down the house in a comedy
by the late Mr Robertson but it is not the talk of rustics.'

55 (p. 177). *'King Arthur he had three sons'*: according to a letter of
Hardy's dated 1 Sept. 1889, the first verse of (see copy) this ballad used
to run as follows:

> King Arthur he had three sons,
> Big rogues as ever did swing,
>> He had three sons (by) wh——s
>> And he kicked them all three out-of-doors
> Because they could not sing.

Hardy also recorded another version:

> King Arthur ruled the land
>> And a mighty ruler was he;
> He guarded sure both rich and poor
>> And eke virginitie.

> He had three sons by wh——s
>> Big rogues as ever did swing;
> And he kicked them all three out-of-doors
>> Because they could not sing.

He went on to tell his correspondent (unidentified; possibly J. J.
Foster): 'This song, as sung in this neighbourhood, has always been a
coarsely humourous one – and as far as I know – orally transmitted
only... The tune was a rather monotonous one, as I heard it; but where
it can be obtained I am unable to say.' Published versions of the ballad
can be found in C. J. Sharp, *One Hundred English Folk-Songs* (No. 80) and
The Oxford Song Book (I, No. 67).

56 (p. 179). *mumbudgeting*: taking by surprise, without notice.

57 (p. 180). *chammer*: bedroom.

58 (p. 181). *Queen's scholars*: this is an anachronism. The period of
the novel is supposed to be about 1840, but there were no Queen's
Scholars before 1846.

59 (p. 188). *emmet*: ant.

60 (p. 190). *traypse and wamble*: walk aimlessly and unsteadily.

61 (p. 195). ' "*Though this has come upon us let not our hearts be turned back, or our steps go out of the way.*" ': Cf. Psalm xlv, 17–18.

62 (p. 203). *Grey's Bridge*: the stone bridge over the River Cerne outside Dorchester on the main road to London. It is mentioned in *The Mayor of Casterbridge, Far from the Madding Crowd, The Trumpet Major*, and several of Hardy's poems.

63 (p. 209). *'The knot there's no untying'*: the title of this chapter is a quotation from Thomas Campbell's poem, 'How delicious is the winning.'

64 (p. 211). *coling*: cuddling.

65 (p. 213). *ting*: make a ringing noise. This is supposed to induce bees to swarm. Bees swarming on a wedding day were a good omen if they belonged to one of the married couple.

66 (p. 213). *chammers*: chambers, rooms.

67 (p. 219). *Weatherbury*: Hardy's 'Wessex' name for Puddletown, near Dorchester. The stocks were in the square by St Mary's church.

68 (p. 224). *put the stuns upon*: check, hamper.

ECLOGUE
A BIT O' SLY COORTEN

—

John and Fanny

—

JOHN

Now, Fanny, 'tis too bad, you teazen maïd!
How leäte you be a' come! Where have ye staÿ'd?
How long you have a-meäde me wait about!
I thought you werden gwaïn to come ageän.
I had a mind to goo back hwome ageän.
This idden when you promis'd to come out.

FANNY

Now 'tidden any good to meäke a row,
Upon my word, I cooden come till now.
Vor I've a-been kept in all day by mother,
At work about woone little job an' t'other.
If you do want to goo, though, don't ye staÿ
Vor me a minute longer, I do praÿ.

JOHN

I thought you mid be out wi' Jemmy Bleäke,

FANNY

An' why be out wi' him, vor goodness' seäke?

JOHN

You walk'd o' Zunday evenèn wi'n, d'ye know,
You went vrom church a-hitch'd up in his eärm.

FANNY

Well, if I did, that werden any harm.
Lauk! that *is* zome'at to teäke notice o'.

JOHN

He took ye roun' the middle at the stile,
An' kiss'd ye twice 'ithin the ha'f a mile.

FANNY

Ees, at the stile, because I shoulden vall,
He took me hold to help me down, that's all;
An' I can't zee what very mighty harm
He could ha' done a-lendèn me his eärm.
An' as vor kissèn o' me, if he did,
I didden ax en to, nor zay he mid:
An' if he kiss'd me dree times, or a dozen,
What harm wer it? Why idden he my cousin?
An' I can't zee, then, what there is amiss
In cousin Jem's jist gi'èn me a kiss.

JOHN

Well, he shan't kiss ye, then; you shan't be kiss'd
By his girt ugly chops, a lanky houn'!
If I do zee'n, I'll jist wring up my vist
An' knock en down.
I'll squot his girt pug-nose, if I don't miss en;
I'll warn I'll spweil his pretty lips vor kissèn!

FANNY

Well, John, I'm sure I little thought to vind
That you had ever sich a jealous mind.
What then! I s'pose that I must be a dummy,
An' mussen goo about nor wag my tongue
To any soul, if he's a man, an' young;
Or else you'll work yourzelf up mad wi' passion,
An' talk away o' gi'èn vo'k a drashèn,
An' breakèn bwones, an' beäten heads to pummy!

If you've a got sich jealous ways about ye,
I'm sure I should be better off 'ithout ye.

JOHN

Well, if girt Jemmy have a-won your heart,
We'd better break the coortship off, an' peärt.

FANNY

He won my heart! There, John, don't talk sich stuff;
Don't talk noo mwore, vor you've a-zaid enough.
If I'd a-lik'd another mwore than you,
I'm sure I shoulden come to meet ye zoo;
Vor I've a-twold to father many a storry,
An' took o' mother many a scwoldèn vor ye.
                    [*weeping*.]
But 'twull be over now, vor you shan't zee me
Out wi' ye noo mwore, to pick a quarrel wi' me.

JOHN

Well, Fanny, I woon't zay noo mwore, my dear.
Let's meäke it up. Come, wipe off thik there tear.
Let's goo an' zit o' top o' theäse here stile,
An' rest, an' look about a little while.

FANNY

Now goo away, you crabbed jealous chap!
You shan't kiss me, – you shan't! I'll gi' ye a slap.

JOHN

Then you look smilèn; don't you pout an' toss
Your head so much, an' look so very cross.

FANNY

Now, John! don't squeeze me roun' the middle zoo.
I woon't stop here noo longer, if you do.
Why, John! be quiet, wull ye? Fie upon it!
Now zee how you've a-wrumpl'd up my bonnet!

Mother 'ill zee it after I'm at hwome,
An' gi'e a guess directly how it come.

JOHN

Then don't you zay that I be jealous, Fanny.

FANNY

I wull: vor you *be* jealous, Mister Jahnny.
There's zomebody a-comèn down the groun'
Towards the stile. Who is it? Come, get down
I must run hwome, upon my word then, now;
If I do staÿ, they'll kick up sich a row.
Good night. I can't staÿ now.

JOHN

Then good night, Fanny!
Come out a-bit to-morrow evenèn, can ye?

THE SETTLE AN' THE GIRT WOOD VIRE

Ah! naïghbour John, since I an' you
Wer youngsters, ev'ry thing is new.
My father's vires wer all o' logs
O' cleft-wood, down upon the dogs
Below our clavy, high, an' brode
Enough to teäke a cart an' lwoad,
Where big an' little all zot down
At bwoth zides, an' bevore, all roun'.
An' when I zot among em, I
Could zee all up ageän the sky
Drough chimney, where our vo'k did hitch
The zalt-box an' the beäcon-vlitch,
An' watch the smoke on out o' vier,
All up an' out o' tun, an' higher.
An' there wer beäcon up on rack,

An' pleätes an' dishes on the tack;
An' roun' the walls wer heärbs a-stowed
In peäpern bags, an' blathers blowed.
An' just above the clavy-bwoard
Wer father's spurs, an' gun, an' sword;
An' there wer then, our girtest pride,
The settle by the vier zide.
    Ah! gi'e me, if I wer a squier,
    The settle an' the girt wood vier.

But they've a-wall'd up now wi' bricks
The vier pleäce vor dogs an' sticks,
An' only left a little hole
To teäke a little greäte o' coal,
So small that only twos or drees
Can jist push in an' warm their knees.
An' then the carpets they do use,
Bën't fit to tread wi' ouer shoes;
An' chairs an' couches be so neat,
You mussen teäke em vor a seat:
They be so fine, that vo'k mus' pleäce
All over em an' outer ceäse,
An' then the cover, when 'tis on,
Is still too fine to loll upon.
    Ah! gi'e me, if I wer a squier,
    The settle an' the girt wood vier.

Carpets, indeed! You coulden hurt
The stwone-vloor wi' a little dirt;
Vor what wer brought in doors by men,
The women soon mopp'd out ageän.
Zoo we did come vrom muck an' mire,
An' walk in straïght avore the vier;
But now, a man's a-kept at door
At work a pirty while, avore
He's screäp'd an' rubb'd, an' cleän and fit
To goo in where his wife do zit.
An' then if he should have a whiff

In there, 'twould only breed a miff:
He can't smoke there, vor smoke woon't goo
'Ithin the footy little flue.
    Ah! gi'e me, if I wer a squier,
    The settle an' the girt wood vier.

FOR THE BEST IN PAPERBACKS, LOOK FOR THE

In every corner of the world, on every subject under the sun, Penguin represents quality and variety – the very best in publishing today.

For complete information about books available from Penguin – including Pelicans, Puffins, Peregrines and Penguin Classics – and how to order them, write to us at the appropriate address below. Please note that for copyright reasons the selection of books varies from country to country.

In the United Kingdom: For a complete list of books available from Penguin in the U.K., please write to *Dept E.P., Penguin Books Ltd, Harmondsworth, Middlesex, UB7 0DA*

In the United States: For a complete list of books available from Penguin in the U.S., please write to *Dept BA, Penguin, 299 Murray Hill Parkway, East Rutherford, New Jersey 07073*

In Canada: For a complete list of books available from Penguin in Canada, please write to *Penguin Books Canada Ltd, 2801 John Street, Markham, Ontario L3R 1B4*

In Australia: For a complete list of books available from Penguin in Australia, please write to the *Marketing Department, Penguin Books Australia Ltd, P.O. Box 257, Ringwood, Victoria 3134*

In New Zealand: For a complete list of books available from Penguin in New Zealand, please write to the *Marketing Department, Penguin Books (NZ) Ltd, Private Bag, Takapuna, Auckland 9*

In India: For a complete list of books available from Penguin, please write to *Penguin Overseas Ltd, 706 Eros Apartments, 56 Nehru Place, New Delhi, 110019*

In Holland: For a complete list of books available from Penguin in Holland, please write to *Penguin Books Nederland B.V., Postbus 195, NL–1380AD Weesp, Netherlands*

In Germany: For a complete list of books available from Penguin, please write to *Penguin Books Ltd, Friedrichstrasse 10 – 12, D–6000 Frankfurt Main 1, Federal Republic of Germany*

In Spain: For a complete list of books available from Penguin in Spain, please write to *Longman Penguin España, Calle San Nicolas 15, E–28013 Madrid, Spain*

THOMAS HARDY

THE WOODLANDERS

Introduced by Ian Gregor
Edited by James Gibson

First published in 1887, at the mid-point of his output as a novelist, *The Woodlanders* is in many ways Hardy's most representative achievement. The author himself came to regard it as his favourite novel and it does, unquestionably, mark a moment of distillation in his writing career: nowhere does he seem more confidently in control of his material, or more certain of his tone.

For centuries the small community of Little Hintock, set on the edge of Blackmoor Vale, had been sustained and protected by the surrounding woodland. But the lives of the villagers are now caught up in a web of intense and consuming emotion: the unspoken love of the peasant girl Marty South for Giles Winterbourne; his own devotion to Grace Melbury; and, at the heart of the web, the troubled relationship between Grace and the ambitious young doctor, Edred Fitzpiers, which vividly captures the complexity of sexual feeling which Hardy was to explore further in *Jude the Obscure*.

THOMAS HARDY

FAR FROM THE MADDING CROWD

Edited by Ronald Blythe

Far from the Madding Crowd was first published in 1874 and was sold out in just over two months, surprising even the publisher. The critics were not quite so enthusiastic, though they all agreed on its power, and Henry James wrote: 'the only things we believe in are the sheep and the dogs'.

Henry James was wrong. *Far from the Madding Crowd*, perhaps the best-loved and most humorous of Hardy's novels even though the familiar themes of suffering and betrayal are evident, is the product of Hardy's intimate and first-hand knowledge of the attitudes, habits, inconsistencies and idiosyncrasies of rural men and women. It would be very difficult indeed to match his portrait of mid-Victorian Dorset before the railway.

The mainspring of the book, nonetheless, centres around Bathsheba Everdene and her three suitors. And, in portraying her caprice and wilfulness gradually crushed by bitter self-knowledge and rejection, Hardy makes his own point about sexual love: 'Romance', he says, should grow up 'in the interstices of a mass of hard prosaic reality.'

THOMAS HARDY

THE RETURN OF THE NATIVE

Edited by George Woodcock

The Return of the Native, both powerful and sombre, is sometimes considered the most representative of Hardy's novels. It tells the story of Eustacia Vye, Thomasin and Mistress Yeobright, and the men who influence and alter their lives – Diggory Venn, the reddleman, Damon Wildeve and the returning 'native', Clym Yeobright.

It is set in Egdon Heath whose lowering, 'titanic' presence dominates the men and women who live on it, and whose menace and beauty Hardy so surely and superbly evokes. Against this changing backdrop, that represents the impersonal forces and eternal verities that manipulate us all, the fates of beautiful, passionate Eustacia and the others are inexorably played out. As Eustacia despairingly cries: 'I was capable of much; but I have been injured and blighted and crushed by things beyond my control.'

Hardy's closely observed local detail and dialect give the novel a firm and realistic foundation and provide a rich, and often humorous, counterpoint.

THOMAS HARDY

TESS OF THE D'URBERVILLES

Edited by David Skilton and introduced by A. Alvarez

Thomas Hardy used to speak of Tess as if she were a real person, and once he wrote: 'I have not been able to put on paper all that she is, or was, to me.' It is true that in Tess he created one of the most striking and tragic of his heroines, whose sufferings cannot fail to grip the imagination long after the book is finished.

As a boy Thomas Hardy had been no stranger to poverty; and he unfolds his story of Tess, struggling to overcome the pitfalls that poverty and ignorance strew in her way, with peculiar intensity. In doing so, he mounts an assault on conventional Victorian society's pharisaic morality, its unforgiving religion and rigid class system, and mourns the desecration by the machine of traditional agricultural life.

THOMAS HARDY

THE MAYOR OF CASTERBRIDGE

Edited by Martin Seymour-Smith

The Mayor of Casterbridge fully confirms the sombre note in Hardy's work. Gone are the comic touches and the 'country laughter' of *Far from the Madding Crowd*: instead it is a powerful character study of a man whose past refuses to be buried, and who is caught by changing conditions of rural commerce.

From the stunning opening wife-selling scene (at one time a not uncommon phenomenon in England) to the final playing out of his tragedy, Michael Henchard proves to be violent, selfish, greedy and crude. At the same time he possesses magnanimity, humility and a grandeur of passion that echoes Shakespeare – a comparison that always pleased Hardy.

Whatever his sins, Henchard impresses the reader with his robustness and life-force, and with his refusal to by-pass life's possibilities. In depicting a man who overreaches the limits, Hardy once again demonstrates his uncanny psychological grasp and his deeply rooted knowledge of mid-nineteenth-century Dorset.

THOMAS HARDY

JUDE THE OBSCURE

Edited by C. H. Sisson

'None but a writer of exceptional talent indeed could have produced so gruesome and gloomy a book', wrote a reviewer in 1895. Victorian delicacy notwithstanding, *Jude the Obscure* is undoubtedly the most outspoken, the most powerful and the most despairing of Thomas Hardy's creations, despite its haunting love story. It is a novel, too, that is uniquely connected with Hardy's own history, although it possesses a peculiar tone which outlives all mere reminiscences.

Jude Fawley, the stone-mason, whose academic ambitions are thwarted by poverty and the indifference of the authorities at Christminster, appears to find fulfilment in his relationship with Sue Bridehead. Both of them have fled from previous marriages, and together they share a 'two-in-oneness' rarely matched. Ironically, when tragedy strikes it is Sue, the modern, emancipated thinker – the last and greatest of Hardy's heroines, ranking with Emma Bovary and Anna Karenin – who is unequal to the challenge.

Its literary qualities apart, *Jude the Obscure* is also a rich source of social history, accurately reflecting within its pages the encroachment of the modern, developing world on the rural traditions of England.

THOMAS HARDY

THE DISTRACTED PREACHER
AND OTHER TALES

Edited by Susan Hill

Thomas Hardy's short stories reveal a literary persona, a creative intelligence and an imaginative vision uniquely and unmistakably his own. Those contained within this volume are among his finest and most representative and include 'The Withered Arm', one of his best known and most gripping; 'Barbara of the House of Grebe', said by T. S. Eliot to portray 'a world of pure evil'; 'The Son's Veto', regarded by Hardy as his best story; and, of course, 'The Distracted Preacher', possibly the most flawless of all.

Like the novels the short stories reveal Hardy's pre-occupation with affairs of the heart; with love requited and frustrated, fulfilled or doomed. They contain many of his most powerful portraits of women: they are streaked with the grotesque, the macabre and bizarre: and they are permeated by that atmosphere, narrative power and vivid sense of place and its intimate relation to character which are the essentials of Hardy's genius.